T0148345

Mountain Mystique

A.T. Hartley

iUniverse, Inc.
New York   Bloomington

Mountain Mystique

iUniverse books may be ordered through booksellers or by contacting:

iUniverse
1663 Liberty Drive
Bloomington, IN 47403
www.iuniverse.com
1-800-Authors (1-800-288-4677)

Because of the dynamic nature of the Internet, any Web addresses or links contained in this book may have changed since publication and may no longer be valid. The views expressed in this work are solely those of the author and do not necessarily reflect the views of the publisher, and the publisher hereby disclaims any responsibility for them.

ISBN: 978-1-4502-2316-4 (sc)
ISBN: 978-1-4502-2317-1 (ebk)

Library of Congress Control Number: 2010904693

Printed in the United States of America

iUniverse rev. date: 04/22/2010

Chapter 1

Becky was eighteen years old, stood five foot zero, and was a hundred pounds of bubbling energy. She had chin-length, straight, dark chestnut hair cut in a bob. She rubbed her head softly on her husband's chest, snuggling closer to her Monster. Twenty-four year old Kyle was a veteran of the first Gulf War, an ex-Marine sniper with two hash marks on his sleeve. He was 240 pounds of ripped muscles, stood six foot three, and had Germanic white-blond hair. At Becky's urging, Kyle was moderating. He was letting his hair grow out to a regulation long style so Becky could run her fingers through it.

Kyle guided his restored sky-blue GTO with white racing stripes down the center, northward on I-95. Becky's ear rested against Kyle's chest. Their hearts now beat as one. She faced him, sitting comfortably on his lap. She was as content as a woman could be. His clean manly scent heightened her feminine senses. She was aglow although relaxed. In an instant she was asleep. She hadn't slept well the night before, as she'd been too excited. Her tribal wedding planned for that morning had gone off beautifully.

Since the weather was warm, she'd chosen a yellow tube top with white short-shorts for her traveling outfit. As they were in Florida, it only seemed sensible to be as cool as possible on their drive, but she had forgotten one thing.

She felt a massive hand snaking its way into the gap of her short-shorts that amazingly grasped a good portion of her tiny bottom. Her right eye opened as she felt a finger toying with the string of her white lace thong.

"Kyllle," she purred, "don't you be startin' something you're not gonna finish…"

Becky felt her husband's hand stop, and then dispassionately withdrawal. Becky's other eye opened as she sat up to face her new husband. "Is something wrong, Kyle? I *wasn't* telling you to stop."

Kyle's face showed deep concern, "I just had a really bad feeling, hon. It's like when I was in combat and my instincts warned me of danger. I learned the hard way not to ignore my intuition. The last time I did, I rushed into an old farmhouse by myself to rescue a captured American pilot. I was nearly stabbed to death from behind."

Becky realized the seriousness of Kyle's mood. She surely didn't dismiss his feelings. She leaned back to look up at her husband's face, but the medallion around his neck captured her eye. It glowed with a smokey blue-white light. " W h e r e are we going, Kyle?" she asked trying to read the inscription. The Aztec-looking lettering, that circled the pendants' edge attracted her attention.

"Well hon, you know we're going to Colorado, to Granite Bluff. Snowy's family has a ranch there. I want to return his medallion to them."

Kyle examined his premonition, "I have this urgent feeling that we need to get to the ranch as quick as we can. I sense trouble there."

Becky leaned toward her man, "Kyle, you know best about these things. I trust your instincts. That's why we're still alive."

Kyle gave her a hug and said, "We'll cross Florida through Orlando and pick up I-75, heading north until it reaches I-10. Then we'll head west until we reach Baton Rouge. There we'll go north through Dallas, west to Amarillo and onto Santa Fe and finally north into Colorado. In Pueblo we'll go northwest to Canon City. Just past there we should come to Granite Bluff." Kyle had the whole route mapped out in his head.

"This is a much nicer trip than the first one I took on the bus alone from Chicago," Becky said. "I love this seating arrangement," she smiled at him.

Little more than two days later, a dusty sky-blue GTO approached Granite Bluff that wasn't much more than a crossroad. There was a sign outside of the town that boasted a population of nine, with a line drawn through it. A hand-painted five stated an adjustment. The town had a gas station, a café, and a lawyer's office. Kyle drove into the filling station. He got gasoline and directions to the Walter's ranch. Kyle missed the frown on the man's face as he drove off.

The gas station attendant shook his head as he walked back into the office. "No use tellin' him," he muttered to himself, "he'll find out soon enough…"

After leaving the filling station, Kyle turned the GTO onto the highway and looked around. "Wow, Snowy said he grew up in a fly-speck of a village, but from all this brown, over-grazed countryside, he was being optimistic."

Becky gaped at the vastness of the high valley, with the ever-present mountains looming in the distance. She recited the directions, "Five miles north on route 9, turn right onto state highway 724. A little farther on the right is where the Walter's place will be *for now*," was what the gas station attendant told them. The area looked like it'd been hit by a seven-year drought. Pictures of the 'Dust-Bowel' era of the Great Depression flashed before Becky's eyes. Even the few tumbleweeds blowing around lifelessly seemed lonely.

Becky pointed out to Kyle, "There's a mailbox with H. Walters stenciled on the side." A red-dirt road went from the highway to a weather-worn two story farmhouse. There was a porch that ran across the front of the house, sheltered by a decaying green asphalt shingled roof. Behind it was a run-down old barn. To the right of that was a small single-story structure that must've served as a bunkhouse decades ago, from the look of the peeling white paint.

Kyle looked at Becky as he saw a brand-new crew cab pickup truck in the front yard. Three huge men with side-arms stood facing the front porch. What caught Kyle's attention was that the armed men were dressed in civilian clothes! A man in a suit was shouting and pointing at an older man dressed like a typical rancher, wearing worn jeans with a long-sleeved white print shirt and cowboy boots. His wife wore an old, one-piece A-line dress, with black Mary-Jane shoes. She worriedly clutched her husband's right arm, standing slightly behind him for protection. Her face showed her fear.

Kyle looked at Becky, as he became KIS, his nickname from the military. "You stay here, but don't let them see you. If you've a need, my pistol is in the glove box. If someone comes to the car and it's not me, shoot first and let God sort out the innocent.

He parked the GTO on the other side of the driveway, stopping before he reached the pickup. Kyle could hear the suited man shouting at the older couple, "You better sign, Walters, or you'll get nothing at all. *Nothing.*"

"Oh don't sign, Harold," the old woman moaned. "If only Snowy were here, but he's dead and buried"

"I feel the same, Laverne," the old man comforted his wife, then looked back at the suited man. "Mr. Stanley, I know the Sheriff will foreclose on our ranch by the end of the week, because we're behind in our taxes, but miracles can happen. I'm not gonna sign. Not like this! You're too pushy."

The suited man was going to keep yelling at the old couple, when KIS interrupted, "Mr. Walters? Harold Walters?"

The old man answered KIS, "That's me, mister."

"*Who are you?*," the business man angrily demanded.

KIS noted that the man in the business suit wasn't wearing a shirt and tie. Rather, he wore a polyester, open-necked casual shirt under the jacket.

Ignoring him, KIS questioned, "Is there trouble, Mr. Walters?"

Harold was bolstered by the intrusion. "The Sheriff's gonna throw us off our land by the end of the week. We're two years behind in our taxes. Of late, I ain't made enough money to pay the store man for flour, let alone pay the tax bill. This here slick-willie and his henchmen, are tryin ta strong-arm us into signing our deed over to them now. He fronts for a business group who's been buyin up every ranch in the basin. He bought out my cousin Frank's ranch earlier this year. Now, he's after my land. "

The fancy dude's question had been ignored. He wasn't gonna ask twice. Mr. Stanley snapped a finger at the lead mercenary, for the merc to take care of Kyle.

KIS didn't appear too threatening, though he was fairly tall and all lean muscle. His white t-shirt and faded jeans over square-tipped boots with two-inch wooden riding heels with spur shelves made the head merc think he was some nosey rancher. KIS stood his ground and waited.

The huge mercenary, a head taller than KIS, saw that he wasn't armed, and thought he'd be easy ta whip bare-handed. Heck, the merc hadn't had a dog to kick all day. This no-account farmer would be good practice. 'This fight wouldn't last long,' the bully thought.

Trusting his intimidating size, the lead merc walked threateningly towards KIS. The large man swung his ham-sized fist in a brawler punch, swinging wide to gain momentum. His crude fighting technique was to use sheer force to beat his adversaries to death. He loved hearing his victims whine.

KIS hunched down and caught the merc's right fist in his

two hands. He savagely twisted the mans arm and a piercing *crunch* of wrist bone was heard by all. Instantly the merc screamed in pain. The next mercenary started to run at him so he knew he needed to finish the first man quickly. From training, KIS instinctively kicked down hard with his wooden boot heal. He expertly popped the knee cap of the first merc's left leg.

KIS released him as he fell to the ground in agony. He prepared for the second merc to get within range. By this time the second merc knew he wasn't facing any *farmer*. The second merc dropped into a karate stance when he was within an arm's length of KIS. Immediately, he shot a lethal front punch straight from his right shoulder aimed directly at KIS's heart.

KIS blocked the thrusting arm with a sweeping right hand. He grasped the second merc's right wrist, twisting the arm behind his back as the sound of snapping cartilage filled the air. The attacker's right arm was torn savagely from its socket. KIS was getting mad now. He grabbed the thug's shirt, running his head into the side of the brand new pickup, denting the freshly polished metal. Reaching down, KIS pulled the automatic pistol from the man's holster and turned to face the third merc, who stood firmly in place.

KIS looked at him with fire in his eyes, but didn't say a word.

Mr. Stanley witnessed his two best men maimed and defeated. He seethed at his remaining henchman, *"Kill him!"* he ordered, his voice hinted with an accent.

KIS waited for the third merc's move. The merc stood stock still. His hands were close to his holstered gun, held in a tie-down tactical rig on his right side.

Cocking his head to one side, "Force-Recon?" he asked.

KIS relaxed a touch, "Close," was all KIS answered.

"Special Weapon's?" was the next question from the last merc.

From the twitch in KIS's jaw, the man had his answer, "What's your name?" the merc asked, cautiously.

"KIS," was all Kyle answered.

The remaining merc jerked, "As in the Special Weapon's - KIS of Death?"

Again the jaw twitched, "I've been called that, *yes*," KIS answered, this time, there was death glowing in his eyes.

The merc's right hand flew up and away from his pistol, as if he had just been burned, "Semper Fi" was all he said.

The death in KIS's eye dimmed, "Right on Brotha," KIS answered. "You fell in with the wrong crowd, I think. You best look to your hold card and pick another game." KIS looked at Stanley and then back to the third merc, "Let the rest of your bunch know that *if anyone* comes out here like this again, I won't be friendly. Understood?"

The merc nodded his head. To him, KIS looked like death on two legs and he wasn't interested in seeing him when he was *really mad*.

KIS asked, "Do you need bus fare somewhere?"

The merc cautiously reached into his pocket for a cigarette and lit up, "I'm thinkin about reenlisting. This mercenary stuff isn't as glamorous as it appeared. Oh, it started out ok, but I'm not into forcing old people into signing away their ranches for pennies on the dollar. There's no honor in that."

Mr. Stanley was crazy with rage, "I told you to *kill him*!" he seethed.

The remaining merc looked at KIS and unbuckled his holster. He tossed it to his boss, "Well Mr. Stanley, if you want *to try* to kill this ugly gyreen, be my guest. I know I can't. Take this as my notice. *I quit.*"

Mr. Stanley caught the pistol belt and blustered, "You better get out of here!" KIS turned to face him silently with the automatic pistol now in his hand. This was a face-to-face fight. KIS knew this wasn't Stanley's style. He had others do his dirty-work for him. If he had to do it himself, he'd be a back-shooter. KIS pegged him for a coward.

After a minute, KIS gave a warning look to Mr. Stanley and turned with the pistol still in his left hand and hoisted the first merc over his right shoulder. He carried him to the bed of the pickup, and none too gently, threw him in. The third merc did the same with the second thug. Fuming, Mr. Stanley stamped over to his truck, got in, and started the engine, dying to say something threatening but held his tongue. He sent a stream of dirt and stones flying from behind the churning truck tires as he angrily drove off toward Granite Bluff.

KIS looked at the third merc, who said, "I could use some money for the bus if you don't mind, KIS. Don't know if I can repay it. I'm going to make my way back to twenty-nine palms and see if I can find a home again."

KIS reached into his pocket and peeled off a handful of cash. He handed it to the surprised ex-merc, "Do you need a ride to where you can catch a bus? Take this pistol too. Maybe you can hock it to cover the back wages you're not going to get."

Shaking hands, the ex-gyreen answered, "No, it's a nice day to be alive. I can walk."

Harold called out, "If you turn right at the highway and go two miles down the road, a bus ta Denver or Santa Fe comes by twice a day."

The ex-mercenary starting walking, 'Yep, it is a good day to be alive.'

"OH-MY-GOD," CATHY GASPED AT BECKY, "Can ya believe this?"

Becky, watching from inside the GTO, was startled to hear from her imaginary friend. "I'm glad you're still with me, Cathy. I was *so* scared. Kyle is very capable and I know he can handle just about anything, but it happened so fast and there was *four of them* to *my* one!"Becky exclaimed.

"He certainly is exciting to watch in action," Cathy commented.

"I thought you were gone. I hadn't heard from you since the wedding," Becky said.

Cathy chuckled, "I wanted to give you two love-birds some time to yourselves, but I'm around when you need me. Is that ok?"

"Cathy, you're my best friend, besides Kyle of course. You're welcome with me anywhere I go – except – in the bedroom that is," Becky answered.

Cathy chuckled, "Spoil sport. I still want *details.*"

As KIS WALKED SLOWLY BACK to the car, he mentally returned to being Kyle. When he reached the front of the car, he was careful to call out, "It's me hon. Come out and let's meet Snowy's parents."

Becky got out of the car, "Are you alright, Kyle?" she asked worriedly.

"Of course your Stud is fine, Becky," Cathy assured her friend. "KIS went through those toughs like a fox through a henhouse."

Kyle saw Becky's confused look and asked, "Is Cathy back? I was starting to wonder. She's been so quiet lately."

Becky walked up beside her husband, "Oh, she's around. I guess she's getting used to the new arrangement, is all."

Kyle rolled his eyes, but leaned down to kiss his angel. Even though it was a quickie, Laverne noticed that KIS got a raised leg effect from his female companion. *'What a man"* she thought.

Kyle walked with Becky up to the older couple standing on the porch. "Mr. and Mrs. Walters? I'm Kyle Swoboda. You'd know me as KIS from Snowy's old outfit back in the Corp. I prefer to be called Kyle now, if you don't mind. I'm *trying* to leave the violence behind me."

Becky moved to Kyle's right side and held his arm. She had a big smile on her face. This is how she dreamed her life would be. She and *her man*.

Laverne moved to her husband's right side, "*Oh yes*! I remember Snowy saying how proud he was to be in your squad. That you were a Real Operator."

"I'm Harold, Kyle, Snowy's dad, God rest his soul," he breathed heavy. "We appreciated your letter after Snowy was killed in action, but never thought you'd come all the way out here to see us." Harold looked at Laverne, "With Snowy gone, we've hit upon hard times, *yes sir*. The Mrs and I were counting on Snowy taking over the ranch. Then we could slip into our retirement years." Harold looked at the surrounding landscape, "As you can see, we've had a fierce drought and nary a blade of grass grows now. In the old days, this plateau was lush." He sighed, "There was a time when a good cow-man could run maybe four head to an acre, but I think those days are gone." Harold lightly touched Laverne's arm, "We're forgettin our manners woman. Let's invite these young folks in ta the kitchen for a glass of iced tea. They've come far and they're our guests."

Kyle indicated Becky, "Mr. and Mrs. Walters, I'd like to present my wife, Becky to you. She's the love of my life and the sunshine on my face."

Laverne lit up like a Christmas tree, "You come in dear. It ain't every day I'm blessed with female company. It's not that I don't appreciate Harold. It's just I've been alone with him, way out here, for the last forty years. With Snowy gone, our conversations don't stray far from the weather or our daily constitution." Laverne looked Becky all over, "Yes child, you're in the flower of womanhood. Kyle is fortunate to have you for a wife. I can see that right off."

Becky didn't know what to say. She was starting to look

at the two Walter's, as she had with her grandparents. The Walters were old, common folk, but they were genuine in their affections and thoughts.

When all four were seated around the kitchen table, Kyle spoke quietly, "I wanted to come and tell you both, that Snowy didn't suffer when he died, and was a Marine doing his duty. You both can be proud of him."

Laverne toyed with her iced tea glass, stern faced, "He might've been doing his duty Kyle, but it's little comfort when the wolves are howlin at the door. I didn't bring Snowy into this world to just have him die in a far-off desert, in a fight over stinkin oil or religious differences."

Kyle blinked, then looked at Harold, "I hope I didn't cause you two any trouble when I came up. Those men didn't give me much choice except to fight."

Harold looked at Laverne, "I'm a thankin ya, Kyle, for standin up to those thugs like you done. They surprised me," he groused. "From now on, I'm gonna wear my 44 on my hip, in case those rattlesnakes come back.

Becky asked, "Did I understand correctly, that the Sheriff was going to confiscate your ranch and auction it off by the end of the week?"

Laverne looked at Becky, "Yup, we don't have the money to pay our taxes. They're gonna steal our ranch, sure as shootin. And that Mr. Stanley, isn't what he appears either. He spoke with an eastern European accent. There's somethin fishy going on here."

Becky lit up, "Tell me about your ranch, if you don't mind. My father is a genious at real estate."

Harold looked around in wonder, "Don't know what to tell ya girl, except this ranch has been in the Walters family since the middle of the 1800s. My great granddaddy, was a share-cropper from Louisiana. After the Civil War, he headed to Texas. Then one year he came north on a cattle drive and learned there was land aplenty. One could claim all the land he could protect. I guess we have a little over four sections. All the land surrounds a mountain in the center. My family said there was gold in that mountain. My granddaddy, his name was Ned, had a mine somewhere up yonder. Its location died with him, when he was killed in a cave-in. He claimed he was getting close to finding the mother lode just before the disaster. It never did us any good. Was like spirits conspired to keep him from cashin in on that treasure."

Becky was guided by inner instinct, "Do you mind showing Kyle and me around the ranch, Mr. Walters?"

Harold indicated the ancient Jeep CJ with the soft top folded down, in the back yard. "Do you mind ridin in that? Some of the back roads are rough. I have wide, aggressive tires on it, so we won't get stuck. The four-wheel-drive comes in handy on the steeper slopes."

Becky looked at Kyle, "I'm game if you are."

Kyle nodded, "Let's go."

Laverne declined, "I've seen all the sights around here before. I'll put a meatloaf in the oven and make a fresh loaf of bread. You'll work up an appetite by the time you get back."

Becky eyed Laverne, "Can you make Italian or French bread, Mrs. Walters? Those are Kyle's favorites."

"Crusty I-talian bread is simple to fix," she nodded, "I can do that."

Harold got up and put on his summer, straw cowboy hat, as he sauntered out the back screen door. "Laverne used to cook for ten men when we were first married. They used to stay in the bunk house over yonder. She and I were planning on movin over there. Fancy people call it somethin, but I can't remember the name," he hesitated.

"An in-law's house?" Becky interjected.

"Yeah, I guess that's what they call it," Harold said. He climbed into the Jeep and fired 'er up. Kyle helped Becky into the backseat and he took the front, which had more room to fit his tall frame. "We were gonna let Snowy an his wife, when he got married, have the big house. The Mrs. and I don't need all that space anymore, now that we're getting up in years. Goin upstairs every night is getting ta be an unpleasant chore," he sighed.

Becky raised her eyebrows at Kyle. He caught her meaning.

"How much land do you have here, Mr. Walters?" Becky asked him again.

"Please call me Harold, Becky," Harold requested. "We've close to four sections."

"That's 640 acres of land to a section," Becky recalled from memory. "That's over 2500 acres of land!"

Harold spoke over his shoulder to Becky, who rode in the back, "That sounds like a lot, but out here with unpredictable rain, the land can get overgrazed real quick. It's not like being back east." Harold added, "There was a time when we rented grazing rights from BLM, that's the Bureau of Land Management. After Snowy left to join the Marines, our luck up an went with him. I couldn't afford to pay the taxes after he left, but before that, we could make a living out here. Mind you, few farmers make a load of money. It's the independence we crave. We're willing to get by on poverty level incomes, to work for ourselves."

"Can we see the mountain up close," she asked.

Harold scratched under his straw hat, "Sure. I can head over that way. Not much to look at and no-body lives close by. Just prairie grass and a few clumps of trees. There is a nice granite cliff with a stream falling over it."

Becky nodded, but she didn't say a word. Kyle was lookin at all the land. There were gullies and open fields. Then they could see the flat topped granite cliff with a waterfall that steeply dropped into a ravine. This had been cattle country in the past, but the drought killed the good grazing.

Harold pointed toward the mountain, "That's the cliff, I was tellin ya about".

"STOP THE CAR," Cathy shouted to Becky. "There's an

old man and a burrow over there. He's beckoning me to him!" Cathy jumped out of the jeep and ran up to the prospector. She lovingly patted his donkey as they talked.

"Stop the jeep, Harold, please. I'd like to look at the cliff," Becky called out. When the jeep came to a stop, Becky scrambled out of the little vehicle. "Kyle, can I talk to you, please?" she called back over her shoulder.

Kyle followed his little woman as she ran about fifty yards from the jeep. She shielded her eyes, looking at the cliff.

"Are you ok?" Kyle questioned, worriedly.

Becky dropped her hands to her side, but spoke quietly to Kyle. "Cathy told me to stop. She said there's an old man and a burrow standing near a stand of trees. She went up there to talk to him.

Kyle blinked in wonder, "Wow hon, you're full of surprises! Your imaginary friend is attracting spirits, like they're stray dogs? This is all starting to sound really crazy, even for me."

Becky put her tiny hand on Kyle's chest. "Relax sweetheart. Cathy's never steered me wrong yet. Let's see what she has to say." Changing the subject, Becky wondered, "What do you think about all this land? It sure is a diamond in the rough, but it's a ranch, like what you've talked about".

Kyle fidgeted, "Oh hon. I feel like a fish out of water. Now that I'm out of the Marines, I don't know where I fit in anymore," he confessed.

Becky looked at her husband, "What do you want to do, Kyle? Do you have *any* idea what you like?"

He looked down at her, "The only things I was any good at was killing people, working with machines, and farming." He laughed, "What a combo, eh?"

"Well, this is a ranch and the Walters could use some help. I know that much," she thought out loud.

Kyle had to agree. The older couple was going to lose their home by the end of the week unless something was done.

Becky waited as Cathy made her way back to the couple. "Well, what happened, Cathy? I don't see anyone up there!"

Cathy grinned at her friend, "It was really crazy, Becky. Suddenly, this old prospector appeared out of nowhere! He said his name is Ned Walters and his donkey's name is Jezebel. He said he was the great granddad of Snowy. He'd spent most of his life in the mine on this mountain. He was very close to finding the mother lode, but then he died in a cave-in, about 1895. He said he was so upset that he never found the vein of gold when he was alive, that he stayed here, waiting to tell someone where it was. As a spirit, he can walk through rock. He said he was called out by Kyle's adventuresome vibrations. That he and Kyle are kindred souls."

Becky told Kyle what Cathy explained to her about Ned as he was unable to see or hear her himself. She waited to see his reaction.

Kyle chucked, looking at his goddess, "Life with you surely isn't going to be boring, Becky. I'm glad you made me wait to hear the full story. That there's gold in this mountain really makes me interested in this place. Not to mention I *love* history. This whole area is dripping with stories from the past, for sure."

Becky looked at Kyle, "What do you think, darling? Would you want to see if we can buy the ranch from the Walters, before they lose it? They can move into the bunkhouse like they'd planned and can be caretakers of the house for us. We can see if Laverne is a good cook when we get back. My father is a real estate master. I can give him a call if you want me to."

Kyle nodded, "Please phone your dad. This place calls out to me. I'd like to get back to ranching. Maybe pick up some horses and cattle. Set aside a field or two of alfalfa and timothy for feed. If you don't mind, I'm interested in this ranch if you are as well."

Becky looked up, "That house looks pretty run down.

We'll probably have to demolish or remodel, but then I can plan an office I'd like when we rebuild. Today with phone lines and satellite link-up, I can have my international office with the Internet right here. I'm ok with the location, although it's really isolated. I'm a city girl at heart, as you found out in the swamp," she smiled.

Kyle kissed her. "I'm working on that. I've got a couple of ideas. Maybe we can talk again after dinner," he said as they turned and walked back to the Jeep.

After they got in, Harold started the engine, "You two look like you just saw a ghost."

Kyle laughed, "You could say that. It's beautiful up here and the sky feels bigger here than on the east coast."

Harold agreed, "Yes, plenty of breathing room. There isn't much more to show you. The biggest city around here is Colorado Springs. We go there every few months, when we need groceries. Laverne grows most of her own vegetables and does a lot of canning," he said as he stopped the jeep in the backyard.

"Dinner's on the table," Laverne announced as the trio marched through the back door. I can hear the sound of that old jeep's engine a mile away. Old habits are hard to break. Only time my man comes home is when he's hungry, or wants a little slap and tickle," she teased as she kissed Harold's wrinkled cheek.

Harold blushed, "*Woman*, have you *no shame*?"

Laverne winked at Becky, "They're a wedded couple, Harold. I'd say she's learned about the birds and the bees by now. Besides, I feel like we're family already," she grinned an impish smile.

Becky washed her hands at the large white porcelain sink as she tried to suppress a giggle. Then she let Kyle seat her. Becky looked at the Walters, "Did you ever want to move away from this ranch? To go somewhere when you retire?" she asked.

Laverne looked down like a deflating balloon, "Golly Harold, I never thought about leaving this place. I was born three miles down the road on my parents' farm. My only brother was killed in a farming accident years ago. My father gave his permission for me to marry Harold when I was sixteen. I inherited what my parents had and we added their acreage onto this place. We're in our fifties, and I wouldn't know where *to go*. I was hopin I could live out my days around here. Now that the Sheriff is gonna auction our place to recoup the taxes, I guess we'll have to move into a town somewhere? She brightened, "*Or,* we could squat on some land, high up, like Frank did?"

Harold solemnly took some mashed potatoes and then handed the bowl to Becky. "Laverne's right. We wanted to live out our days here in these mountains," he wiped some moisture from the corner of his eye, "but I guess we can't."

Becky took the meatloaf and laid some on her plate. She poured some brown gravy over it. She added some snap beans and then took a piece of the piping hot Italian bread Laverne offered her. After a few bites from her plate, she had her answer. Becky looked at Kyle, who nodded his head. The place was starting to grow on them both. Its charm had worked its magic and they felt they could be at peace there.

"How much would you want for the ranch?" Becky asked. She added, "You could stay on the ranch, and do pretty much what you're doin now? Like Laverne doing the cooking and cleaning. Harold, you could be the ranch foreman? We could work out a salary for you both aside from the ranch price."

Laverne's eyes lit up and she put down her fork. She looked at her husband with great anticipation and held her breath. This was a dream of her's come true. A new family *and* stay on the ranch! '*There is a God,*' she thought.

Harold took a long time to butter his fresh bread. He talked as if to himself, "The land ain't worth much, but there's a bunch of it." He took a pencil from his shirt pocket, wet it with the tip of his tongue, and wrote a figure on his paper napkin. He pushed it toward Becky and Kyle. Then he added, "I wouldn't mind helping out around the ranch. It's just that I'm getting too old to shoulder all the business stuff. I never was much good with figures, no-how."

Laverne anxiously added, "I'd love to cook and keep house for a family again. Who knows," she looked at Becky with a twinkle in her eye, "maybe I could help you change diapers, come spring? I wouldn't mind that *one bit*."

Becky blushed to her core, totally embarrassed. "Laverne," she breathed, "I haven't thought about having a family *yet*. I *just* met Kyle. It felt like, in a blink of an eye, we were married. I'm not complaining, and I love Kyle deeply, but I'm still just trying to get used to my man, plus *all* that goes with him."

"Don't you worry none about that, Becky. It seems ta me, you got yourself a right good man, and nature, she'll take her course. You'll see. It'll all fall into place," Laverne smiled confidently.

The Swoboda's looked at the figure, then Becky looked up. "I think that's possible, but after dinner, I'll make a phone call."

Kyle told the Walters, "Becky is the business whiz of our family. We inherited some money before we were married. We have what we need to do the things we want."

As soon as Becky was finished, she and Kyle walked out to the GTO. She got the satellite phone from the glove box. Kyle lit a cigar while she punched in a number from memory, "Jeffrey? Hello, this is Becky….you know… *Rebecca…* your daughter?" Kyle could only hear half of the conversation.

"No Jeffrey, I'm not dead, *but* you mustn't tell mother that I'm alive," Becky admonished. She laughed, "Yes, I didn't think you'd have a problem keeping a secret *from her*," Becky smiled. "I need a favor, Jeffrey. You see, I'm married now, and we've found a ranch in Colorado that we'd like to buy."

Kyle walked away as Becky outlined the property. He looked at the old buildings and kicked the sick looking grass. After a moment, he walked back.

Becky explained, "The house is run down and needs modernizing. The land is pretty worn out. It's a diamond in the rough, you might say. The value can only go up from here." Becky held the phone from her ear as Kyle could hear laughing. Becky asserted, "Be that as it may, Jeffrey, my husband and I want to buy the property. We don't want to travel to Denver. There's trouble about a land swindle around here. A fight broke out the minute we arrived."

Becky looked at Kyle, then spoke back into the phone angrily with fire in her eyes, "You know I don't judge you Jeffrey, but as my father, *I expect* your help! Do you know an attorney who'd be willing to travel to us? We aren't far from Colorado Springs."

Becky listened intently. Jeffrey's tone changed after he heard violence had occurred, along with Becky's plucky outburst, demanding his help.

Becky brushed back her hair nervously, curling it behind her ear, "That would be wonderful, *but*, the Sheriff will auction off the ranch by the end of the week. The current owners are behind in their taxes. Can you have your friend call me tomorrow morning?"

She smiled, "I appreciate your help, Jeffrey. Please give my best to William," Becky added, as she ended the call.

Becky looked at Kyle, "Daddy has an attorney friend in Denver, who owes him a favor. He said he could have the attorney, whose name is Robert, call me tomorrow morning. He'll travel here to us, as a favor to Jeffrey, with all the paperwork. Colorado Springs is the county seat. Robert can register our title and mortgage papers there on his way back to Denver.

"I'm glad your Dad can help us," Kyle said. "Time is not on our side."

Laverne came to the front door, "I made up the bed in the Snowy's old room. You're going to spend the night with us," she announced.

"Thanks, Laverne," Becky called back. "It's been a really long day and we could use some rest." She and Kyle wearily walked arm in arm to the house.

Chapter 2

The next morning Becky was awakened by Kyle getting dressed at dawn. The sound of his belt buckle made her crack open one eye.

"What time is it?" she groaned.

He came to kneel by her side of the bed, "Almost five. Laverne's probably got breakfast agoin already, if I know her."

Becky's one eye opened fully as she motioned with her finger between her husband and herself. "We're going to have to work out some rules about getting dressed at this unholy hour, ya-know. I'm *not* gonna be woken up before dawn each morning, honey."

Kyle gently moved the hair away from her face. "This is farm life, love. I'm sorry if I woke you," as his hand snaked its way under the covers to feel her soft warm body.

Becky's eyes flew open. She warned, "Kyle, don't you be startin somethin you're not going to finish…"

Kyle withdrew his hand gently. "I guess we've got too much work to be done this morning, what with all those people coming. Farmers are usually night-time people, when all the chores are done," he grinned.

Becky frumphed in frustration as she started to realize what farm life entailed. She understood the logic but her sleep cycle didn't like it.

Kyle handed her robe to her as he gave her a quick kiss. She answered his peck dispassionately with her own lips. She slid into the pink robe and slippers, following her husband downstairs. She shuffled into the old wooden kitchen in her pink pom-pom adorned slippers while Laverne was busily moving between the stove and the table, getting a huge farm breakfast prepared.

"How many eggs do you want, Kyle?" Laverne demanded like a short order cook. "Coffee's on the table. Help yourself," she announced.

Kyle was right at home in this kitchen gathering, since he'd lived the farmer's life back in Lancaster, Pennsylvania. Becky wasn't used to all these family meetings. She didn't have anything like this to relate to growing up. She was starting to enjoy the mealtime conversations. At times, the subjects tended to wander away from the socially acceptable, like animal husbandry, or roundup chores. Laverne simply would clear her throat and shake her head as if to say, "Not at *my* table you don't." The men would then quickly change the subject.

Harold was dressed in his usual casual cowboy attire, nursing a cup of steaming coffee that was black as midnight and strong as sin. He silently raised his index finger away from his coffee mug as his silent greeting.

Kyle looked at the old man, "You been nippin at the jug, Harold?"

Harold didn't deny a thing, but just smiled and raised his eyebrows. He wasn't hung over in the least.

Laverne answered for him, "Ole Harold likes to sample his moonshine from time to time. There is a copper pot still in the bunkhouse. He has white lightening distilled farther back than we've been married. It's stored in wooden casks out there, labeled with the year it was made. But honestly, our bodies are just taking longer to limber up in the mornings, the older we get.

"Takin a nip at night," Harold confessed, "helps me sleep plus wards off sickness and pestilence," he smiled a toothy grin.

Kyle knew Laverne would curtail any excess Harold might lean towards, so he didn't worry. Becky shuffled over to Laverne and she looked at the huge skillets on the ancient eight-burner propane stove.

"Don't you look darling, as pretty as a newborn calf," Laverne looked at her sleepy young friend. "What you gonna have this morning, suga?" she asked.

Becky pointed over at the table, "I'll have coffee and toast," adding, "I'm not much of a morning person."

Laverne chucked, looking at Becky, "If you're gonna live on a ranch, your schedule might change, darlin."

Becky could see this as she poured herself a cup of coffee. She looked at Kyle, who was wolfing down his six eggs, a pound of bacon, four huge flap-jacks, toast with preserves, and all washed down with the biggest cup of coffee she'd ever seen. The mug must've held close to *a quart* of liquid.

True to his word, Harold was starting to move about. It just took Harold's body a little while to unkink after years of hard work. Even though he only ate half the quantity of food Kyle did, they both finished at the same time.

Kyle looked at Becky, "Harold was going to run me over to his Cousin Frank's cabin down the valley a way, to see some horses. Do you mind?"

Becky shook her head, "No, I don't mind. It'll give me a chance to take a shower before you get back."

The men helped clear the table then walked outside to the jeep. Becky heard the now familiar sound of the ancient vehicle. She could see why Laverne said she could recognize the jeep's engine a mile away.

She felt increasingly at home here. She liked the routine. Farmers' lives follow the seasons of the year and weather conditions. It felt nice to be close to nature.

"Can I help you with the dishes, Laverne," Becky asked.

"Naw, but thanks for askin," Laverne brushed a wisp of graying hair away from here eyes. "It does my heart good to have a purpose again, a reason to live. Harold's and my life seemed to have no direction before you and Kyle showed up. I'm enjoying the simple things now. I feel like I have a family once more." Laverne seemed irritated with herself, "You go along now darlin, get your shower before your man shows up and gets you messy again. Men have a way of a-doin that to a girl, ya know?"

Becky put her hand on Laverne's arm, "I'm learning that," she giggled and headed off towards the stairs, that led to the second floor bathroom.

After her shower, she dried and combed her chin length dark-brown hair. She dressed in a lightweight pink collared, cotton sleeveless shirt, slid into hip-hugger jeans and completed her outfit with black flat shoes. She then made her way back to Snowy's room. She sat in his light-brown leather armchair just perfect for reading. Her legs were propped up on the paired ottoman. She heard Kyle came up the stairs to be with her after he and Harold returned from Cousin Frank's.

The phone rang in Becky's purse. Picking it up she answered, "Hello." Kyle could only hear half the conversation as usual.

"Yes, Mr. Edwards. Ok, I'll call you Robert. I'm glad to hear from you. I appreciate your prompt attention. We need to conclude this transaction before the end of the week. The Sheriff's sale is scheduled for Friday and there's been an attempt to force the owners to sell to a mysterious buyer from back east. We believe we've settled on a fair price for the ranch. My husband and I deal with a bank out of Freeport in the Bahamas. Can you draw up the sale papers, work with a title company, and arrange a mortgage to transfer a title that fast?" There was a pause as Becky listened, then laughed. "Yes, I know that's a tall order and oh, one more thing, I need you to come to us. There's a ruthless businessman, a Mr. Stanley, who had mercenaries come with him to the ranch. We don't want to leave here until the sale is complete."

Kyle let Becky finish the details as he walked about the large house. Laverne and Harold had gone out to the bunkhouse to start to clean. The place hadn't been occupied for at least four years.

"Kyle?" Becky called out from Snowy's room.

"Here," Kyle called back from down the hall.

Becky followed the sound of his voice. They joined up and looked about. There were three bedrooms, an attic, and upstairs full bathroom circa 1940s on the second floor. Downstairs, the kitchen was a 1950s version, the living room was dingy at best. There also was a storeroom that Becky felt could be an office, a downstairs half bath, plus a large pantry completed the structure.

"Looks like I'll have my work cut out for me this winter," Kyle sighed. "Still happy we're buying this place, hon?"

Becky looked at Kyle. She knew they'd love this land as much as the Walters. She was happy to allow the older couple to stay on the place plus have them help run the ranch. Becky asked, "Will it be too much to repair the house? Can you handle it, or do you want to hire a contractor, or just start over?

Kyle looked around, "I don't know. If you think we can afford it, maybe you'd be more comfortable with a new house. I'm not sure what style home you want. Can we talk about this again? If you could give me a budget, then I can offer some options."

"Sure, I can do that," Becky responded. "I think the question we need to ask ourselves is, do you really want this place? It's *a dump* from a real estate perspective."

Kyle walked around the kitchen. "Hon, I'm not really sure where I fit into life, but I feel this land calling to me. I guess I really do like farming or ranching like how you discovered you enjoy business. We're far enough away from most folks that the drug cartel won't know we're here, if we keep to ourselves."

Becky sat down looking at Kyle. "I'm a city girl, but I can see the love you have for the land. I wouldn't mind living out here if we can also have a townhouse in Denver? I want a place where we can stay, when we go on shopping trips in the big city, or if we wanted to go to the philharmonic. It's exciting that Boulder has a large campus we could affiliate with, to learn of cutting-edge technologies. Young people with vibrant minds live around college towns. Its fresh ideas, hopes and dreams, that are the basis for businesses of the future."

Becky got up and looked out the window, "I'd love to catch a revolutionary invention, so new, no one knows about it. I'd like to discover Joe Schmo, the geek inventor of a gizmo or process, that he thought up and perfected out in his garage workshop as his hobby. It'd be thrilling to me, if in time, this new idea would revolutionize civilization, like the invention of the telephone. I want to buy some stock in the next Ma-Bell corporation! I'd love to help people, but at the same time, watch our savings pile up. That'd be the best of both worlds for me."

Kyle walked up behind his tiny princess, "I can see that, hon. I'd like to help you do that. College towns are full of people who like to think and research."

Kyle was more practical minded and he spoke his mind, "I can also see we'll need transportation. I think we need to get a pickup truck, and probably a jeep Wrangler of our own. Most of our supplies can be delivered, but a 4X4 crew cab pickup will be handy to haul small loads from the stores back here. The jeep would be awesome to move around the ranch, without having to borrow Harold's keys all the time. I was thinking about getting a helicopter too, so we could travel quickly from here to Denver for a night on the town. There are all sorts of helicopters in different price ranges. I'm not sure what we can afford. I'm like Harold. I'm not into business as much you are. My technique of striking a bargain, is a little different than yours, I imagine."

Becky looked at him with shielded eyes, "Yesss," she hissed, "I imagine your idea of negotiation is burning bamboo sticks under the salesman's finger nails until he agrees *to your* price? I need to work on your people skills."

Kyle looked at the ceiling, then at his fingers. Becky changed the subject.

"Hmmm, a helicopter?" Becky tasted the idea. "We'd need to get one that could carry a lot of packages, for when I go SSSSShopping. Do they make one, like a flying station wagon?"

Kyle warmed to the conversation, "Anything is possible, hon, if you've got the cash. You just need to give me a price range I can haggle within," he winked. "I want to buy some saddle horses to start. That way we can ride around and camp out under the stars," he smiled. "After we buy the ranch, we could go up to Cousin Frank's cabin. Harold says he's the best 'horse man' in these parts. I thought about getting a cow for milk, but I don't know if that's such a good idea. I don't fancy getting up at four am on a cold snowy morning to milk the cow. Doing that once or twice might be fun, but milking her *every day*, 365 days of the year, sounds like a drudge. Laverne already has chickens for eggs. Of course we'd have to fix up the barn, and I want to build a garage/workshop for the cars and farm machinery," Kyle listed his wants.

Something told Becky to turn around. She looked into Kyle's face. She could see that he was happy. She also saw the little boy in Kyle, peeking out. It made her feel good. Kyle was a farmer-rancher at heart. He was earthy in spirit.

Kyle looked impishly at Becky, "Do you think we can drive out to where Cathy saw that old prospector, again? I'm excited to look around."

Becky thought a minute, "Robert Edwards won't be here until after noon. He'll stay here overnight and then travel to Colorado Springs to file the title at the courthouse tomorrow. I'll ask Laverne to make up a bed in the guestroom for him. He'll just have dinner and breakfast with us, then he'll be gone.

Both Becky and Kyle walked out to the bunkhouse. "Mind if I borrow the Jeep, Harold? We want to look around some more, if you don't mind."

Harold stood up, tossing the keys to Kyle, "Golly Laverne, it feels like Snowy's home again."

Kyle straightened as he took the medallion from his neck and held it out to Harold. "The main reason we came back here was to return Snowy's lucky pendent to you both. He dropped it in the desert the day before he was killed."

Harold looked at Laverne, and turned back to Kyle. "Son, all things have reasons for happening. Maybe it was Snowy's time to go and you were spared. The fact that you're here, helping us, is just like our son coming back from the dead. We have what we want out of life."

Laverne echoed, "You keep the pendant, Kyle. Maybe it was your time to carry it. Harold and I are at peace that Snowy is ok. Soon we'll join him, but for now, we're happy with the arrangements we've made. You've bailed us out of hot water, and we're obliged."

Becky asked Laverne, "Can you make up a bed in the guestroom for Mr. Edwards, the attorney, who's coming this afternoon from Denver? He's going to manage the sale of the ranch. He'll bring all the papers we need to complete the job."

"No problem," Laverne answered. "I've got a few more things to do out here, then I'll make sure the room is ready him."

Kyle gave the elderly couple a wave, and then he helped Becky get into the Jeep. The roof of the Jeep was made of canvas. The doors were off their hinges, and laid on the back seat, in case it rained.

Kyle started the engine and spied a large 500 gallon gasoline tank with an electric pump beside the barn. He stopped. Beside the tank was a long dipstick. Quickly, Kyle learned that the tank was nearly empty.

He got back in the jeep and started off toward the spot where the prospector, Ned, was last seen. "We'll have to get the fuel tank filled soon, Becky. There aren't many places to get gas out here. I want to stay away from that town as much as possible. It gives me the gibblies an makes me wary."

"I'll call around and see what can be done," Becky assured him.

As the Jeep neared the clearing, Cathy mysteriously appeared and chirped, "*There he is again.*"

"Where, Cathy? I don't see a thing," Becky complained.

Kyle stopped the jeep. Cathy grabbed Becky's hand and pulled her towards the edge of the woods on the left side of a large field. Kyle got out and followed.

Cathy looked at the old prospector, "Hello, Ned. This is Becky and Kyle. They're going to buy this ranch from Laverne and Harold. The Walters can still live here as long as they want while they help the Swobodas run it."

"It's right nice that Laverne and Harold are going ta be taken care of," Ned nodded. "Are these new folks interested in the mine or the gold?" he asked Cathy.

Cathy pointed Kyle out to Ned, "This is Kyle, Becky's new husband. He says he *loves* gold mines and prospecting. I think the mine is one of the things that interested him in the ranch, but yet he's a farmer at heart." Cathy whispered to Ned, "They can't hear you, so I'll translate what you say to Becky. She and I are old friends."

Ned looked at Kyle, although Kyle couldn't see him. "There's a mine with gold close by. If they can find the location of the mine, then tell them to look for Neptune's Fork. The mother lode is just behind it."

Cathy told Becky, who told Kyle. Kyle felt this was a strange way to carry on a conversation, but he was thankful for the information. Kyle was starting to open up to the spiritual world. Becky already was comfortable with it.

Kyle asked the open space around them, "Cathy, can you ask Ned, the location of the mine? Will he show us where the gold is?"

Ned heard Kyle, but Kyle didn't see Ned's reaction as the

color drained from his face. "Cathy, tell your friend he'll have to find the location of the mine on his own. The entrance is not easily seen as it blends into the landscape and *NO*, I'll *not* go back in that mine! *It's haunted* by *horrible beings!*"

Becky looked wide-eyed into the field. Kyle knew she was listening to Cathy.

"Ned says he has a cabin back in the mountains. He was wondering if I'd like to visit with him and watch the sunset?" Cathy giggled to Becky.

"No! You're not? Are you?" Becky gasped at Cathy, "I want *details.*"

Cathy looked indignantly at Becky, "You little twerp! You wouldn't say a thing about your night of adventure with Mr. Stud there, Rebecca!"

Becky suspiciously eyed her long-time best friend. "Cathy, I've been wondering. If you are my imaginary best friend, how can you see a spirit? I didn't think you could, unless…you were a spirit yourself?"

Cathy leaned close to Becky and whispered into her ear, "I'm really your guardian angel, honey. Up until now, I didn't think you could handle knowing the truth. Your grandmother asked me to watch over you, since she couldn't. She didn't want you to fall under the same evil spell your mother did. After she turned bad, your grandmother prayed and prayed for help. I was sent to her. Your grandma loved you very much and so did your grandpa." As an after thought, Cathy whispered, "Look around Snowy's desk in his room. Twist the handle on the upper right side drawer…"

Kyle patiently waited while Becky and Cathy talked. He was getting used to these weird conversations.

Becky then grabbed Kyle's hand, leading him back to the jeep as she called back over her shoulder, "Thanks Cath. You and Ned have a great time. We're doing fine here."

"Where's Cathy going?" Kyle asked.

"She's going to visit with Ned for a bit," Becky said.

"Now I've heard it all! Maybe someday you'll explain this to me?" Kyle said looking completely confused.

Cathy waved goodbye to Becky as Kyle drove back to the ranch. As soon as he stopped the jeep at the back step, Becky flew up to the second floor. Kyle was wondering where she was going and followed quickly behind.

Once inside Snowy's room, Becky went over to the desk by the window. She twisted the handle on the upper right drawer, like Cathy had told her to do. Both Kyle and Becky heard a latch release under the top surface of the desk. Becky looked underneath and saw a secret compartment with a ledger in it. She pulled it out and opened the book.

"It's Snowy's diary!" she gasped, showing the book to Kyle. "Do you mind if I read some of the entries?

"Go ahead, see what you can learn about the mine. I'll relax outside where I can hear you," Kyle said.

Kyle walked over to the balcony, went out on the Captain's Watch and lit a cigar. Becky flipped through the pages of the diary. Suddenly, she exclaimed, "Kyle, there's an entry from October 19, 1984, when Snowy was sixteen. He describes meeting a stranger far up in the woods. The stranger said he wasn't from around here. He appreciated Snowy sharing his dog with him, so he could pet him for a few moments. The stranger said he missed being able to feel the soft fur of his pet." Becky read on, "He said he asked the stranger where he lived, and all he would say was that he lived close by. The stranger asked if his family knew of a mine? Snowy, answered yes, but the location had died with his great grandfather. The stranger answered that the mine was, very pleasant to an Englishman, but it certainly wasn't in Piccadilly. Now what does that mean?" Becky wondered aloud.

Kyle snuffed out his cigar and came back into the room. He sat down on the desk chair and ran his hand through the half-inch long, white-blond, hair. He gave himself time to think about recent events.

Becky watched as many emotions crossed Kyle's face as he

thought about how amazingly his life had changed in so short a time. Only a month before, he'd been so lonely he'd thought about doing himself in. He'd turned into a dirty hermit, living alone far back in the wilds of the Everglades Swamp. But now, he was hopeful for the future. He was blessed with a gorgeous, petite woman to share his life. He was about to purchase a huge Colorado ranch, complete with a gold mine! He'd inherited Snowy's good natured parents and life had never been better. Kyle's heart beat faster than any other time in his life. He had so much to look forward to.

He couldn't stop himself as he went over and picked Becky up in his arms and gently crushed her to him, holding her like she was his life itself. He softly, tenderly kissed her lips, tasting her, giddy with excitement as he held her to him and smelled her fragrant hair. Becky forgot all about the diary as it slipped from her hand and landed on the floor.

Awhile later, Becky leaned back in bed. With a content smile on her face, she confessed to her husband, "*That* cowboy, is what I call a *close encounter…*"

Chapter 3

Kyle's satellite phone rang in Becky's purse, as she sat in Snowy's room reading his journal. She picked it up, "Hello?" Becky straightened. "Hello, Robert. Yes, we're all here waiting for you. You have the building inspector with you? Wow, that's great! That means we can complete the finances today and all you'll have to do is register our deed at the county seat." Becky ran to the front porch, "Yes, I can see your convertible now."

Robert Edwards turned onto the red-dirt road that led to the old farmhouse. Robert looked at the large muscular, dark haired man sitting next to him. He was an ex-construction foreman, turned building inspector. He now worked for a large mortgage firm in Denver.

"Goodness, Phillip," Robert said, "you'll have your work cut out for you with this *dump*. I don't know how my friend's daughter ever got mixed up in this disaster of a property. I never would've dreamed that a relative of Jeffrey Wells could be wooed into such an apparent misadventure."

"Yup," Phil Hadley answered his cosmopolitan associate. "This place needs a lot of work. Not just the houses, but all around the ranch." He looked beyond the obvious, "Although, with some investment, this place could be something special," he confessed with admiration at the young couple's courage.

Phil looked towards the east at the Rampart Range Mountains in the distance. "I've heard rumors that a consortium of investors wants to build another recreation park, with a massive hotel capacity in and around this area. I don't think this valley is right for another ski resort or snowboard pipe." He looked at Robert, "I've also heard that another group wants to put in a solar farm around here. This plateau is high enough to receive pure sunlight."

Phil thought out loud, "What this young couple needs to do is modernize the house and clear the land of scrub brush that sprouted up from the over-grazing. Then they can reseed the acreage with a hearty pasture grass, fertilize it, and leave the land over the winter. Come spring, this place would be ready for some cattle." Phil nodded his head, "I think the place has potential. The ranch could employ people from around here, get them back to work. That's what we need in this country today, more visionaries for local industry!"

Robert stopped his silver BWM 640i convertible in the front yard. The two dissimilar men got out.

Kyle walked down the porch steps, looking like a typical rancher. He was dressed in a short sleeved cotton western shirt with collar, comfortable boot-cut blue-jeans, and western boots with spur shelved riding heels. Becky followed closely behind him. "I'm Kyle Swoboda, and this lovely lady, is my wife Becky. We appreciate you both coming so quickly. The Sheriff is anxious to auction this ranch off and put our friends off their land. We'd like to buy the property before that happens.

Phil, being in his mid-thirty's, 5 ft 10, a muscular 180 pounds, wore a yellow short sleeve collared polo shirt, work blue-jeans with tan construction boots. He judged Kyle rugged enough for him to relate to. "Kyle, why don't you show me around, so I can make some notes? Off hand, this place needs *a lot* of work, but it has hidden assets, possibly a diamond in the rough I think."

Kyle walked towards the front door. He and Phil started talking, "Becky and I feel this place has potential," Kyle began. "I was wondering, Phil, have you heard of a group who's buying up properties in this area? A slick-willie and his thugs were out here the other day. They tried to force my friends into selling cheap, before the Sheriff's sale," Kyle explained.

Becky and Robert watched the pair of men walk and talk as they disappeared into the house. When the two men were gone, Robert looked at Becky, "Well, I declare, Rebecca! You've grown up since I last saw you."

Surprised, Becky confessed, "I don't recall seeing you before, Robert."

Robert reached into the back seat of his eye-catching sports car for his soft brown leather briefcase. He stood 5 ft 6 inches tall, weighing a trim 128 pounds. He was magnificently dressed in a sharply cut gray tweed sports jacket over a freshly starched powder-blue, open collared shirt. Carefully tailored cream trousers and cordovan penny-loafers completed his outfit. His expensive cologne was out of place, competing with the scent of dry sage and dust.

"Jeffrey and I were in college together," Robert explained to Becky. "*We were* - close friends, you could say. I used to come to those opulent parties your conniving mother threw to impress her bosses. They were enough to make me gag," he ground out tersely. "Even back then she was shunning Jeffrey, but that was her loss, and our gain."

Becky agreed, "I had enough of my mother and found a new life of my own. I'm happy with my husband, and what we're doing," Becky confided.

Robert's eyebrows rose almost imperceptibly, "Oh darling, I can surely understand, but yet, your man is *so big*. You two remind me of beast and the beautiful."

Becky didn't say anything about the analogy, but she agreed. She took Robert's arm and walked him into the house. Harold and Laverne were nervously sitting at the kitchen table. Becky introduced Robert Edwards, the prominent attorney from Denver, to the Walters. Shortly, they were joined by Phil and Kyle.

Robert looked expectantly at his associate, "What's your recommendation to the bank for the mortgage, Phillip?

Phil leaned back in his chair looking at a paper with the asking price for the ranch written on it. "I can only guarantee half of this price to the bank," he sighed. "From the run down condition of the buildings and the pastures, I can't value this place higher than that," he shrugged his shoulders.

Robert nodded and thought, 'Now somebody's showing some sense around there. We're in the middle of *nowhere*. The passes back here can get snowed in for six months out of the year. There's *no* guarantee that the roads will get plowed. I'd walk away from this disaster, if it were me.'

Becky beckoned Kyle for a private meeting. Laverne and Harold sat nervously at their kitchen table. Sure, the place was run down, but the Walters never dreamed their homestead would be valued so low!

Becky looked at Kyle, "Do you want this place? We could throw in some of our cash to close the deal, but this is a real estate nightmare, I have to be honest. Chances are we'll have to bulldoze most if not all of the buildings."

Kyle rubbed the back of his neck, "It would make a nice start toward a new life for me. Plus I can pay back Snowy, for his sacrifice, by making sure his parents have a roof over their heads till they leave this earth. I vote we make up the difference with our money."

Becky patted Kyle's arm, "I know we talked about this, but I want to make doubly sure we're on the same page. I'm game. Let's do it." They walked back to the table. Four pairs of expectant eyes bore into the young couple.

Becky looked at Robert, "Kyle and I *want* the ranch." She took a piece of paper and wrote numbers on it. Pushing the paper to Robert she told him, "We'll take the mortgage at 5.4 % interest for thirty years. On the paper is our account and phone number of our bank. Kyle and I'll make up the difference in cash. We want to close the deal today. Can we do that?"

Robert got up frustrated, to make his phone calls. "You're both crazy in my opinion," he said. In less than ten minutes he returned to the table, muttering under his breath, "*I hope you know what you're doing.*"

Robert looked at the Walters, "Between the Swoboda's bank and the mortgage company, you're asking price has been secured. We have to pay your back taxes off from that money first before the sale can be finalized. The rest of the money will be yours. I can open a bank account for your deposit."

Harold and Laverne grabbed each other's hands and bounced for joy. Never in their wildest dreams did they think they'd have this much cash, but they did now!

Robert pushed the transfer of title paper over to the Walters to sign. The bulk of the signing fell to the buyers. When all the legalities were complete and Robert was satisfied, Phil looked at Kyle and Becky.

"I think you can make something of this place with reasonable planning," he offered. "My suggestion would be to let the old house go. Use modular, green construction, partially underground, if you choose not to remodel." He offered Kyle and Becky a card. "Here's the name of a builder in Denver I'd recommend. You can also contact the University's Agricultural Extension Service for their advise as to good grass seed. Heck, there might be grant money, to reseed your pastures. This will revitalize the area, for free," he offered.

Robert looked at Phillip, somewhat disgusted. "I want to get on the road soon if you don't mind. In an hour, we can be in The Springs, file the papers, and be sipping a cocktail in the hotel bar in two. What do you say, huh?"

Phil looked at Kyle, who shrugged. Phil agreed, "Let's go." He didn't want to be with Robert much longer. These men were cut from different bolts of cloth.

Kyle and Becky waved as the foreign sports car sped down the road. In a final gesture, Robert gave Kyle that mornings copy of the Denver newspaper.

Walking back to the house together, Kyle glanced at the front page and one story caught his eye. 'Hitch-hiker, mysteriously shot in the back of the head, execution style, on state highway 724, sometime yesterday. The victim, identified as Blake Thompson, currently unemployed and without permanent address, was found laying along side the road. He was pronounced dead at the scene by the county coroner. The reason behind Mr. Thompson's death is under investigation.' Kyle frowned, folded the paper and placed it under his arm.

When they entered the house, all was eerie and quiet. Becky called out, "Laverne? Harold?"

"Up here," Harold's hushed voice reached her ears.

Becky went up the steps. The drawn look on Harold's face worried her, "Where's Laverne?"

Harold motioned up towards the attic, "I'm giving her some space, but I'm sure she'd appreciate another woman's company. We've lived out here all alone. It was just Snowy and me with her for all these years. We had no daughters, though we tried and tried. Laverne's life has been lonely and lacked female company. For that, I'm truly sorry. There're dang few females around these parts. Mostly, it's just us mangy men and cattle," he confessed.

Harold went downstairs to keep out of the way. Becky climbed the stairs up to the attic. She heard Laverne sobbing softly.

Becky saw Laverne on her knees beside an ancient bassinet. Laverne clutched the crib like it was her child. Like her life, the bed was empty, only memories remained.

Becky's heart went out to the older woman. Her only son had been killed in combat. The trauma of this week, selling her ranch, leaving the large house for the last time as her own. All of this was too much for her!

Becky kneeled down and hugged the sobbing woman. Laverne cried into Becky's shoulder. Sharing her grief with another woman was comforting. It wasn't that Laverne minded selling her home and ranch to Kyle and Becky. On the contrary,

Kyle was like her son finally come home and Becky was the daughter she never had. It was just too many changes so fast, but then, life is like that sometimes.

Laverne dried her tears and dabbed her nose with a dainty, laced hanky. "The crib did me in, Becky. I so wanted to have a little girl. I grew up on a farm with one brother and my father. My mother died birthing me. Then I married Harold so young, and we had Snowy, but no girls. Oh my God. How I ached to have another female around, someone I could confide in. To brush her hair, kiss her soft cheek, to share recipes and to pass on womanly secrets I've learned."

Becky didn't know what to say except to hug the older, sweet woman. She brushed a kiss against Laverne's weathered cheek. She tasted Laverne's salty tears. In a minute, Laverne stood up and took a deep breath. "I'm a pioneer woman! I come from sturdy stock!" she sternly told herself.

Laverne hugged Becky to her and relished the softness only a woman could offer. Looking down into Becky's bright blue eyes she whispered, "If you have a baby, I'd love to help you with her or him." From the surprise in Becky's eyes, Laverne clarified, "It's not that I want to control you or your child. I just know how hard it is to do *everything* by yourself. To keep a husband happy, to run a house, to pay the bills, and to watch and teach a youngster. It's just too much for one person to manage *alone*. It was very hard and lonely for me. I wouldn't want that for you."

Becky hadn't had a real female friend since Blanche. Wela had been sweet, but the two women hadn't been that close, yet. Cathy was her confidant but she couldn't touch her. With Laverne and the arrangement they'd forged here, Becky knew that Laverne and she were going *to be close*.

Becky shyly confessed, "Laverne, I haven't even thought of a child. I don't even know if I can have one."

Laverne fixed Becky with a concerned look, "Is everything ok? Are you irregular? Maybe we should get you checked out by a doctor."

Becky enjoyed having an older, experienced woman to talk with about things. She assured Laverne, "I'm in good health and all is normal, best I can tell."

Laverne sighed in relief, "You gave me a start, child."

Becky spoke quietly, ""That's just it, Laverne. For years, I've been treated like a child. My mind hasn't caught up with my body yet." A little timidly Becky shared. "I've only known Kyle, or *any man*, for about a month. Our courtship was a whirlwind you could say. I'm not used to all this yet. It's just that a girl sleeps alone for eighteen years of her life. Then *one day*, she gets married. After this special day, she's supposed to reverse all the No-No speeches she's ever heard. She's supposed to be completely comfortable, having a large man sleeping in her bed, next to her!"

Laverne hugged Becky, "I understand. I didn't mean to belittle you as a woman. It's just you're like the daughter I never had. I didn't mean to rush you about having a child, either. It's that I miss my baby and feel alone inside. Does that make any sense to you?"

Becky laughed, "Heavens, I understand completely. I'm a woman too!"

Laverne smiled, "I rest my case," she laughed in relief.

Becky said, "I just hadn't given having children any thought." She imagined in her mind, 'It would be wonderful to have a life blossom from Kyle and my love. To feel that life grow inside me, for me to nourish him or her, to give something of myself to the babe.' She decided, 'Yes, I can see that would be exquisite.'

Suddenly, Becky heard a rifle shot. She gasped, "Now what?" and then flew down the steps, and out the back door. She ran towards the now familiar sound of the gunshot.

Becky ran up to Kyle, who was laying on an old rug with his M-14 sniper rifle. "What happened, Kyle? You scared me to death!"

Kyle carefully laid the rifle down and rolled over, looking

up at the tiny princess who stood close beside him. A strange smile and laugh lines formed at the corner's of his eyes.

"Wwwhat?" Becky questioned, looking down at her Monster.

Kyle's smile broadened, "I was just imagining you standing over me, with you wearing a dress."

Becky knelt down, straddling her man. She pinned his shoulders to the earth with her arms. She lowered her head, "Oh you rutting beast! Is that *all* you ever think about?" she laughed.

Kyle didn't answer. Becky already knew his reply.

Kyle moved to plant a kiss on her tiny lips. The kiss lingered, as he savored the taste of her. His arms encircled his goddess. "I confess my lady, that you tempt me to the core. When you're near me, I want to be totally with you, to feel your warmth."

Becky changed the subject, gasping, "What are you doing with the rifle?"

"Target practice. I'm getting rusty," he explained, becoming serious.

Becky looked around, "Where's the target? I can't see a thing."

Kyle lifted her off to kneel next to him, "See that hill out there?"

Becky nodded. Still she couldn't see the paper he'd shot at.

"At the base of the hill is a fence post. I nailed a target to it," he pointed.

"What made you decide to start shooting again?" Becky questioned.

Kyle went over to his equipment bag and pulled out the newspaper. "Robert gave me this," he said. He pointed out the article.

As Becky read, her face tightened, "Is this who I think it is? Is he the third merc who walked away from here? How could this happen?"

Kyle shook his head, "I don't know what we've fallen

into, Becky, but there are major players here. People just aren't murdered, without a reason."

A worried Becky looked at Kyle, "Is there a way of finding out what's going on? I don't want to live my new life in fear."

"I could make a phone call to Montana. He has many connections, but I could be opening another can of worms, if I call," he confessed.

"Would a phone call cause that much trouble?" Becky wondered. "If you can make a call, without a commitment, then I'd say do it."

Kyle picked up his phone and punched in a number from his black book. "Hello, Montana? This is KIS. Can you talk for a minute?"

Kyle listened, then answered, "Becky and I are in Colorado and bought Snowy's parent's ranch. Someone was trying to muscle them into selling out before they were foreclosed and put off their land. I was attacked by some mercenaries when we first got here. I maimed two and let one ex-gyreen go. Then I saw in the newspaper where the third merc was murdered. He was just walking along a country road, to catch a bus."

Kyle listened, "Ok, so your contact, who's interested in me, is with The Agency? This sounds like an organized crime problem to me. That would be Bureau's turf, right?"

Kyle looked at Becky, as he listened further. "All right, so you want me to take Cobra's phone call and go from there? OK, then, make the call. You have my number," he said and disconnected the call.

Kyle stood up and started walking to his target. Becky followed. Where they were shooting from was northwest of the farmhouse. Kyle's target was over 600 yards and two pastures away. The couple strolled over the four inch high mixture of summer wildflowers and thin pasture grass. In the distance, square clumps of evergreen trees defined the boundaries of pastures. The mountains were off in the far distance, veiled by a bluish-gray, mist.

"Montana said there's a man, codename Cobra with The Agency, who's interested in my skills. Cobra would be my contact. He'd coordinate any calls to the Bureau on our behalf." Kyle looked over at his wife, "Montana said that if Cobra were going to delve into our problem, then I'd have to take an assignment, to return the favor."

Becky asked, "I don't understand. What is an assignment?."

Kyle looked at his tiny treasure. "An assignment would be a fire mission in the bush."

Becky couldn't believe her ears. This touched a visceral nerve in her. "*You mean* you'd be sent to shoot someone? You'd return to being a sniper?"

Kyle shrugged, "Well hon, that's what I do."

Becky shook her head violently. She didn't agree! "That's what *you did*, Kyle. That's not what you're doing, *now*."

Kyle stopped and looked at his wife full on. "Well hon, with all of your business knowledge, you tell me what you want to do. I did what I thought was needed, to protect us."

Becky was at a loss. "I don't like it," she confessed.

Kyle walked ahead, "Neither do I honey, but the enemy that we face has many heads. There's no local police out here. I doubt even the state police would know what to do, *or* could protect us. That merc we let go wasn't *stupid*. He was highly trained, but they surprised and executed him, just the same."

The satellite phone rang. Kyle answered, "Hello? Yes, Cobra. You've got the KIS of Death," Kyle spoke into the phone.

Kyle listened for awhile. Then he replied, "I understand what you're saying Cobra, but I'm not ready to ask for your help, *yet*. The land swindle, the muscle tactics, seem like organized crime to me, and that's Bureau," Kyle insisted.

Kyle moved his feet around the ground, not making much headway. Then Kyle answered firmly, "I'm going to stand firm for now. You send your package. I'll be around the ranch. Ok, I'll expect a messenger later this afternoon. If I need you, I'll call. I have your number. Out."

Kyle looked at Becky. "You heard all that went on. I didn't lock us into anything. Cobra wants me to look at something he's sending out here. We aren't under any commitment until I ask for help."

Becky took her husband's hand as she worriedly looked at him. "I hope we don't need their help, because the cost is too dear to me."

Kyle retrieved the target. An eight inch group at 600 yards. Not bad, but he needed more practice. A group that size just *wasn't* good enough.

As the couple started back to the house, Kyle sighed, "Trouble finds people, Becky. Sometimes it's fate. I'm glad we helped Snowy's parents. They were really in need. If we hadn't come along when we did, they might be dead by now. Something really serious is going on here.

Kyle wanted to break the tension. "Want to go back out to the pasture where Cathy saw Ned? I want to look around a little. What-do-you-say?"

Becky was a little hesitant, but she thought getting away for a bit wouldn't be a bad idea. "I can see it will be handy to buy our own jeep. You go get the keys from Harold. I'll wait by the house."

Becky was standing on the back deck when Kyle drove up. She hopped into the ancient CJ. Kyle drove around randomly looking at the ranch that he and Becky now owned. He made his way over to the pasture where they'd spoken to Ned. Kyle went a little further and parked the jeep in a stand of pines. This hid the vehicle from view.

Kyle climbed out while Becky came around the jeep to meet him. He took her hand and led her over to the granite cliff. "Remember the entry in the diary? The part that only an Englishman would enjoy the location of the mine? What do you know about Englishman?" he asked Becky.

She thought, "They like fish and chips? They like their gin or bitter ale?" she guessed.

Kyle smiled, "They always seem to carry an umbrella don't they, for when it rains?"

Becky nodded, "But it hasn't rained for a long time around here."

Kyle agreed, "But rain falls from the sky. Does that give you any clue?"

"No, not really," Becky complained. I've never been good at twenty questions."

Kyle walked Becky over to the side of the cliff and pointed to the small stream that fell from above them. "And this area sure isn't Piccadilly Square."

Kyle made his way down the side of the cliff leading Becky and helping her over the steep areas. Kyle nosed around near where the stream fell over the cliff and disappeared for a minute behind the waterfall.

When he emerged, he was soaked. "The mine entrance is behind the waterfall," he told Becky. Kyle grabbed her hand and pulled her into the frigid down flow. Becky squealed when the ice cold water hit her.

Once inside the hidden mouth of the mine, Kyle found an old rusty kerosene lantern. He took out a strike anywhere match and lit the lamp.

They hadn't gone more than ten paces, when the earth seemed to shudder, like an earthquake was moving through the hillside. As the couple went on a few steps further into the mine, Kyle glimpsed a trident shaped deposit of rock. As he inspected the fork, the opposite wall seemed to come alive!

Becky screamed her surprise at not being alone in the mine. She bolted for the waterfall not knowing what was behind her. Kyle didn't mind a fight, but had no choice but to follow his frightened wife, as she made a hasty retreat. Neither Becky nor Kyle saw the iridescent blue eyes that stared after them, from the dark interior of the mine as they fled.

Once outside, Becky made a beeline for the jeep. When Kyle got in the CJ, Becky nervously gasped, *Did you see something?!*

Kyle tried to mentally recall what he'd seen. "It was hard to see clearly, but it looked as if the wall of rock just melted away. In place of the rock, was this, *this thing*. It looked like rock, but had hairy tuffs growing out of its elliptical body."

Becky agreed, shivering with fright. "That's what I thought I saw too. I'd never seen anything like that before, have you?"

"Nope, that was a first for me. It didn't seem like it wanted to hurt us. It just stayed where it was. If I didn't know better, I'd say it was as surprised as we were to stumble onto each other," Kyle offered.

"We better not act weird when we get back to the ranch," Becky advised. "We don't want to scare Laverne and Harold. It'd be a horrific shock to know you've been living around a haunted mountain!"

Becky clutched herself, "Next time we go away from the ranch, Kyle, I want you to carry your pistol. There are too many weird things going on around here. I'm getting *way past* scared!"

Kyle nodded, "Gotcha." He didn't have a problem packin iron, especially when conservative Becky demanded it. He quietly made his way back to the farmhouse, following a zig-zag pattern. After parking the jeep in the backyard and walking through the back door, Laverne called out from the pantry, "Are you two hungry?"

Kyle blurted out, "I could eat a horse, if we had one."

Laverne was apologetic, "Hope you two don't mind leftovers. Our cupboard is pretty sparse right now."

"Leftovers are fine, Laverne," Becky answered, adding, "Can you make a list of what we need? Do you have a freezer? Maybe we can buy half a steer along with the everyday things."

Laverne brightened, "I've died and gone ta heaven, darlin. Sure I can write out a list. The bill might be hefty, though." She added, "No, we don't have a freezer. The last one died a year after Snowy joined the Marines."

Becky didn't blink, "Make out a list of supplies, Laverne. I'll call it into some stores in Colorado Springs. A messenger can deliver our groceries out here. I watched my mother's secretary do this for an executive weekend once. It was a secret meeting way out in the woods, for about twenty people. They needed a ton of stuff."

"Colorado Springs is called, The Springs, by locals, darlin. Just to let you know," Laverne shared.

Becky nodded as everyone sat down for a tasty meal. As soon as they cleared the table, Harold looked up, "Someone's coming up the drive. You expectin company, Kyle?"

Kyle nodded to the affirmative and went out to meet the plain black government sedan. He took a case that looked like it held a trombone and a square metal box from the trunk. As soon as the cases were delivered, the car drove off.

Kyle went into the living room and Becky joined him. He opened the large case and blinked when he looked inside. He pulled out a *huge, long* rifle.

"What is it, Kyle?" Becky questioned him.

"This darlin, is the long arm of the law!" Kyle soberly replied. "It's a fifty caliber, bolt action sniper rifle, with a bipod up front. It fires ammunition used in B-17 bomber machine guns, back in World War II. The cartridges are huge. This weapon has a muzzle break on the end of the barrel, to reduce the monstrous recoil. It has a five shot box magazine plus a scope. With this weapon, I can accurately hit a target a mile away. At least I'll have something to practice with. There are all kinds of ammunition to get me started. They included a powerful spotting scope too."

Becky didn't reply as her face showed how much she disliked this entire situation. She figured to keep her comments to herself for now.

Becky looked out the windows at the fading pink sunset becoming twilight and stifled a yawn. She turned to Kyle, "I'm going to bed, sweetheart. I can't keep my eyes open any longer."

Kyle looked at her, "I'll be up in a little while. I'm going to rework this rifle."

Becky was amazed, "But it's brand new, Kyle! It *isn't* broken."

Kyle looked up tolerantly, "Yes love, it's new, but I need to file some of the rough edges smooth. Then I need to learn this tool, inside and out. That's what marksman do."

Becky's eyes flared as she brushed Kyle a kiss goodnight. She purposely pounded her way up the stairs. Laverne met her on the second floor hallway.

Laverne whispered to Becky, "Boys and their toys."

Becky was a fuming, "I'll give boys their toys!" Then she seethed, "He's got a new toy *right here*, and she'd like her bed warmed by her man *thank*-you, *very* much!"

Laverne squeezed Becky's hand. As they turned into their respective rooms, Laverne said, "As soon as we can, Harold and I'll move out to the bunkhouse. I know how it is wanting to howl at the moon with in-laws across the hall. I always hated having to be quiet when I didn't want to. I don't want to inhibit you with a couple of old fogies close by. I'm hopin we'll be sewin diapers come spring."

Becky blushed and gave Laverne a wave, "Last I heard, it takes two to tango," she grumped.

Laverne straightened, "Want me to go down an knock that galoot upside his head? My Harold can be dumb like that every once in awhile. I just give him a good slap, that rattles his eyeballs. That usually clears away his cobwebs. He gets right attentive after that," she winked.

Becky looked angrily down the stairs, "I'll take a rain-check on your offer Laverne. I see I can learn a lot from you," she winked. "G'nite," and turned into her room, slamming her door.

Laverne tiptoed into her room and quietly closed the door. Harold was taking off his shirt. "I heard a door slam. Is everything ok?"

Laverne calmly sat at her dressing table. She started

combing her hair. "The newly weds are having a tiff and Becky was tellin her new husband, she's *not happy* with him." Laverne looked at Harold, "She's just setting limits, Harold. Don't fret."

Harold opened the door, then looked back at his wife, "I forgot to brush my teeth. Do you think it's safe to venture into *the war zone*?"

Laverne's shoulders slumped. She stared wide-eyed at her husband of thirty-seven years. She didn't say a word, but thought, *'Men!'*

Harold had seen 'that look', before. It usually meant he was going to sleep alone on the couch if he didn't watch his step. He didn't say another word. He did what he needed to do, then quickly climbed into bed, and turned off the light.

Chapter 4

Dawn broke with a kaleidoscope of colors filling the eastern sky and gradually illuminated Snowy's old bedroom. Becky's eyes slowly opened and she realized that her man wasn't in bed with her. Kyle was sliding into his jeans and then sat down in the plush arm chair near the door and pulled on his boots.

Becky rolled over pulling the covers up to her neck. "Did you get any sleep last night?" she asked worriedly.

Kyle sighed, "A little. Not more than a half hour at a time. Same as usual." He looked at her softly, "You're relaxing me, honey, but it's taking time. I'm sorry I made you angry with me last night. I didn't mean to do that."

Becky pushed back the pillow, keeping the covers defensively below her chin. "I was, and still am, angry that you ignored me over that darn rifle, Kyle."

He looked around, at a loss for words. "Becky, I'm not sure what I've gotten us into. This is really bigger than I can handle alone. I'm not used to talking and dealing with women. The rifle - I know."

"That's a little of what I'm afraid of, Kyle!" Becky confessed. "I don't want you going back to your old, violent life! We're married now. Laverne is talking to me about wanting us to have a baby. She's offered to help me with it. This new life is exactly what I've always dreamed of. I don't want to take any chances on losing you now," she choked back a sob.

Kyle sat back in the soft reading chair. He was taking in

her words. 'A baby?' he thought. 'He hadn't ever thought about children. It'd be great to have a son to go hunting and fishing with, or a little girl, with her mother's nose.' His eyes twinkled with excitement. 'This part of the country would be perfect for a boy to grow up in. However, a girl, she'd want something more civilized. We could buy a townhouse in Denver, close to shopping and the University. Either way, it'd work out fine.'

Becky studied her husband. She wasn't used to his moods or looks yet, but she was learning.

"Look, Kyle," she offered, "Why don't you go and do what you need to do with that rifle. I've got some chores around here. When I'm finished, I'll come find you, unless you are finished before I'm done. Either way, we'll meet up, ok?"

Kyle slid into his shirt and sat on the side of the bed as he buttoned it up. "That sounds fine. I'm sorry about being jumpy and ignoring you last night." He leaned down and kissed his goddess, "I was confused. I knew I couldn't sleep very long, and I wanted to smooth out the action on the new weapon. I might need it to protect us.

"Kyle, with your post traumatic stress disorder, do you need to see a doctor? I read there are medicines that can help. You can either make an appointment with the veterans' administration clinic, or we can get a private doctor," she suggested. "I don't want to live my life like this, where you can't sleep with me. Think about seeing a doctor, please?" she urged.

Kyle leaned down and kissed her, "Ok, I'll think about it." He then got up to go downstairs. He started to open the door, but stopped and turned. "I'll be out at the range with Harold if you need me."

"Thanks, darling. At least I know where you'll be," she smiled. "I can follow the sound of the *big boom*, right?"

"Right," Kyle managed, smiling somewhat weakly as he closed the bedroom door behind him. He had a lot to think about. He always thought best between shots at the rifle range.

Laverne was clearing away the breakfast dishes when Becky

entered the kitchen. The men had had a fast meal of venison steaks and eggs. They quickly gathered their equipment, walking out to what was becoming Kyle's rifle range.

"Did your argument end well dear, or is it still smoldering?" Laverne asked at her tiny companion. "Can I get you something to eat?"

Becky absent-mindedly looked up at Laverne, "Just coffee will be fine."

Laverne brought a cup of steaming coffee to Becky. She sat down with her new friend. This looked serious, "Are you alright, dear?"

"I'm still learning about Kyle," Becky explained, "He came from a simple background. I came from the big city. We were raised very differently."

Becky stirred in three teaspoonfuls of sugar as Laverne's eyes widened. Then Becky briskly sloshed in some milk as she continued her story.

"Kyle can't sleep more than a half hour at a time," Becky said. "If he does, he relives the last two days with his squad, when they were all killed."

Laverne gasped and put a hand to her mouth, "Oh Lordy! I never dreamed, but surely this can happen with combat vets. I've heard the old women in my day, talking about their men coming home from World War II. Then there were the Viet Nam vet's wives of my time." Laverne shook her head, "Mercy, we've got our work cut out for us, darlin. Will Kyle see a doctor about that?"

Becky shrugged, "I asked him that this morning. He's thinking about it."

Laverne put a motherly hand on Becky's arm, "I'm so sorry, sugar. I had no idea."

Becky finished her coffee and shook off her mood. She looked at Laverne, "Do you have a telephone? A land-line?"

Laverne gestured towards the resident model Ma-Bell, circa 1963, "Thar, she be."

Becky gasped, "Laverne, that phone needs to be in a museum!"

Laverne shrugged, "That's all I got, sugaplum. Take it or leave it."

Undaunted, Becky rose to the challenge. She assumed the duties of Mistress of the House. "Do you have a phone book of The Springs and did you make the list of groceries for me?" Becky asked Laverne.

"Got it all right here, Becky. I'm ready for you," Laverne beamed.

Becky took the sheets of paper from Laverne, scanned it, and then added a few items of her own. Laverne gave Becky the old tattered phone book from the kitchen drawer.

Becky immediately turned to the pages in yellow. She laughed, "I'm not sure if I should call a restaurant supply store or a grocery store. Some of the quantities are staggering. I never bought fifty pound bags of flour or sugar before!"

Laverne looked lovingly at her young friend. "Welcome to ranch country, darlin. Out here, the skies are huge and so are our men's' appetites. We don't have a store just down the street. These old farm houses have pull-out bins in their large pantries that hold fifty pounds of flour and sugar. We use flour every day to make our bread, not to mention on the weekends. Then we might spice life up and make Johnny Bread or Bear Claws."

Laverne said, "Reminds me, Becky. The way your man likes Italian bread, you better get me another fifty pound sack of bread flour and another sack of all purpose flour. We don't want to run out. If the winter comes early and the passes close, it can be two or three months between trips to the food store. I've seen that happen a time or two."

Becky held up her credit card, "I've got my plastic. I'm ready to do battle."

The telephone wouldn't reach to the kitchen table so Laverne brought Becky a small desk to put the phone on. There was enough space to write and place the phone book as well."

Becky worked efficiently as she called the restaurant store that had a meat department. She chose the deal that threw in a new freezer with the purchase of a full steer, various cuts of chicken, and several whole turkeys. Next came the executive purchasing service. They'd to go to the grocery store and buy the smaller items that they needed. Next, she scheduled a delivery group to bring the grocery store items out to them. The restaurant supply store had it's own delivery truck complete with a refrigerated section in it.

Becky learned that regular gasoline went into the large fuel tank by the barn. She called an oil company and they agreed to come out and fill the tank with regular plus drop off a 250 gallon tank to be filled with high-octane gasoline for the GTO. On a whim, she asked if the company provided aviation fuel? The secretary assured Becky her company was a full service firm and could provide whatever she needed.

Becky stood alone in the kitchen checking her to do list when Cathy spoke, "How's it going, Beck?"

Becky was a little startled when her old friend made her presence known. "You surprised me, Cathy, but it's always good to hear from you."

Cathy announced softly, "I've been concerned. You've been worried of late. I didn't want to butt in, but I wanted you to know, I'm still with you."

Becky blinked, "I'm glad you're still here. It's always comforting to have a good friend close by." She hesitated.

"What's the matter?" Cathy asked. "You're troubled and I feel your fear."

"It's Kyle, Cathy. He has PTSD and he can't sleep. He needs to see a doctor, so he can rest," Becky confided.

A blast sounded from the field outback and Laverne returned into the kitchen. Cathy whispered, "We'll talk about this again," and she faded away.

Out in the field, Kyle was sighting in the 50 cal. Harold was spotting for him like Owl used to do.

Laverne asked Becky, "Do you have any more calls to make?"

Becky answered, "Nope, I'm finished for now."

Laverne took Becky's arm and walked out the back door. Both women shielded their ears from each loud blast when Kyle fired. They walked up on the two men.

"Harold," Laverne announced, "I need your help in the house. Can you come back with me?"

Becky saw Laverne's eyes, motioning her to Kyle. "Kyle," Laverne interjected, "Can Becky help you with the spotting? Do you mind, Becky?"

She answered, "I don't mind. It's just I never did this before."

Kyle looked at Laverne, not being totally dense, "Sure. It isn't hard."

Harold had been sitting on a picnic table that he and Kyle moved over to the rifle range. Kyle was laying on a rug that covered the ground. The good-sized 50 caliber rifle was resting on the two legs of the bipod that spread out from the body of the rifle. Kyle gave Becky a pair of ear protectors.

Harold eyed Laverne knowing she was getting him out of the way so the couple could talk alone. He got up switching places with Becky. "Okay woman, show me what you need me to do fer ya," Harold said. Laverne put her arm through his and the two walked back to the farmhouse.

Becky looked around, "Where is your target now?"

Kyle pointed at a distant hill, "I moved the target over there. This rifle has a farther reach."

"I didn't think a rifle could shoot that far," she blurted out.

"This gun is a big step up from my 30 caliber sniper rifle I used when I first met you," Kyle explained. "Look through the spotting scope. You should be able to see the target pretty clearly."

Becky put her eye to the scope. Suddenly she could see the man-sized target way in the distance. She stopped for a moment.

Kyle stood and gently encircled his goddess in his arms, picking her up completely off the bench and turned her so they were eye to eye. Becky toyed with her man's lips, making a little girl face.

Kyle sighed. Looking at her sweet face and feeling her in his arms, he knew he loved her completely. He had to tell her, "I've been thinking about seeing a doctor about my condition. The reason I haven't, is because if I take medicine, my medical clearance to fly will be canceled." He paused and kissed her lips tenderly. "I've wanted to fly for the longest time," he confessed. "Now that we have the money so I can fly any kind of plane I want, I have to take medicine to sleep, and then can't fly! Great choice, eh? It's just frustrating." He added without hesitation, "but I want YOU _more_, _than_ I want to fly."

Becky now understood his hesitation about seeing a doctor. Also, she realized the importance of his decision. He was turning away from a passion, to preserve his love for her. Her heart melted and she hugged him as hard as she could. She made a mental note to work on the problem.

She played with Kyle's big ears as she nibbled on his neck. "I've been a busy girl this morning," she said as she softly rubbed her face against his cheek. "I ordered our groceries and they'll be delivered late today. I called for regular gasoline and arranged to have a 250 gallon tank of high-octane fuel for the GTO delivered. The fuel company said that they could supply us with jet fuel A, A-1, JP-4, or aviation gas. Whatever we need."

She looked confused, "What's the difference between them all?

Kyle smiled, "Jet fuel A, jet fuel A-1 are civilian versions of a kerosene based fuel gas-turbine-engines burn, like to fly helicopters. The difference between the two civilian jet fuels is the temperature at which they freeze.

Becky smilingly blinked, "OK. I guess that makes a difference or _What-Ever_," she waggled her body.

Kyle laughed. He was appreciating this little lady *and* her huge sense of humor.

"Well, IF we were flying in our twin, gas-turbine engine helicopter, at 15,000 feet over Colorado in winter, it gets *pretty cold* that high up. I wouldn't want you to experience a fast drop and a sudden stop, if our gas line froze."

Becky sobered. She saw why Kyle was concerned with the details.

Kyle softened, "*What* did I do, to be blessed with such a beautiful and intelligent woman such as yourself?" he said as he squeezed her to him.

When Becky got her air back, she whispered, "Right question, *Buster!*" She didn't need to see the smile on his face. She knew *she* was the one who put it there. She felt proud of her work, too!

Becky felt her teasing was having the effect on her husband she'd hoped for, as she hung plastered against his body. He held her prisoner in his massively muscular arms. She wiggled and giggled as they talked.

Kyle looked at her surprised, "Rebecca Allison. Don't you be startin somethin that you're not going to finish…."

With a twinkle in her eye, she pushed back so she could see her man's face. She looked directly into his eyes, "Kyle Ibsen, *I…don't* start *anything* I'm not gonna finish. Can we leave this stuff here and come back out after lunch?"

Kyle turned toward the house, still carrying his little lady in his arms. Walking through the kitchen toward the stairs, Kyle looked at Laverne, who was sitting at the table with an open-mouthed Harold. "Laverne, can we have lunch, say in an hour?"

Laverne winked at Kyle, "You two take your time. I'll keep the lunch warm while *you and she* make up."

Becky hid her face in Kyle's chest. Laverne caught Becky's impish smile, as The Monster from the Black Lagoon, carried her upstairs. She had some things she wanted to say to her man. She wasn't *about* to be denied.

Later, Becky and Kyle walked into the kitchen. Their lunch had been kept warm in the oven. There was a note on the table. "Harold and I are in the bunk house. See you two at supper. Love, Laverne and Harold."

Becky sat at the table as Kyle served her. This was their arrangement. Kyle asked Becky, "Do you mind going out to the mine again? I've a feeling that someone was watching us, the last time we were there."

Becky was hesitant, "I know. The hairs on the back of my neck were standing up!" In a minute she answered her husband's questioning look.

"I'll go with you, but you *go armed*. I'm getting tired of being afraid on my own land. I want to start fighting back," she fumed.

"OK," was all Kyle answered, as he went upstairs for his pistol and 30 caliber rifle. Kyle saw the jeep keys hanging by the back door. He'd have to thank Harold for being so thoughtful. This way, Kyle wouldn't have to ask him every time he wanted the keys to the jeep.

Becky felt safer now that Kyle was armed as she got into the old CJ. Kyle purposely drove a meandering, unpredictable path to the granite cliff. This was in case they were being watched. He hid the jeep in the dense stand of pine trees.

Kyle led the way behind the waterfall and stepped into the mine entrance. There he lit the kerosene lantern as he walked deeper into the mine. They walked closer to where they'd seen the Neptune's fork on the right side of the tunnel. Kyle found an old pick leaning against the wall and grabbed it.

With the first strike into the rock that first appeared to be granite, the stone proved to be quartz, a different kind of rock in composition. Immediately, Kyle saw a small bit of gold color!

Becky heard Cathy in her head, "Ned says that he looked for the gold all his life, but could never find it," she explained. "He said that after he died, he could look through the rock as if looking through glass. Then he could see the gold behind the surface of mine wall. Just to let you know, the Mother Lode is where he told you. There's got to be a ton of gold in there, he says."

Becky stood with Kyle, but her eye was drawn to the pendant around his neck. "Kyle, the medallion is really glowing," she told him.

Kyle picked up the medallion from around his neck and tapped it to see why it was glowing.

Instantly, both Kyle and Becky heard a footsteps behind them in the darkened mine shaft. The hairs on the back of Kyle's neck stood up.

"Snowy? Is that you?" a soft, voice called out.

Kyle whipped around, facing the sound and brushing Becky behind him for protection. He also drew his pistol in the smooth action of a trained professional. Becky peeked around her husband's side. She was rooted to the spot in terror.

"Who goes there? Kyle demanded.

The footsteps instantly stopped. "I detect that you're not Snowy. I see there is a new player in our game. What is your name, stranger?" the mysterious voice questioned in an *educated* British accent.

"I'm Kyle Swoboda, and this lady is my wife, Becky," Kyle answered.

"Where is Snowy and why do you have his pendant?" the voice asked.

Kyle explained, "I was in the Marines with Snowy. He lost this medallion in the desert, the day before he was killed in combat."

The stranger walked out of the darkness and stood within five feet of Kyle. He sadly looked down after hearing the news. Kyle and Becky heard the stranger almost whisper, "What a waste…" Then he looked up, almost as if to say, "Life must go on."

The man in the mountain, looked human. It was almost like encountering a stranger on the street. He didn't look much different than any other person. He stood about five feet four inches tall, weighing near 115 pounds, had translucent bluish skin, with bright blue eyes. He had the slight body frame of a woman, but looked like a male, since he didn't have much of a chest. His hair was thin and sparse, old looking, but with a young looking face.

"Please put your weapon away," the stranger urged. "You have nothing to fear from me. You may call me, Adam."

Kyle stood gawking, "Whoahhh," he breathed. He usually took things at face value, but unsure, he looked at Becky. "Am I seeing this, *or*, is this one of my paranoid dreams?"

Becky crossed her arms over her abundant chest nervously, "He appears real, *or* I'm in the same strange dream with you, Kyle," she answered stiffly.

Adam straightened, smiling tolerantly. "I have this effect on people," he joked. He added softly, "That's why I've stayed hidden, for *many* years.

Becky gravitated to Kyle's side. She hugged Kyle's arm for security, looking at Adam.

"Are you from around here?" she smiled. Becky tried to be pleasant and not make the small man feel uncomfortable.

Adam viewed Becky and smiled back, "You can say, *I'm not* a local."

Kyle stood his ground, but wasn't aggressive. He tried to understand what was going on. "You have an English accent. That's unusual for around here."

Adam looked up at Kyle, almost as if to study him. "Awhile back," Adam said, "I met an Englishman. He stayed with me for *some time*. He helped me understand many things of the world. He was from Oxford, I think."

Becky couldn't help herself, "So you live in this mountain? By yourself?"

Adam's bluish eyes, looked at Becky, as he answered, "Pretty much."

"Kyle and I were in this mine the other day and encountered something strange. It was hard to see, but looked round with tuffs of hair growing out of it's body!"

Adam smiled, "That's my mifflin, my pet. She's what you might consider a dog, but please don't touch her! Her skin is very acidic and she moves through rock like we walk through air."

Becky was amazed, "I've never heard of such a creature. I read the complete encyclopedia. I've a photographic memory. I don't recall any mention of a mifflin here on earth."

Adam's eyes were kind, "Becky, Kyle, do you think you're the only beings the Creator made? The universe *is vast*." Adam let his statement sink in. "Please be assured there are many different life forms on this planet, beyond humans and plants. They are, what you call paranormal. There are spirits, black shadows, and shape shifters just to name a few. They are usually very hard to see and you need to be looking *for them*. People tend to see only other humans. They don't recognize subtle images, that don't look familiar. Humans seem to overlook a lot. There are also interdimentional planes," Adam offered. "To see within these areas, one needs to be specially educated."

Kyle and Becky were stunned speechless. They tried to grasp the meaning of what Adam just said. They wondered, 'Is this possible? Could other life forms live here on earth without humans being aware of it? They were intelligent enough to *not ignore* that possibility.

Becky and Kyle had identical thoughts. 'It is astounding to meet someone not of this planet, but, Adam wasn't threatening in any way, not in appearance or speech.'

There was a silence as Adam considered the couple. Kyle and Becky looked at him, likewise. It was as if Adam could read their minds. Adam relaxed.

"I see you are new to this area," Adam said to the couple.

Becky explained conversationally, "Yes, we just bought the Walter's ranch. They were falling onto hard times."

Adam looked at both new comers. "That was very kind of you." He seemed to see something in Kyle, "You seem to have an interest in gold mines?"

Very openly, Kyle admitted, "Yes. Old places and history *intrigue me.* Also, gold is a way of gaining wealth, of making a living."

Adam noted his statement. Then his attention was drawn to Becky, who seemed to have lost some of her fear.

"And you Becky, what are your interests?" Adam asked.

Becky hesitated for a minute, looking up at Kyle, but then back to Adam. "I like numbers and business. I like to find inventions that can help people and then market the ideas."

Adam eyed her, "Then we have something in common. I want to help people, too."

"How?" Becky asked.

"Let me explain," Adam said, "I am a Professor of Anthropology at a university. My passion is human history. I see a parallel between your culture and mine." He sighed, "I want to help people. I've learned things that can elevate their lives and their quality of life. I see how things can be better, but I have a problem."

Kyle looked at Adam, "Which is?"

Adam shrugged, "My appearance puts people off. I am searching for one or two people I can work with. To act as my agent, between myself and others."

Becky offered, "You mean like a liaison?"

Adam shifted his weight, "In a way, but I want to give of myself to your people. At the same time, I don't seek attention. I want to start a foundation that will help people, to feed them, to make their lives here on earth more pleasant. Also, I want to try to change practices that are harmful to the earth and society."

Kyle looked a little confused, but Becky tried to read between the lines. "You want to start a philanthropic foundation? To help people?" she asked Adam.

Adam looked at Becky, "Yes, that puts my idea into words."

Becky looked uncomfortable as Kyle viewed his wife. Adam looked confused, "I don't understand. Is there a problem?"

Kyle smiled, "Even I know something like that takes *a ton* of money. Helping people doesn't come cheap," he gave his opinion to Adam. "Even millions of dollars would just be a drop in the bucket, to feed people. It would probably take billions maybe trillions of dollars, to elevate the quality of life, of poor people around the world. It's an unfortunate fact, but poor people today, don't just live in third world countries. There are plenty of starving and homeless people right here in America, for example."

Becky raised her eyebrows, "He's right. Helping people is an expensive proposition. The way this country is today, with all the regulations and control, bringing even a simple idea to market is costly. It's getting that life is so complicated, I think the only solution would be, *alien intervention*," Becky said with a smile. Emotionally, she waved her hands, looking at Kyle, "I'd first wipe out all the bureaucrats and War-Lords of the world. *They* hold up progress!"

Adam jerked, "E-Gad, that statement is blunt, but astute, my dear."

Becky cringed a little, "Sorry, I can be blunt at times. It's just that I get emotional about helping people. *It isn't* a game *to me.*"

Adam looked at Kyle, "And what about you, sir? Do you have other interests than gold minds, flying, and mechanical things?" he said with a smile.

Kyle looked stunned. He was like a deer fixed by a headlight.

"I was a farmer before I joined the Marines. That's one reason we bought this ranch. I want to try farming or ranching, while I pursue my gold mining interest. This area is rich in gold and other precious things."

Adam nodded, "Yes, I've explored this area and farther out, thoroughly. You are correct in that this country is rich in natural, valuable resources. I estimate the value of hidden treasures, to be staggering."

Adam looked at Kyle, "What crop do you want to raise?"

"Land around here is pretty arid" Kyle admitted. "There isn't much water and the winters are long. People here abouts, raise cattle."

Adam put his hands on his hips as he thought to himself. Then he looked at Kyle, "Why do people raise cattle?"

Kyle looked surprised, but explained, "We eat meat for protein."

"But there are crops that are a source of protein. Plants don't harm the land with toxins. Plants participate in photosynthesis, to help oxygenate the air and take carbon dioxide, a pollutant, out of the atmosphere," he explained.

Both Becky and Kyle could see Adam was amazingly intelligent. Becky viewed him with keen interest. His ideas appeared brilliant. They were out of the box. Kyle rose to the challenge as he and Adam began a staccato conversion.

Kyle started off, "Crops suck the nutrients from the land."

"Crop rotation cures that, without the need for fertilizer," Adam countered.

Kyle frowned, "People are meat-eaters. We like the taste and texture of it."

Adam jerked, laughing, "A throw-back to your caveman days?"

"I'm not partial to tofu, soy burgers, and such," Kyle confessed. "People like to eat: bread, meat, and potatoes. That's when we're happy."

Adam brightened, "A problem I see with poor people, is that they're diet mainly consists of carbohydrates. This makes them fat, slow moving, with impaired intelligence. If we fed poor people inexpensive, easy to grow *protein*, we could reverse that." Adam tilted his head as a thought occurred to him. "If someone was sluggish and stupid, do you think their population could be easily controlled?"

Kyle and Becky looked at Adam. Is there was a master plan here?

Adam smiled, "What if I could give you two plants? One, a grain plant that will grow in arid soil, taking water from the air, at dusk and dawn to grow, and is perennial. It was originally intended for the arid desert of the Andes mountains in Peru. That area has a dense fog in the morning and at night. That's the only water the plant would get. It will give you three cuttings a season: spring, summer, and fall. The grain is protein and not carbohydrate. It can be ground into flour to make protein bread or any other product you make with corn-like flour."

This possibility grabbed both Kyle and Becky. It was too good to be true.

"The second plant grows in swampy soil, similar to what rice is grown in." Adam explained, "Plant two grows perennially as well. You plant it once and forget it. Just pick the fruits. The pods grow on their own each year. The fruit or pod is about the size of a chicken breast or a New York strip steak. It is protein as well, no carbohydrates. The pods can be flavored to taste like different meats, and are fibrous. The pulp of the pod has the texture of flesh."

"I'd say there are no plants like that in the world," Kyle smiled confidently.

Adam smiled in return, "And I thought you were a history buff. What if I told you there were plants that were offered to the Inca, Aztec, and Mayan Indians, that did what I've described?"

"Why hasn't anyone made a bundle of money from this? Those ideas are perfect in so many different ways," Kyle exhaled.

Adam squinted his eyes, "I told you I was an Anthropologist. Those two plants were offered to these early people, to feed their civilizations. There is written evidence of these plants on their temple walls. Alas, these Indians were more interested in corn. They turned away from these foods and then these plants disappeared as did these old cultures. And you know the old saying?"

Kyle recited, "History will repeat itself?"

Adam looked at Kyle with new interest. Becky wouldn't be taken lightly either.

"Helping people is a lofty idea, but we don't have enough money to invest, not yet at least," she explained.

Adam grinned, "I like that last part, Becky. And what if I told you I had a donation to start our project? The first installment of funds?"

Becky chucked, "I'm all ears, Adam," she stated confidently. She was loosing her initial fear of the little man. Maybe it was his small size that was making the difference or his calming tone of voice.

Adam motioned to Kyle, "Follow me please," as he led the way just beyond the circle of light.

Becky looked nervously at Kyle. The lantern rested on the floor of the mine tunnel near her feet.

Kyle looked at Becky, "Stay right there. I'll keep you in sight. Don't worry."

Becky blinked. She felt growing apprehension in her body.

Kyle moved into the darkness several feet and reached where Adam directed him to look down. Kyle touched three, fair sized burlap bags. Each bag weighted about twenty pounds.

Adam pointed to one bag, "Please give that one to Becky. Kyle, the other two bags are for you."

Becky's fear disappeared as she saw Kyle walk back to her. He handed her one of the burlap sacks. She heard the sound of tiny crystals rubbing against each other as she took the bag from Kyle. She untied the string at the top and dipped in and then pulled her hand out. She gawked at what she saw.

"Are these, what I think *they are*?" Becky gasped.

Adam shrugged, "They are perfectly cut diamonds. My English friend was quite agog over them, I must say. They are of *little* value to me. Rather, they are more of a nuisance than a blessing. I have rooms full of those bags. I search for a rock called Formalite. Formalite puts off a sonic vibration that is food for my soul. The diamonds are primary, occurring in volcanic funnels, and surround my Formalite deposits, *like warts* on a beauty." Adam stated with distaste.

Kyle exclaimed calmly, "I've heard some people believe the vibrations from rocks have healing properties. You say, the formalite is a food for you?"

Adam didn't say anything more. He just nodded.

Becky was bewildered, "There are only five or six cities in the world that specialize in cutting diamonds. You have a huge bag of what you say are perfectly cut diamonds worth millions, possibly a billion dollars?"

Adam corrected, "I have bags of those stones. They are *worthless* to me. If we could use these stones to help the people of the world, I'd be very happy."

"But who cut the stones? The best diamond cutters are in Amsterdam," Becky pressed.

Adam was tolerant, "I have a tool that cuts the Formalite for me. It needs to be calibrated. Once tuned, this tool precisely cuts my precious Formalite, to give perfect light reflection and vibration. I use the diamonds to calibrate this tool. It is similar to you using a knife sharpener to sharpen your kitchen knives."

Adam looked at Kyle, "The bag with the blue tie hold seeds for the grain plant. The bag with the red tie is seeds for the pod plant. My English friend told me about patents. I'd suggest you patent the seeds, so they can be protected. It will assure that the people of the world, will benefit from these gifts."

Adam looked at the couple, "Will you help me in my efforts?"

Becky bubbled with enthusiasm. "Oh Kyle, *I'd love* to do something like this! To make a positive difference in the world."

"It would be a complete switch to my former way of dealing with people," Kyle chuckled.

Becky looked at her watch, "Oh! We'd better be getting back."

Adam agreed, "Yes, your supplies will be arriving shortly, Becky."

Kyle and Becky looked at Adam, "If you ever need to contact me, please feel free to do so. Simply come to the mine as you did and tap the medallion three times. The vibration will beckon me to your side. If you can't come to the mine, then only at night, I can come to you. Sunlight is very uncomfortable for me."

Adam shook Kyle and Becky's hands. They noticed his skin was cool, almost as cold as the surrounding rock. Also, when they touched, surprisingly, the hair on the back of their arms raised, as if caused by a static electrical field. Becky had the feeling Adam was *marking them* somehow.

Adam looked at his new friends, "I look forward to a long and fruitful association. To answer your question, please feel free to compensate yourselves for your cooperation. I sense I can trust you two. I just ask that you primarily use the money to help poor people. It's like being on the Honor System."

Becky smiled, "We can do that. I understand what you're saying."

Adam winked at Kyle, "I'm gonna like working with this girl."

Kyle shook Adam's hand one last time, "She is my life, the air I breathe," he confessed.

Adam solemnly nodded, "I understand your sentiments, sir. I look forward to working with you and your wife."

Adam walked the couple to the entrance of the mine. After waving good bye, he merely drifted back into the darkness, shying away from the sunlight."

Kyle helped Becky back into the Jeep. He rounded the car and got in himself and started the engine.

"Can you believe all this?" Becky gasped excitedly.

Kyle shook his head once, "It's hard to believe, but that monstrous bag of diamonds isn't a joke! Neither are those sacks of seeds."

"We need to get the diamonds to the bank in Freeport. But, how can we get them there, without going through commercial airliners?" Becky wondered.

She saw the twinkle in Kyle's eyes, "*No!* I'm not letting you build another Screaming Eagle to fly us to Freeport. It's too far! We'll have to come into the new millennium and find a modern way of transportation. She looked at Kyle, "I know a person who could help us!"

Chapter 5

Becky asked Kyle, "Do you mind if we call Siegfried Henkle at the Swiss bank? Maybe he can give us an idea how we can get to him."

Kyle drove the old jeep to the crest of a hill and pulled out a cigar. As he lit the expensive stogie he shrugged, "Be my guest. You're better on the phone than I am. I'll just sit here quietly and enjoy the scenery."

Kyle looked at Becky, "Will Siegfried help us? Do Swiss banks extend varied services to their established clients who have large bank accounts?

Becky was confident, "Sure they do. Just as businessmen extend varied services to good customers in order to increase the customer's business."

She picked up the satellite cell phone and called Siegfried's private number. In a minute, her call was answered, "Hello Siegfried, Becky Swoboda here. Yes, everything's fine, but I need your help. Do you know of a private jet charter company that could pick my husband and I up in Denver, Colorado? We want to make *another* deposit. *Yes*, we think it will be worth your time!"

Becky listened then laughed. "Yes, we are fortunate in locating valuable resources. We need to be able to come to the bank without a lot of red-tape, if you know what I mean? Yes, that's right. I don't want to get bogged down in customs at the airport." She smiled, "No, Siegfried, we still aren't doing anything illegal. Kyle and I are just unusual people, but from your bank's perspective, we are still profitable.

She looked around the beautiful countryside. The smell of sage permeated the air. "I'm glad you know a charter company. We need your protection until we reach your bank. Can you have them send a helicopter to our ranch? We're about five miles northeast of Granite Bluff, Colorado, just west of Colorado Springs.

Kyle sat forward, "Can you tell Siegfried I want to get checked out in a HJH-65 Dolphine helicopter?" His eyes twinkled, "I've had my eye on that bird for some time now. Also, I need to get licensed to fly a medium-sized business jet." He smiled, as he took a puff on his cigar. He was starting to enjoy the benefits of having money!

Becky spoke into the phone, "I want a flight instructor onboard who could help my husband transition into not only a HJH-65 dolphine helicopter, but also get some flight time in a medium-sized biz jet. We plan to start traveling around frequently. Oh, you think you can? That would be lovely! Can you also reserve our suite at the yacht club? Yes, the room overlooking the dock on the beach. Maybe we should lease that room," she said, half laughingly, half serious. "You have my phone number where I can be reached." She went on, "I'll await your call. We'd like to be picked up here at the ranch at 10 am and leave from the Denver airport at noon. Many thanks, Siegfried." Then she signed off.

Kyle put the 3 bags in a backpack that he had on the rear seat of the jeep. He pulled the CJ around the back of the farmhouse and jumped out to help Becky. They took the backpack inside and went up to Snowy's room.

As soon as Becky walked into the room, she looked at the desk and then at Kyle and whispered, "I could hide the diamonds in the secret compartment where I found Snowy's journal. Sound good?"

Kyle straightened, "Seems like a great place to me. Great thinking, hon."

Just then the phone rang and Becky answered it. "Hello

Siegfried. Great!" she answered looking at Kyle. He'd laid down on the bed looking at her. "The dolphine helicopter will pick us up here at the ranch at 10 am. The biz jet will be waiting for us at the corporate terminal at Denver's airport, at noon."

Kyle nodded at her questioning look, "Sounds perfect. Let's do it."

"Ok, Siegfried," Becky spoke into the phone. "The package we're bringing this time, is the shape of a medium sized jewelry box." She paused, listening, "Wonderful, you have a way to by-pass customs at least initially? This way, we'll get to the bank without exposure to outside eyes. What we're depositing isn't illegal, just unusual. Oh, I forgot. Can you have a gemologist with you tomorrow night when we get to Freeport?" She nodded, "That would be grand. Look forward to seeing you tomorrow night. Thanks for all of your help, Siegfried. We really appreciate this. We think you'll be pleased too. G'bye."

Kyle smiled up as Becky walked around the edge of bed to place the phone on the desk. She shrieked as he grabbed her and tossed her over his body to lay beside him. "I'm a starting something...*okay?*" he laughed.

"As long as you finish what you start, *I'm happy*," Becky purred back.

AWHILE LATER, BECKY AND KYLE came down the stairs and went into the kitchen. Laverne appeared as if out of nowhere. She looked at Becky's rosy cheeks.

"Worked up an appetite, did we?" she teased with a broad smile.

Becky didn't say a word to her older friend. She just blushed, shyly.

Kyle was looking in the pots left warm on the stove. "What's for lunch, Laverne? I could eat an elk, I'm so hungry."

Laverne pushed Kyle to sit near his precious. She put a pot

of hearty Irish stew on the table. He took out a round loaf of freshly baked bread from the oven.

"Eat up you two, Laverne ordered. "I want you both to keep up your strength," she teased, as she winked at Becky. "I'm going over to the bunkhouse with Harold. We're getting that place cleaned up."

Kyle offered the pot to Becky, who put a ladle's worth on her plate. She passed on the bread, "I've got to watch my figure, Kyle. Now that I've got what I want, I don't want to lose you to some young thing, because I let myself go," she smiled cautiously.

Kyle raised his eyebrows, not commenting. He took four scoops of stew and a hearty chunk of bread. Becky poured each of them a cup of cowboy coffee. She took one sip and whispered to Kyle. "Laverne says she make's her coffee strong enough to put hair on my chest. I'm gonna water this down by half," she wrinkled her nose.

When the couple finished their meal, Kyle got up to take care of some business. This left Becky alone in the kitchen.

Cathy whispered to Becky, "I *heard* about a doctor visiting Denver, from Germany. He's experimenting with metaphysical acupressure. He's staying at the airport hotel. Call there. I think you can get an appointment with him, before you board the jet tomorrow. He's evidently able to treat PTSD without using medications. Give it a try, hon…"

Becky called out thanks to Cathy, but didn't hesitate. She dialed the hotel room immediately. "Hello, I'm Mrs. Swoboda and I'd like to make an appointment with the doctor to see my husband tomorrow at 11 am at the airport? My husband has PTSD and he's not able to sleep, but it's essential that he doesn't take medications, since he is on flight status. Would the doctor be able to help my husband?" There was a pause. Then Becky hesitated, "Oh doctor! I'm so sorry to intrude, but my husband's suffering terribly and can't sleep." Another pause, "That would be wonderful, doctor. I appreciate your time."

Kyle came back into the kitchen, "Who were you talking to, hon?"

Becky looked hopefully at Kyle, "I found a doctor who's staying at the Denver airport hotel. He's experimenting with acupressure to treat PTSD. He thinks he can help you, without you having to take medicine!"

"Wow, hon, that'd be great if it'd work," he sighed. "I can't remember the last time I had a decent night's sleep."

Becky was relieved. "I was worried you'd think me too bossy. I made an appointment for you tomorrow morning at 11 am. That's before we get on the jet to Freeport. The helicopter will pick us up here at 10 am," she explained.

"I'll try anything to treat this problem. Especially if I won't lose my flight status," Kyle told her. "Thanks for thinking of me! You're very thoughtful."

Kyle kissed her. "No love, I don't feel threatened by you being helpful. I'm comfortable with my masculinity. You're a great help to me. We seem to compliment each other in our abilities. I like that. It seems like you have everything covered. I'm a lucky man to have you with me."

A loud engine interrupted them as Becky ran to the front window. Laverne and Harold heard the sound too and came to see what was happening. It was the restaurant supply truck!

Becky ran out front and joined Laverne. Then she walked over to the driver and his assistants. "I want the freezer to go in the house, in the pantry. Mrs. Walters will show you where she wants it. Then you can stock it with the frozen items. After that, she'll tell you where the dry goods go."

Things were starting to jump at the ranch, but Becky was comfortable and in her element. Two other trucks arrived coming up the front drive. "Kyle," Becky gasped. "That's the fuel tanker and a truck with the other gasoline tank. Can you show them where they need to go?"

Kyle smiled, "Sure, no problem."

Laverne was clapping her hands together and dancing a jig. "Oh, Becky! This is like Christmas in the summertime. I can't remember when the pantry was last full. I don't know how to thank you two."

Becky hugged her older friend. "We're all helping each other. That's what families do."

As the restaurant supply truck turned around in the drive, now empty of its cargo, it headed out the dusty road and onto the highway. Waiting its turn to come into the lane, a panel van lumbered up to the house.

Laverne shouted, "Another truck? Good heavens, Becky, what are *they* bringing?"

Becky spoke quietly, "The regular groceries, like TP and other smaller items. The executive service went to the supermarket for us. You can show them where to drop off the packages."

"You've thought of everything!" Laverne said honestly. "Bless you for the TP. We were getting low and I was startin ta worry."

"Do you think we can have steaks for dinner tonight, Laverne? With baked potatoes and sour cream?" Becky asked.

"If we have it, I'll cook whatever you want, darlin," Laverne smiled.

The tanker and flatbed truck rumbled by the house having made their deliveries by the barn. Kyle walked up to Becky at a saunter.

"Are you expecting any more deliveries, hon?" he asked.

She grinned, "I think we've gotten it all now."

"Can we get back to the rifle range? I need you to spot for me," he said.

"Sure darling. I just want to get a glass of iced tea," she replied.

Expectantly, Kyle asked, "In all those supplies, did you happened to get a supply of Dr. Peper or any orange soda?"

Becky smiled, "I'll grab a bottle of the Dr. for you, when I get my tea."

"I'm going to fill up the jeep with fuel. I think it was running on fumes. That gasoline got here just in time. Thanks for taking care of all these things for us," he said thankfully as he bear-hugged her.

After giving his darling a substantial kiss, he gently put her down and climbed into the jeep. Then he drove off towards the barn and the gas pump.

After that, Kyle drove the jeep up to the back porch as Becky stepped out under the stoop with a glass of tea and a bottle of pop in her hand. Kyle reached out and unscrewed the top. He downed the whole bottle in one *long* pull.

Becky looked amazed at her giant. Calmly, she asked, "Would you like to take another bottle of Dr. with us?"

Kyle gave her his innocent look. She laughed and turned back into the kitchen. Laverne was standing in the doorway.

She held out a bottle, "I told you darlin, our men out here have large appetites and thirsts." She laughed, "Don't be surprised if he waters the plants out there. Country men are prone to do that," she giggled. "Grown males are like little boys, but men shoulder the weight of responsibility. This country separates the men from the boys mighty quick. Especially, when the temperature drops to minus ten degrees on a cold winter's night. Then life gets serious, *real quick*."

Becky thanked Laverne for both the pop and the western lecture. Then she stepped into the jeep. Kyle had thoughtfully pointed the CJ at the house with the passenger side close to the back stoop.

The afternoon passed delightfully as Kyle got used to the new rifle. He shot burgundy-tip tracer ammunition. It was surreal for Becky to see the flight of the bullet, streaking out to the target, almost a mile away.

Kyle took the cartridges from the metal box that came with the rifle. The ammunition was separated into different compartments. She saw that Kyle took out bullets with different colored tips.

"What do the colors on the bullets mean, Kyle?" she asked.

Kyle took out a black-tipped cartridge, "The colors tell us what the bullet will do. This black tipped bullet is armor piercing. The silver-tip is an armor piercing incendiary. The red/silver tipped one is an armor piercing, incendiary, tracer. The burgundy tipped is a tracer alone."

Kyle sat up and lit a cigar. He was pleased that Becky was interested in his life.

"Guys in the armory can link different bullet combinations together in what we call an ammo belt. That is for a machine gun, for example." He paused, "A usual mix is one tracer bullet in every five cartridges. More tracers than that ratio can burn out your gun barrel, real quick."

Becky sat down and looked at the bullets as she frowned. Kyle instantly saw she was troubled. This wasn't Becky's usual mood.

"What's wrong, hon?" he questioned.

Becky shrugged, "It's kind of you to explain all this information about the bullets. I have to say, I'm sad our society has gotten so involved in war. I think it's a huge waste of resources and energy," she frowned. "That's just my opinion. Maybe I'm in the minority," she shrugged. Then she brightened, "I'd rather try feeding people." She confessed, "I want to see if there isn't a way of bridging our differences somehow, without resorting to violence. There's so much hatred in the world."

Kyle puffed on his cigar and examined the glowing tip. "You know I like flying and mechanics, but another passion of mine is history."

Becky leaned closer, "I heard you mention it. Tell me more.

He shrugged, "One of the last things my mom made me do, before she was killed in the accident, was to read a biography of Thomas Jefferson. He was one of the early U.S.

presidents. That's how I got interested in history." He thought then shared with her, "Did you know President Eisenhower, in his farewell address, warned Americans against letting the military-industrial complex dominate our society and lead us away from peaceful, civilian endeavors?"

"Wow," she admitted, "I didn't know that! Isn't that what's happened?"

Kyle raised his eyebrows, "Yep, pretty much. We've shipped our manufacturing jobs overseas. Most research and development today is military related. I think our leaders have made a wrong turn somewhere. Of course, a few are getting their pockets lined, while the average Joe is pinching pennies." Kyle shrugged, "That's just my opinion. That and sixty-nine cents will buy you a cup of coffee."

Becky looked into the distance, seeing where cattle used to graze, "With our new foundation, I'd love to develop those plants Adam gave us. We can come up with a plentiful protein other than animal. We could help the ranchers move into a different kind of agriculture, without losing their livelihood or the way of life they love. If it's profitable for them and easier, I think they'll get onboard." She looked at Kyle, "That's the same with any company. If we can show people a cheaper, easier way of doing things, that's green, that's more profitable, they'll convert their factory without losing any jobs. To me, that would be the ideal situation."

Kyle pointed out, "You know, our country has tried for years to feed the poor in the world. Somewhere along the line, some greedy War-Lord diverts or controls the flow of food to the starving." Thinking in a different direction, he sighed, "I'm not sure how to solve the hatred coming from religious differences as that's a really serious issue. People are being killed over the different names of God. That's sad! I agree with you, hon. I wish the people of the world could move into a calmer way of life. To focus on caring for each other, rather than trying to control each other."

Becky nodded. That would be lovely. A more caring way of life.

Kyle finished his cigar. "Wow, that was a long discussion, but I like talking about current events."

Becky looked at Kyle, "Laverne wants me to think about having a baby. I have to admit, I'm afraid of bringing a child into the world filled with hatred and death. I want to give him or her a better future than that," she confessed.

Kyle nodded and kissed his wife tenderly, "I agree. Although Teddy Roosevelt said, 'Walk softly, but carry a big stick.'"

Becky slapped Kyle's arm, "I'll Big Stick you!"

Kyle stuck his tongue out at her, in mock protest. Then he laid down and took a few more shots. Becky learned to work with Kyle to adjust his shots, so that he was getting an eight inch group, at a mile away. She was amazed that Kyle was just happy, but not satisfied with his grouping.

"I need to get a three shot group into a five inch circle at a mile, to be effective," he told her.

Becky didn't say a word. She just mouthed, OK, and left it at that.

Kyle drove the jeep close to the house, so they could unload the equipment. Then he parked it in the old weathered barn. Kyle appeared at the back door. Laverne shouted over her shoulder, "Go wash up, Kyle. The steaks are about ready. How do you like your's cooked?" she asked.

"Well done with some charcoal on it, if possible," Kyle answered.

Becky already told her she liked her steak medium rare. Harold and she liked their beef, medium. Four happy, but tried campers, ate their dinner quietly. Everyone turned in early with full bellies. Laverne even had time to bake an apple pie for desert. She felt rich with a full larder and fully stocked freezer. With Harold by her side, life didn't get much better than this.

Kyle had excused himself and skipped desert. Laverne looked at Becky, who shrugged as if to say, 'I don't know…'

After dinner, Becky went upstairs to Snowy's old room. Laverne and Harold wearily made their way up to their bedroom down the hall. The bunkhouse wasn't ready to move into yet.

Dusk was turning into night as Kyle walked into the room. He came over to Becky, putting his hands over her eyes.

"I have a surprise," he said softly with a big smile on his face.

Becky let Kyle lead her out onto the balcony. '*That's* why Kyle skipped desert!' she thought

Kyle presented an old, upholstered love seat, he'd found in the storage area of the barn. He'd hoisted it up to the second-story balcony with a rope. He swept his arm out and said, "A little something for you to lounge upon."

"Oh, Kyle. How *thoughtful*. I love it." Becky sat on the soft cushions and looked up at the night sky. "The stars are beautiful out here. We're so far from civilization. It's like being in a planetarium."

"I thought so. I wanted us to see them together."

Becky got up to change for bed. Kyle waited for her to get into her night gown. She came back to her Monster who remained sitting on the sofa. She sat on his lap facing him as she drifted off to sleep. It wasn't ideal, but at least he was with her, when she fell asleep. It'd been a long and busy day. Within minutes, she was breathing softly with Kyle's heartbeat in her ear.

Chapter 6

When Becky's eyes opened, the room was bathed in the soft glow of dawn. Kyle, still fully dressed in old jeans, a white t shirt and white athletic socks sat in the comfortable armchair by the window. She smelled the rich restaurant grade coffee that wafted from his steaming, oversized cup.

"Did you get any sleep last night, darling?" she asked her husband. She held her head up in her hand, making a triangle out of her head and her arm. She'd kept her chestnut brown hair short, chin-length in a kind of a bob style that she could easily pin up in burettes.

Kyle took a sip of coffee and looked at his petite bride, "I got some, here and there. Pretty much the same as usual. Even so, I enjoyed watching you sleep. Your breathing is so gentle and delicate, so much like you," he said with a gleam in his eye.

"Wwwhat?" she hesitated. She was getting more used to him and his humor. It was so quirky. Mostly, males think about lusty musings, she knew.

He blushed. He was shy to confess his inner thoughts.

"Kyle, what?" she urged. "Don't tell me I drooled."

He laughed. Mistake number one!

She glared at him ferociously. Then a look of panic overtook her, "Oh my God. I'll kill myself, if you tell me I snore!"

Kyle blinked, "No darling, you look like an angel when you sleep."

"*Kyle Ibsen*, tell me what you were smiling at, when you watched me sleep," Becky demanded.

Kyle held up his hands defensively, "I was just watching your…chest, rise and fall with your breathing, while you sleep. They look like gentle waves. Your body is so…interesting," he smiled reflectively.

She was off and running, "Well, you like these pillows so much, I'll strap them *on you*, and see how you feel!" she fumed. "You wanna talk about psychotic? I'd *kill*, to have a night sleep on my tummy."

Kyle blinked again, "Whoa there darlin, calm now."

Becky put a hand to her head and mentally tried to calm herself down. "Sorry Kyle," she sobbed, "I get really cranky, about this time…"

Kyle concerned look softened. "All I wanted to tell you, honey, is you've made me very happy that you married me. I know I'm a super lucky guy for you to have allowed me into your life. I wanted to say I love you more than I can express. I'm not really good with words."

"Ahhhhhhh," she gasped, "that's so sweet to wake up to, Kyle." She got out of bed in her white-cotton, floral-print, thigh length nightie. She walked barefoot over to sit on the soft arm of the upholstered chair. She was getting used to her husband. Now that she wasn't intimidated by his size. 'I can look him right in the eye when he *crushes me* to his *massive, muscular chest*,' she thought. With an impish grin, she stole his coffee cup from his hands and daintily sipped the coffee, sugar and cream. The couple eyed each other as Becky sipped the steaming brew. A set of petite blue eyes blinked in innocence. The huge set of ice-cold blue eyes scanned her completely head to toe. The little one wasn't afraid anymore. She was completely at ease now, with her Monster.

The coffee reminded Becky of Blanche, of Miami, of Café con Leche and of Little Cuba. She thought of how far she'd come and how much she'd gained in leaving her gilded prison, almost a year ago. She'd gambled her life, to gain much. The cherry on top was her Monster from the Everglades Swamp.

She felt a massive hand touch her soft, golden thigh, as she smiled into the huge coffee cup. Like a little boy with a toy, Kyle's hand was creeping upward. Her eyes sparkled with life.

"Kyllle," she stifled her giggle, "Don't you be startin somethin you aren't going to finish," she warned.

Kyle gently took the coffee cup from his goddess. He picked her up in his massive arms and carried her over, alongside their bed. Gently he put her down. She carefully removed her gown and scurried between the covers.

She watched as her giant, her beast, with muscular limbs and triangular torso unveiled his treasures. He first removed his shirt, then his socks. Next he looked down at her as he unbuttoned his trousers. She feasted her eyes. She thought, 'I wonder if he knows how much I like seeing him do this?,' she giggled. Her laughter was cut short as her beast rounded the bed to his side and slipped beneath the sheets. Then he reconnoitered, as he sought out his prey.

She yipped, "You've got cold hands, cowboy!" she complained.

Kyle smiled and looked into her sparkling blue eyes, "Then warm my hands my love. My heart beats only, *for thee*."

She shrieked, "*Yep*, that'll do it!" as she climbed on top of him. Smiling a sultry smile she said with a husky voice, "You know how to push my buttons."

Kyle arched his right eyebrow as he nipped at her lower lip. He was gentle not to bruise his treasure, but firm enough for her to know she was being taken. He laid a kiss on her that made her toes curl.

When he finally let her take a breath, she screamed, "Yeehaa," and cowgirled up.

Down the hallway, Harold was holding Laverne tenderly in his arms. They quietly laid in their bed, savoring the peace and quiet, of early dawn. Both jumped when they heard Becky yell.

Harold said, "You thinkin what I'm thinkin?" he laughed, disbelieving what he heard.

Laverne gently kissed Harold a soft good morning kiss, "Never you mind, *Mister*. I'm thinking I'd better get breakfast cooking. The kid's will be down shortly, and I want to keep up their strength. I'm countin on a full bassinet come summer. I'm startin ta knit a white blanket with a pink border."

Harold pushed himself up, leaning back against a pillow as Laverne crawled out of their bed. "Now don't you get your hopes up, gal. They can't promise a little one. Heck, we don't even know if they're tryin or not."

Laverne stopped dressing and laid her fists to her hips, her bra still in her hand. "Sure I don't know if they're tryin, BUT they're sure *practicing* a lot!" she giggled.

Harold feasted his eyes. He'd seen this girl at age six, then at fifteen. He married her when she was sixteen. Now that she was fifty-four, she still looked *mighty fine* to him. He couldn't help himself, "Why don't you come a little closer darlin, and give me your lecture," he grinned.

"Oh *you!* You *old horny toad*," Laverne gasped with exasperation. "You still haven't learned how to romance a girl and after thirty-seven years of tryin! I've about given up…"

Harold got the hint. He climbed out of bed in his long-underwear bottoms, with bare feet and chest. He early-morning soft-footed over to his frustrated wife. He noticed, she hadn't moved.

He carefully pushed back her graying-black, long hair, and kissed her lips. Gazing softly into her eyes, "Do we have to get up yet? I'd love to hold you in my arms a little longer. The smell of your hair with your head against my chest is ambrosia to me," he smiled, softly rubbing her back.

Laverne thought for a minute, then started dressing again. "Not bad bucko! You're on the right tract, but your timing isn't right yet," she admitted. Then a glowing smile spread across her face, "The kids will be gone after 10 am. After that, if you're still interested in a little slap and tickle, come back. Then tell me how much you like the smell of my hair." She winked and finished dressing. Then she hurried downstairs to get breakfast started.

Harold angrily snapped his finger mumbling, "Almost, but *no cigar.*"

Becky and Kyle walked into the kitchen as Laverne was making fresh coffee, "Oh, Becky, this Bund coffee maker and three pots is *wonderful*. I would've never thought to order food through a restaurant supply store. The coffee maker, with the packets of coffee can make two pots of coffee, and pot of hot water for tea as fast as I can pour water into the reservoir." As an after thought, she added, "The coffee is a might weak, for my taste, I've gotta say."

Unfazed, Becky walked over and poured a cup, blew on it to cool it a might and sipped it, sighing. "Laverne, the rest of the world is more used to coffee *this strength*. But, for you hearty pioneer types, just put two packets in the basket. That way you can make it stronger." Becky joked, "Just put a skull and cross bones for the universal poison sign on that pot. Then I'll know the coffee is for you and Harold."

Laverne ignored her taunt and looked wide-eyed at Becky, "Why didn't I think of that? Oh dear, you're *so smart*." Without missing a beat Laverne looked at her adopted son, "And what will Kyle have for breakfast?" Laverne paused, then added, looking at the young newlyweds, with smiling eyes and a raised eyebrow. "Did we sleep well last night?" she questioned.

Becky looked away embarrassed. Kyle blushed, but he was a typical man.

"Well enough, thank you," he replied. Now that he was satisfied, he was hungry. "Can I have six eggs, bacon, toast, orange juice, and do we have any venison steak left?"

Becky blinked at Kyle, who sheepishly admitted, "We'll, *I'm hungry*," he confessed, grinning at his goddess.

This time it was Becky, who blushed. '*Men*,' she thought.

Kyle went into the bathroom to wash his hands. Becky looked at Laverne concerned, "I hope we didn't disturb you," she said hesitantly.

Laverne wiped her hands on her apron. "That's what I like. A young strappin man workin up an appetite before he goes out into the fields. Does my heart good," she glowed. She added, "Leaves his lady whistling all day until he can come home again. Then, he puts another smile on her face, later that night."

Becky stared at Laverne in stunned disbelief. She was surprised at Laverne's openness. She thought it might be because Laverne was a farm girl, living her life so close to nature. What caught Becky's attention was that Laverne appeared to be a two time a day woman. 'No wonder Harold walks with a limp,' she laughed to herself, but noted Harold was always smiling. He doesn't complain one bit.

Laverne grinned, "We don't mind darlin," quickly adding, "but that's why I said, Harold and I'll move out into the bunkhouse, as soon as we can." As an after thought she couldn't resist, "Once you two got busy, it did sound like you were at a rodeo," she giggled. More seriously Laverne whispered, "but then again, with a big galoot like your hubby, he's gonna rattle the windows some, when he gets a'goin," she winked.

Becky rolled her eyes, putting her hand over her face in embarrassment. "Oh golly! Nothin like advertising to the neighbors, we're off to the races…"

Laverne looked sternly at her little friend, "Now *don't you* be ashamed of what you two were a'doin, girl. If every woman was ashamed of being with her husband, then the human race would come to *an end*," she said exasperated. "Makes me angry that society says women can't have fun too in a marriage. It ain't all just goin shoppin and spendin money, either! Girls have feelins, just the same as the guys, you know. We just don't advertise as much as they do. It makes me glad I live way out here, away from town-folk. I don't cotton to some of their Victorian ideas," she huffed.

The thought that Laverne needed to feed a hungry man crossed her mind, and she got busy. An aunt of her's once told her two rules for ranching women. "Don't bother a man when he's workin *and* have hot food on the table when a workin-man comes through the door."

Harold joined everyone for breakfast. Becky outlined the upcoming agenda.

She looked at Laverne, "You have our cell number?"

Laverne answered, "Yup, got it."

"The helicopter will pick us up here at ten am. We have a doctor's appointment at eleven. Then we meet the chartered jet at the Denver airport at noon. We'll be in the Caribbean, for awhile," she explained.

Laverne looked at Becky, "Don't you worry about a thing, darlin. Harold and I have been takin care of this ranch for many a year. We'll be fine and settled into the bunkhouse, by time you two get back home."

Kyle came back into the kitchen and took the chair at the head of the table. Becky sat to his right. Laverne's chair was to Kyle's left, and Harold faced him, at the other end of the table.

Kyle talked between bites of bacon and eggs, "I'm really excited about flying in that helicopter, Becky. I'd like you to take a close look and see if you're comfortable, riding in it." He shrugged, "The price tag is a little stunning, but I'd love to buy one, if you like it too. We could jump between here and Denver. With a pressurized cabin and a service ceiling altitude of 15,000 feet, we could pop over almost any mountain in the Rockies. If you felt like Mexican, we could easily fly to Santa Fe or Phoenix for dinner. And there're *all kinds* of shops in those towns."

"What kind of power is in those birds, Kyle?" Harold asked, being curious.

Becky sat back and knew that Harold had just dropped the dime in the juke box. Kyle was off and running.

Kyle started, "The HJH-65 is flown by the Coast Guard. It can be flown by one pilot, but it's best to have two. Becky, you're going to learn to be my copilot, and help me fly. It has a range of 300 comfortable miles, and its twin engine gas turbines drink JP-4, kerosene-like jet fuel. It has a 291 gallon fuel tank. Maximum airspeed is 165 knots or 184 mph, but the cruise speed is 120 knots. Rotor diameter is 39 feet. Empty mission weight is 6000 pounds. Maximum take off weight is 9000 pounds. To be on the safe side, you can haul home 2000 pounds or one ton of shopping bags, perfect for Becky" he laughed.

Becky was afraid, just a little mind you, at having to learn to fly along with Kyle. She remembered him teaching her how to drive the airboat. How free it made her feel. That Kyle accepted her as not only his wife, but as an intellectual equal, thrilled her. Being able to take the helicopter to go shopping, to a new restaurant, in a far-away city, she wavingly snapped her fingers, "You go, guy!"

Kyle explained he wanted both Becky and he to learn to fly a new class of corporate plane called the super medium jet, like the Citatium King. "It's supposed to carry eight to nine passengers. If we didn't carry that many people, we could convert their weight into available cargo capacity. The article said this jet had a cruise speed of 513 mph, its range was 3315 miles, and so the plane could fly coast to coast non-stop. Also, it can fly from continent to continent and can land in smaller airports. I want to check that plane out, when we can."

Becky finished her coffee and single poached egg, "Sounds fine with me. I have faith in you. I trust you with my life, Kyle."

Kyle winked, "I feel the same way with you, hon."

He knew their time was short so he finished his breakfast.

The young couple went upstairs to gather their things. They didn't have many clothes, only two bags. Becky knew they'd buy what they wanted in Freeport. The flying arrangements Kyle was talking about sounded great.

Becky thought. 'That helicopter would be great if they had to run to the super market in Colorado Springs, when the roads were snowed over. Ouuu, I have all sorts of plans for the helicopter. Now I just have to get Kyle helped with his PTSD without medicine, so he can sleep without fear. I'm not going to keep him around long if he can't rest,' she reminded herself.

Another issue came into Becky's head. She'd started taking birth control pills when they got married in Freeport. 'I wonder when I should stop taking them IF we want to try to have a family? I'll have to make a mental note to talk to Kyle soon. One thing he asked me *not* to do, was to give him *surprises*. When it comes to big decisions, our rule is to talk first *before* acting. *If* no talk, *no* action. That's our deal. Kyle talked to me about the helicopter and the jet. He's practicing one of our cardinal rules of our marriage. I can at least do the same and talk to him, *if* he'd thought about when he wanted a baby.'

Becky's thoughts were interrupted by Laverne calling up the stairs after the phone rang, "Becky! Kyle! That was the helicopter pilot," she hollered. "He said he's about fifteen minutes away. Are you two ready to go?"

Kyle walked into the room. Becky looked around one last time.

"Those two suit cases are what we're taking," she directed. "Can you take them downstairs, please?"

"No problem, hon," he answered. "I'm on it."

The almost imperceptible sound of the corporate helicopter setting down alongside the barn drew their attention. The pilot turned off the turbines as the rotors spooled down.

Becky kissed Laverne and Harold as Kyle carried the bags

to the chopper. The pilot was stowing the luggage when Becky ran up to look into the cargo hold.

"There's loads of space for packages and groceries," Becky announced, as Kyle helped her sit in the rear passenger seat. Becky couldn't miss the broad smile and twinkle in his eye, as Kyle climbed into the copilot's - right seat. He watched as the pilot primed the engines. They whined alive, as he toggled the starter switch. Once the engine gauges settled, the pilot engaged the rotor, which started spinning in ever increasing speed. In a second, the pilot lifted the small corporate helicopter off the ground. He dipped the nose slightly, for the rotor blades to bite into the air, and start their forward momentum.

Becky and Kyle waved to the older couple, who squinted their eyes against the rotor wash. Harold held onto his straw hat as the chopper took off, then disappeared over the horizon.

The pressurized cabin allowed for normal conversation as the pilot explained it'd take a half hour flight time to Denver. Kyle was looking around as the Rampart Range of the Rocky Mountains passed underneath to his right.

Becky leaned forward, talking to the pilot, "Can you drop us at the airport hotel? We have an appointment there at 11 am."

The young, ex-military pilot smiled, "Ma'am, I can put you down on a postage stamp if you want. The hotel at the airport has a heliport on the roof. That's a simple job for me."

Becky and Kyle enjoyed the short ride. At 190 mph, the 100 miles to Denver, as the crow flies, didn't take long.

At the hotel heliport, as soon as their bags were offloaded, a bellhop took charge of their luggage. Kyle kept the twenty pound bag in his backpack. Becky told the bellhop, "We have an appointment in suite 826. Can you take our bags there? We'll call when we've finished, and then we'll need a car to take us quickly to the corporate jet terminal at the airport."

She handed him a hundred dollar bill, "If you see to our needs, there's another two hundred in it for you."

The enterprising bellhop coolly answered, "Ma'am, you have my *undivided attention*. I'll see you get to your flight on time."

Satisfied she had their exit plan established, Becky and Kyle headed for the elevator that would take them from the roof to the eighth floor. Kyle looked uncomfortable but Becky rubbed his arm and said, "Relax darling, everything will work out. You'll see."

They reached room 826 where Becky smartly rapped on the door. A cute young receptionist answered and invited the couple inside.

Becky explained, "We're the Swoboda's. We have an 11 am appointment with Dr. Leonard Reinholz."

The receptionist ushered them into a private room with a plush seating area, announcing, "The doctor will be with you shortly."

Becky patted Kyle's arm, "Are you ok, darling?"

Kyle was stiff with anticipation, "I'm ok, but nervous. I'm excited about buying one of those Dolphine helicopters. What did you think about the ride?"

Becky smiled, "Don't you worry, Kyle. I've got one of those Dolphine's on our To Buy - Short List. That's the *only* way to travel."

The far door opened and an elderly gentleman with silvered hair entered. He was dressed in an immaculate, charcoal-gray double breasted business suit with cuffed trousers and rich, dark-brown wing-tipped shoes. He approached them. "Mr. and Mrs. Svoboda?" he asked, with a High German accent.

Kyle leaned over to Becky whispering, "In German, the W in Swoboda is pronounced as a V."

Kyle stood up, but Becky remained seated. "That's us." Kyle answered.

"I'm Dr. Reinholz," he said as he shook Kyle's and then Becky's hand. Motioning to a soft upholstered chair without arms, "Sit here please, Mr. Svoboda." The doctor pulled up a chair looking at the couple.

"Why don't you tell me what brought you here today?" the doctor asked Kyle. Kyle was having trouble finding the right words and looked to Becky for help.

Becky nodded at Kyle and explained, "My husband was in the Operation Desert Storm and all of his sniper team were killed, except himself. He can't sleep longer than twenty minutes at a time. If he does, he dreams the last two days with his men, which ended in their deaths. He needs to rest, *but*, he doesn't want to take medicine. He's a pilot, the culmination of a life-long dream."

Dr. Reinholz leaned back in his chair as he stroked his chin, looking at Kyle. It wasn't that he was looking at him, but rather, looking *into him*.

"I've been born with a *rare gift*," Dr. Reinholz explained to the couple. "That you are suffering from post traumatic stress disorder is apparent. Treatment with medication is routine and very successful. Your stipulation of treatment without drugs has brought you to me?"

Becky nervously shook her head, yes. The concern in her eyes was evident to the doctor.

Looking at Kyle, "Do you seek treatment, Mr. Svoboda?"

Kyle looked straight into the doctor's eyes, "Yes I do, please."

"May I touch your neck, Mr. Svoboda?" Dr. Reinholz asked.

Kyle shifted in his seat, relaxing, "Be my guest."

Dr. Reinholz came around the chair and placed both thumbs on Kyle's spine, at the base of his head. The doctor took a slow, deep breath and then exhaled as he closed his eyes, concentrating.

The doctor winced as if in pain, then quickly opened his eyes and shook his hands earthward, as if air-drying wet fingers. "Mr. Svoboda, how do you feel?"

Kyle answered, "I felt as if you put your fingers into my brain and massaged a part of it. I feel a little light headed, but relaxed."

Dr. Reinholz returned and sat down in front of the couple. "My gift, is to mentally put my hands in people and surgically do what is needed, *without* cutting into them," he explained. "My methods are unconventional, but I am guided by intelligence of a higher order," he explained. Then he became aware of his surroundings and added to Kyle and Becky, "Of course, you realize this impromptu appointment will not cure you. I estimate that you can now sleep at least four hours, without being tormented by your retched nightmare."

Becky blinked, "Oh, that would be *wonderful*, doctor."

Kyle was like he was waking from anesthesia, still a little groggy. He was glad that Becky was there to hear the instructions.

"Mr. Svoboda will need at least two more *full* appointments to be cured. I scooped out some of the evil in his brain, but touched nothing else. My oath as a healer prohibits me from altering my patient, beyond treating his ailment. In brief, Mr. Svoboda is as he was before he came through my door, except a little less of his bad dream. Do you understand, Mrs. Svoboda?"

Becky nodded, "How do we contact you for follow up appointments, doctor?

Dr. Reinholz stood. The Svoboda's reacted and stood also. The receptionist appeared, ready to escort them out.

The doctor motioned to his assistant, "Marjorie will give you a cell number where I can be reached. You understand, that I travel the world. For further treatment, you will need to travel to where I am." He paused, "I should have helped your husband a little." He smiled a gentle smile, "but from the feel of his brain, I can remove that nightmare with more time. Now I am exhausted and must leave you. Wiedersehen," he said as he walked away without saying more.

Marjorie took the couple to her desk. She pushed the bill to Becky. Becky pushed a card back to her with a number written on it, "That is our Swiss bank account."

Marjorie was efficient and typed the number into her computer. Instantly, the approved notice appeared. She next gave Becky a card with the doctor's cell number typed on it.

Becky explained, "We are traveling now, but when we can, I'll arrange for the other two appointments."

Marjorie nodded, "We'll await your call then. Please have a pleasant day and a safe trip."

The Swoboda's turned and left the suite. As soon as Becky and Kyle opened the door, the bellhop came to attention. He had their two suit cases on a luggage dolly. The young man had been waiting for them.

"There's a car downstairs that will take you to the airport corporate terminal, Ma'am," he explained. "Are you ready to go?"

Becky looked at the time, 11:45, "Yes, we have fifteen minutes to make our way to the terminal."

The bellhop called for the express elevator and within five minutes their bags were in the limo. Becky handed two crisp one hundred dollar bills to the enterprising young man, "Thanks for your help."

The bellhop produced a card, handing it to Becky, "If you're ever at the Denver Hotel, please call me. My name is Jakob Swenson. My cell number is on the card. I'm happily here, to be of service, Ma'am."

Becky took the card and nodded. Within five minutes, they were standing in the corporate terminal of the airport, at the concierge desk.

Chapter 7

Kyle tipped the driver as Becky asked the concierge, "Is there a jet here from a Swiss bank in Freeport?" The dynamic young man, in a crisp dark-gray pin-strip suit, pointed to two pilots sitting against the wall. They're from Strata Airways. He waved the pilots over, "Are you looking for a couple going to Freeport?"

The lead pilot nodded, "Yes, a Mr. and Mrs. Swoboda?"

Kyle stepped in, "What's the name of the man who ordered your flight?"

The head pilot checked his manifest, "A Siegfried Henkle."

Kyle held out his hand, "Right answer. I'm Kyle Swoboda and this beautiful lady, is my wife Becky. A suit case and a B-4 flight bag are our luggage."

The second pilot reached for the bags, "I've got 'em. Let's get aboard so we can keep to our departure window."

The command pilot looked at Kyle, "I understand you want to log some flight time? Have you had any experience?

Kyle pulled out his wallet and showed the pilot his commercial pilot's license. The pilot examined the ticket and handed it back to Kyle.

"We'll let you get some flight time once we're out of the airport's traffic pattern. You'll be in the copilot's seat. Until then you can sit in the flight engineer's seat, to watch our pre-flight routine, and flight ops" the pilot offered.

Becky, Kyle, and the two pilots walked out to the gleaming

silver corporate jet. As they walked out to the aircraft, a ladder was lowered from the rear of the plane. A stewardess stood attentively at the head of the metal stairs.

As Becky climbed into the multi-million dollar aircraft, she was amazed by the expensively decorated interior. She saw that this wasn't the typical passenger airliner. The walls and rugs were a steel gray hue with beige leather seats worthy of a corporate CEO. The passenger compartment was arranged more like a living room. There was a seating area on the left side, with two pairs of wide, first-class seats that faced each other. It was designed so two couples could leisurely chat as they were whisked off to an exotic destination. A polished cider-maple table was between the four chairs. Becky could see from the hinges against the cabin wall, the table could be folded to allow the seats to recline. The stewardess's area, complete with small desk was aft, near the private lavatory. The right side of the passenger cabin had a reverse C-shaped soft leather sofa with an accompanying thin coffee table made of clear glass.

The hostess helped Becky seat herself. Becky chose to sit in the forward facing set of chairs, selecting the seat nearest the window. She was pleased to see from the chair, that she was forward of the plane's wing, giving her an unobstructed view. As she sat down, the whoosh of the seat emitted the rich aroma of carefully crafted leather. She felt the soft texture of the chair's arm as she snuggled back into her seat.

Kyle was talking to the lead pilot as they walked towards the cockpit. He stopped in the isle, close to Becky. "I'm interested in flying a Citatium King sometime."

The pilot nodded, "The Citatium is a beautiful plane. Our aircraft today isn't that different, but our bird can't set down on short-field airports like the Citatium can. We have the same range and also have the twin engines. You flying this aircraft, will be very similar to the one you're interested in.

When all four people were safely aboard, the rear door was

closed and locked. The lone stewardess took Kyle's jacket and offered Becky a drink. The pilot brought out an official looking bank box, complete with lock.

"Herr Henkle sent this box. He gave instructions for you to put whatever you want to deposit in the bank, in here. We'll close and lock the container in your presence. It will stay back here with you, Mrs. Swoboda, until we reach Freeport. There I'll hand it over to the limousine driver who will sign for it. The box will remain unopened until you reach the bank. Once there, Mr. Henkle will open this in the presence of a senior custom's official. The agent will then inspect its contents, in the privacy of the bank. Please don't seal any illegal substances inside. This would violate customs law and will subject you to prosecution. Do you both understand?"

Kyle and Becky answered, yes. The pilot opened the metal container. He and the stewardess turned their backs on Becky and Kyle. Kyle put the large bag of diamonds inside.

"Ok," Kyle told the pilot, once he closed the heavy lid.

The pilot and the stewardess turned around. The pilot locked the box with a special padlock.

Kyle put the box under Becky's feet for safe keeping. The lead pilot told Kyle to come forward to the cockpit when he wanted. Then the couple was left alone.

Kyle pressed his warm lips to Becky's, "Thanks, hon, for doing all these things for me. Will you mind sitting back here alone?"

Becky looked at her hubby, "I lived the first eighteen years of my life *alone*. I'm still trying to get used *to you*. I have to admit I'm becoming more attached to you more each day." She smiled, "I'll be fine. You go play with the pilots, dear."

Kyle walked forward into the cockpit. He sat in the flight engineer's seat, buckled himself in, and put on a headset with a boom-microphone. From there, he could easily see all flight activities. Kyle orientated himself so he could talk to the two pilots, but not interfere with any radio traffic outside the aircraft.

The pilots worked as a team, going through the preflight check-list, and warmed up the engines. Kyle could see that his experience in a single engine plane was similar, but primitive, in comparison to this sophisticated twin engine jet. He saw that he'd have to revise his plan to get flight qualified on this size of jet, which would take some time.

The pilot pushed the COM button on the handle of the control wheel. "Denver ground, Strata - November 642 Zulu, docked at the corporate terminal. I request permission to taxi and take off, for visual flight rules international flight from Denver to Freeport, over."

In a minute the pilot responded, "Rog ground. Take taxiway Delta 6 to light and hold. There I'll contact Denver Tower, for takeoff instructions. 642 Zulu over."

The lead pilot signaled the ground support team to disconnect the electric and com lines from the bottom of the plane and push the aircraft away from the terminal. The crew chief guided the pilot onto taxiway Delta 6 and waved them on, giving a final salute. The lead pilot returned the salute with a thumbs up also.

"Rog Denver ground. Strata - November 642 Zulu, VFR from Denver nonstop to Freeport. Estimated flight time is four hours and ten minutes, over," the lead pilot spoke into his headset boom mike.

The pilot stopped the aircraft at the end of taxiway Delta 6 red traffic light. He acknowledged, "Rog Denver ground. Contact Denver Tower at freq 956.02. Thanks for your help Denver ground. Have a great day, 642 Zulu out." The copilot tuned the radio frequency to 956.02 mh. The lead pilot called, "Denver Tower, Strata November 642 Zulu. Requesting permission to take off. Activate our nonstop flight plan from Denver to Freeport when airborne, over."

Everyone on the flight deck waited. The metropolitan airport was busy. All aircraft movement needed to be coordinated with the Denver control tower. This was for everyone's safety. A large 747 was landing. It would take a few minutes for the jet wash or air turbulence to dissipate from the active runway before they could take off.

"Rog, Denver tower. Strata November 642 Zulu. We have permission to take off runway Beta niner left. Will call when airborne, over."

The pilot looked both ways. Then he taxied the twin engine corporate jet onto the active runway, and he ordered, "Take-off power." Both pilots worked as a team, moving the throttles forward to full power.

The jet started to roll and gain speed. The copilot watched the airspeed indicator and called out to the lead pilot, "Take off speed."

The lead pilot ordered, "Rotate," and both pilots together pulled back on the control yoke. The nose of the aircraft responded to the pilots' control and rose, as the powerful jet engines thrust the aircraft skyward like a rocket.

"1500 feet," the copilot announced.

The lead pilot turned the jet into a gentle left climbing turn and called, "Denver tower, Strata November 642 Zulu, airborne, over."

In a minute, the pilot received the call he was waiting for, "Rog, Denver tower. Strata November 642 Zulu, climbing to 33,000 feet, dialing first omni and will squawk ident 1226. G'day Denver tower, 642 Zulu, out…"

Everyone in the cockpit relaxed a notch now that the aircraft was out of the controlled airspace. The copilot dialed in the first omni navigational radio beacon the aircraft would fly toward. For the next four hours, the pilots would be flying toward a series of radio navigation stations across the US, on their way to Freeport. The navigation stations are like following channel buoys, on rivers.

Kyle told the pilots he'd be back in a little while. Both pilots gave him a nod with a thumbs up which was the sign-language for OK.

Kyle walked back and sat beside Becky, "Wow, that was interesting. There's complete control on the airfield and in the air for ten miles all around it."

Becky looked at him, "Could you get used to flying a plane like this?"

Kyle thought, "I'll have to go to a flight school, to get instrument qualified, multi-engine prop, next jet, then multi-engine jet qualified."

Becky shook her head, "Sounds intimidating."

Kyle smiled, "I *love this*, hon. It's intricate, but exciting to me. It's like giving you a million dollars and telling you to go have fun in the stock market."

Becky nodded, "Ok, I can see what you're saying. It's complicated, intricate, definitely cerebral, but *extremely exciting*, gotcha."

"If someone is going to buy an airliner the size of this one," Kyle explained, "most aircraft manufacturers have their own flight school close by. It might mean that we'd have to travel to a location. We'd spend several months there attending flight school *before* I could take command of a jet like this. Would you mind traveling with me?" he asked.

"Heck no!" she answered. I love to see new places. We could live in a hotel close to the airport. It would be fun. Of course, hotels like that would have Internet connections, so I could take my office with me. I could check my stock market reports and keep in touch with my think-tank people. That's how I get tips on new markets. My team scans news programs and technical journals for promising technologies or inventions. I'll gather people for *my team*, whose passion is research, in a central location, like maybe in Denver. These people are a step away from a gamer. I guess you could call them *info teckies*."

Kyle kissed her, "I love how adventuresome you are, Becky. You're adaptable to changes and challenges ahead. I know I can pass all the tests. It'd just take some time to go through the schooling, the procedures, and the flight exams. Usually if a company is going to sell an aircraft this expensive, they try to make the education part as painless as possible. Then again, we'll have all sorts of choices and decisions as we select the features on our new airliner. So I want you close by. You'll be selecting the luxury options and décor for our aircraft."

Becky lit up, "Ooo that sounds *like fun*. I love to accessorize things. Of course, you'll have to make the decisions about the technical stuff. *Please* pick out a good navigation system *this time?* I'm not up for the - fly by the seat of your pants stuff. I believe in my creature comforts," she tossed and fluffed her hair.

Kyle canted his head, "I'd want to buy the helicopter first, and I'll need to get checked out in that also. I think there's a company near Fort Worth, Texas that sells both the helicopter and a sister plant, that constructs the Citatium King nearby. I could get qualified in both aircraft at the same time." Kyle grinned, "Fort Worth has *some great BBQ* places we could try."

Becky's head swiveled, he *had* her attention now. "Wow! That sounds like a great idea. If we're going to be living in that area for any length of time, maybe we should rent a condo? I don't know, maybe a suite at the airport hotel would be more convenient? We'd have a restaurant, room service, and maids right there. Now that's *my idea* of setting up house. I can contract a limo service to be at our beck and call. I'm familiar with that, from back in Chicago."

Becky interjected, "Kyle, I've been wanting to ask you something."

Kyle looked intently at his wife. She surely didn't ask him for much, "OK."

"I started the birth control pill when we got married. I'll have to stop taking the pill a month or two before we want to try to have a baby," she began. "I never got to ask you. What are your feelings about making a baby? When would you want to start trying, *if*, you like the idea of children?"

Kyle thought for a minute, "You mentioned Laverne was hinting about having a baby. I'm surprised, *but actually* I like that idea. I'd love to have a son to do all sorts of guy stuff together." He frowned, "But I wouldn't know what to do, if we had a girl first."

Becky relaxed, "Laverne says a baby girl or boy are about the same at first. One difference is when you take the diaper off a boy, you have to be careful."

Kyle looked wide-eyed, "*Careful?*"

Becky grinned impishly, "Laverne said when the air hits a boy baby down there and the diaper is moved away, he might try to play fireman and squirt you with his hose."

Kyle jerked, "*No-way.*"

Becky giggled, "Laverne says they're really tricky about it. It's a game he plays with mamma. No harm done. It's just nature. It's only water *and* the baby *is yours*. Laverne says that makes all the difference."

Becky grinned, "A boy would be wonderful, but girls aren't all that hard to get to know at first. It's their teenage years that can be difficult. Raging hormones and all the changes, can make some girls hard to talk to." She took a breath. "Let's not get ahead of ourselves and worry about problems that aren't here yet. I'm a firm believer, that sometimes we can think problems *on ourselves*. I want to think *positive*. That makes good things happen."

Kyle winked, "I knew you were a smart girl when I saw you in the swamp."

Becky laughed, "*No you didn't.* You told me I was a stupid city girl."

"That was because I was dazzled by your attire," Kyle whispered.

Becky slapped his arm, "Oh *you*. You told me I was just trouble, gift wrapped with a pretty brown bow! You told me highway 41, was *up that-a-way!*" She harrumphed, "Go fly the plane. I'd better take a nap." She looked through shrouded eyes, "I've a feeling today is going to be *a long one*."

"Not before you give me a kiss. I want to know that you're not mad at me," Kyle demanded softly.

Becky piercingly eyed her man, but then relented and offered her exaggerated pouted lips to her tormentor. She wasn't going to make it easy for him. He was *a beast*.

Kyle sucked on her lips and nibbled a bit as her eyes flashed open. For a minute, to tell her he wasn't afraid of her, he held the kiss. When he finished, he leaned forward gently and whispered so softly, "I'd love to make a baby with you. If you'd like, you can stop taking the pill. Please just tell me when you do."

Becky flung her arms around her Monster from the Black Lagoon, "I'm stopping *now*," she softly whispered.

Slowly drawing back, debonair Kyle, suavely nodded his head, "And tonight, I'll give you my undivided attention. You have been warned."

With a glean in her eye, she shot back, "*O-K.*"

Kyle looked deeply into Becky's blue eyes and didn't say anything else. He let her have *the last word*.

He gave her one more, gentle kiss on her lips, that bespoke his love for her. Then he walked back to the cockpit to sit with the pilots flying the airplane.

Becky's eyes gleamed and her grin was ear to ear. She took the eye-shields from the stewardess and drifted off to sleep. The descending aircraft woke her up. She looked out the window, seeing the vast blue of the Atlantic Ocean. Looking out the front window, Becky could see the Freeport airport.

In no time at all, the plane was on the ground. A limo was waiting to whisk them to the bank. Becky kept a close eye on the sealed box.

Once at the bank, a receptionist met the entourage at the door, "Yes may I be of assistance?" she inquired.

Becky explained, "We have an appointment with Herr Henkle. He's expecting us."

Becky, Kyle, and the limo diver, who carried the sealed

box, walked down the hall to Siegfried's office. The driver set the sealed box on the now familiar table. He explained their luggage would be taken to the yacht club. He instructed them to call, when their appointment was over, and a car would come round for them. He tipped his cap and left the office.

Siegfried was seated at his desk when they arrived. He stood as everyone came in. He walked around the desk, kissed Becky's hand and then shook Kyle's. He introduced Mr. James from the local custom service to the couple. Also, he presented Ms Elsa Moot, a certified gemologist, who had a long association with the bank.

"I was pleased to get your phone call, Becky. You and Kyle are the most inventive people I know, in acquiring wealth. There is such mystique surrounding your fortunes," he grinned.

Becky motioned with her hand, "Open the box and see what you think."

Siegfried produced a special key, unlocked the padlock and then opened the lid. He looked amazed, but confused by what he saw. "Is this a full sized ham?" he wondered aloud.

Becky reached in, pulled the bag from the box, and untied the string around the top of the bag. Looking around, she saw the desk blotter on Siegfried's desk and carefully poured a few crystals out on it.

"I *don't believe* these are *illegal*, Mr. James," Becky offered.

Mr. James produced an eyeglass from his pocket, examined one of the cut diamonds closely. Satisfied, he gently placed the crystal back on the desk. "No, *not illegal*, but presumably *very precious*." Mr. James looked at Siegfried, "I will leave this matter to you. What they carry isn't a custom's issue. I would say that I believe they are legal, since they were cut long ago, before laser identification was instituted. I assume you will follow International Law insuring there is *no Blood Diamond cash flow?*" With that, Mr. James shook Siegfried's hand and walked out.

Elsa was drawn to the bag of crystals like a moth to a flame. She took out an eyepiece and with excited hands placed it to her eye. She examined the rocks. "Oh mine Got!" she gasped. "Diamonds flawless, and exquisitely cut." She took away the eyepiece, "You know, there are only five cities where diamonds are cut. Each diamond cutter has *a style* that can be seen by the trained eye. I've *never seen* diamonds, so perfectly cut, so precisely virgin in my twenty-five years of experience," she exhaled. "Where…?" but she stopped herself.

Siegfried laughed, "Becky, Kyle, again you've surprised me! I'm glad I can tell my wife, delaying our dinner, was worth the effort." He looked at Elsa, "How much do you think the stones are worth?"

Elsa approximated, "A guess, I'd say half a billion dollars US."

That, made Siegfried gasp. Then he sat down and offered chairs to Becky and Kyle.

"There are two thoughts here, my friends," he began. "First, we have to spread the diamonds throughout the world. We must slowly trickle the gems onto the market, so we don't drop their value. Second, we have to be able to disprove the Blood Diamond test. *That is* verifying that the proceeds from the sale of these diamonds won't go to finance genocide, ethnic cleansing, or war in general. Finally, the bank will require a brokerage fee to coordinate all these activities."

Becky grinned and sat forward. She *loved* this part of the financial game, *the negotiations*. "What are the amounts of all these expenses?"

Siegfried rubbed the side of his chin, "The bank would need two million dollars US, for brokerage and gemology services."

Becky was thinking a mile a minute, "Let us come back and see you tomorrow after we've had a night to sleep. This is too big a decision to make when we're tired. Will you secure these for us carefully, Siegfried?"

"But of course," Siegfried cringed. "How stupid of me Becky, Kyle. You both must be exhausted from your journey. I'll have the limo take you both to the yacht club. I'll call you tomorrow, say tenish?"

Becky stood up taking Kyle's arm, "I'm exhausted Siegfried. Until tomorrow."

The hostess walked them to the front of the bank where a limo awaited. Once moving toward the club, Becky told the driver she'd like to be connected to the yacht club's front desk. The driver handed her the phone.

"Hello, front desk? This is Mrs. Swoboda. What room are we in?" She waited, "Oh that's wonderful. Would you please transfer me to room service?"

Becky looked at Kyle, "What would you like for dinner?"

"A double lobster tail, baked potato with sour cream, green salad with iced tea. For desert, I'd like blueberry pie and milk," he answered pleased with himself.

Becky relayed Kyle's order and then explained she wanted a porterhouse steak, medium rare, mashed potatoes, green salad, iced tea, and chocolate mousse for desert."

Shortly, they were in their rooms. Having food in their stomachs revived them somewhat.

Becky looked at Kyle, "I think we don't have enough money to do all the things Adam wants us to do! Of course, half a billion is a lot of money, but not nearly enough to do *major philanthropic work*. I wish we could talk to him, to hear what he thought."

Kyle looked around and then smiled, "Do you want me to call him?"

Becky remembered if Kyle tapped the medallion, Adam said he would come. She looked at Kyle, "You can try but we're so far away."

Kyle walked around the room, closed all the blinds, and turned off all the lights but one. Then he took out his medallion and tapped it three times.

They stood expectantly not knowing if Adam would come. Just as they figured they were not close enough, there was a knock at their door. Kyle shrugged at Becky and went to open the portal. Adam stood in the hallway, "Is there a problem?" he asked.

Kyle smiled at Adam and ushered him in. Becky offered the small man a chair. "We weren't sure you could come so quickly," Kyle said.

"Distance is in the mind. You are only a thought away," Adam explained. "What do you need from me?" he asked as he settled himself in the soft chair.

Kyle seated Becky and then himself across from Adam.

Becky wasn't bashful, "Adam, we took the diamonds to our bank and they said the bag was worth a lot of money. The stones would need to be trickled onto the market to not deflate their value and not crash the gem market.

Adam nodded, "OK, *and what* does that mean to *a stranger*, my dear?"

Becky explained, "What I was thinking about, was more like a billion dollars to start our charity work. I need to pay for intellectual groups to form and to start a school so Dr. Reinholz can teach his new medical techniques to others. I need money to invest in turning deserts into fertile fields, planting, cultivating, and harvesting the YP-684 grain plus YP-685, pod crops. I want to really make an impact on world hunger! That's not to mention finding jobs for people!"

Adam listened intently, "I'm honored you've embraced my project so seriously, Becky. Clearly, you've given my idea considerable thought. How many more diamonds would you need to accumulate the wealth you estimate we'll need? Your ideas sound wonderful."

"Becky started doing calculations in her head that would fry a computer. She looked distraught.

Adam sat back in the chair, "Becky, Kyle. I *have bags* of these stones, but there are also other sources of income, I haven't mentioned yet. That first bag of diamonds was really a test, to see how you'd handle this tempting challenge. I'm pleased with your efforts and my trust in you two has been confirmed."

Becky sat forward. Kyle looked at Adam closely.

"I have other uses for some of the diamonds. They make wonderful lasers that can do all sorts of interesting projects," Adam explained. "How's this idea? What say I get you another bag of cut diamonds, the same size as the other one?"

Becky asked, "Can you get them here to us, tonight?"

Adam thought, "I can do that."

Kyle quizzically asked, "You can get a twenty pound bag of diamonds, from Colorado to Freeport, *tonight?*"

Adam blinked, "Yes."

Kyle couldn't let it go, "How can you do that?"

Adam looked around the room, "I have my ways," he smiled then stood. "I must be going now. I need my beauty sleep, cherro," and he walked out of the suite's door which closed behind him.

Kyle jumped up and looked outside the door. Adam had vanished.

Chapter 8

Somewhere during the middle of the night, Becky woke up. On her way to the bathroom, she noticed a large canvas bag sitting on the coffee table. The second miracle she saw was Kyle asleep in the arm chair. She looked at the clock and noted that four hours had passed since she'd gone to bed.

Kyle stirred as she neared, "Oh wow. I must've drifted off."

"Did you have a nice rest, darling?" Becky asked as she touched his cheek.

Kyle mentally checked himself, "I feel rested and relaxed. I guess whatever Dr. Reinholz did, allowed me to sleep better."

Becky pointed to the middle of the room, "That's the other wonderful thing that's happened tonight. Look at the coffee table."

Kyle laughed, "I see Adam's been busy."

Becky turned to Kyle, "Why don't you get undressed. I'll be back in a minute. You can come to bed with me. I think you can sleep for four hour intervals, until we see Dr. Reinholz again."

Kyle stood, and began unbuttoning his shirt as Becky turned towards the bathroom. By the time she came back, Kyle was fast asleep on the bed.

'Poor dear,' Becky thought. 'He's dead tired.' She stopped to cover her husband with a blanket. He'd laid down on the bed in his t-shirt and boxers, then crashed. Becky wearily made her way to the right side of the bed and in an instant, she as fast asleep also.

The phone rang. Quickly, it was answered by Kyle's hushed voice. This caused Becky to open her eyes. The sun had fully risen and a breakfast cart sat in the middle of the living room. Kyle was speaking on the phone, with a cup of coffee in his left hand.

Becky pushed herself up in bed and leaned back on a pillow "Who is it?"

"It's Siegfried," Kyle explained. "He was wondering when we're coming to the bank?"

Becky reached out for the phone from her hubby, "Mind if I talk to him?"

Kyle laughed, "Be my guest," as he poured himself another cup of steaming coffee, adding cream and sugar to it."

Becky ran her hand through her short hair, from her forehead back, giving herself a second to think. Motioning toward the huge bag, Becky whispered, "Are they really there?"

"Yup," Kyle laughed in amazement, "One jumbo bag of cut diamonds. *It's unbelievable!* This bag *is bigger* than the first."

Becky nodded, "Siegfried, can you send over an armored limo to the yacht club in an hour? We have another surprise for you."

Becky scooted her bottom back as she leaned against the pillow. Kyle handed her a cup and saucer, which she placed on the night stand, and she took a sip of coffee before going on. "Yes, I know this is getting to be a habit, Siegfried. I hoped you'd be pleased with our little surprises." Kyle could hear Siegfried laughing at Becky's joke. When Siegfried settled down a little, Becky advised, "I'd have Elsa Moot with you again, if you don't mind. Right now, I want a long, hot shower before we meet. Gotta go," she said as she hung up.

Kyle sat down in the arm chair, "You look mar-velous, my love."

Becky daintily sipped her steaming café con leche. "I'm really glad we found Dr. Reinholz. He's seemed to done you wonders. No bad dreams?"

Kyle knocked on wood of a nearby table for good luck. "Not so far," he offered. "Do you want me to wait for you and have breakfast together or should I go ahead and start? I'm famished."

Becky threw off her covers, "No honey," she answered as she went to her hubby. She gave him a lingering kiss. She was blissfully happy as all things appeared to be going well. "You go ahead and have breakfast. I'm going to get ready for our appointment at the bank. I'm not really hungry. Later, I want to *go shopping*. I need to watch my figure because I want to buy some new outfits, shoes aplenty, and makeup by the carload. I just don't have a thing, to wear…"

Kyle blinked. He'd developed a survival mechanism from his sniper days. He kept his mouth shut and just smiled at his wife. Then he started dishing up a *massive* plate of food. The nights sleep made feel him like a new man.

Becky had finished dressing and was putting in her ear rings when there was a knock at the door. The phone rang at the same time. Kyle answered the phone and told at Becky, "Siegfried says his man should be at the door, *now*."

Kyle opened the door, looking at the limo driver and uttered, "Dam?"

The guard looked at Kyle seriously and countered with, "Amster."

Siegfried heard the exchange, "*That's Malcolm*. He's my trusted man."

The couple grabbed their things and followed the guard out to the sleek limo.

It didn't take long to ride to the bank. This time, Malcolm drove them around to the rear of the building.

Siegfried met the group at the rear entrance of the bank, shaking Kyle's hand and hugging Becky, "You two *constantly* amaze me." he laughed. He was dying to ask where the diamonds came from, but it wouldn't be professional. He knew Elsa could tell the diamonds' origin by their chemical composition. She already knew the first batch came from North America, differing, but not by much, from the Canadian-Great Lakes diamond field from the signature crystalline structure. None of the stones had laser cut identification numbers on them, now required by International Law. Therefore, they were cut more than fifteen years ago, at least. Elsa also determined that these stones were primary, meaning they were actually found inside a volcanic vent somewhere in North America. Primary diamonds are the purest of the pure. Not like secondary diamonds, washed away by the action of a stream or river, and found further from their place of origin.

The large bag was taken to a counting room. Elsa Moot was like an excited child on Christmas day, "Oh mein Himmel. Another load," she breathed. "I'm going to be busy for months grading each and ever stone. She'd already started assessing the gems, seeing that they were *absolutely* top quality. Any flaws had been expertly cut away. Each diamond *was perfect*.

Siegfried looked at Elsa, "Do you have any idea how much all of this is worth?"

She busily made calculations, then she gulped, "At the current exchange rate, *and if we don't* destabilize the market, I'd say 1.25 billion dollars US total."

Siegfried's eyes lit up, but he didn't say a thing. He led the couple back to his office where he seated them before his desk.

He looked at Becky and Kyle, thinking as he pushed the fingertips of his two hands together.

"We need to manage these jewels carefully," he cleared his throat. "I'm going to say the bank will need ten million gradually, to orchestrate this deposit. To move the stones around the world wisely and slowly trickle them onto the market."

Kyle looked at Becky. She was the family business expert.

Becky leaned toward Kyle and whispered, "That figure seems fine," she looked at her husband. "I'm glad Adam gave us the extra stones. They'll cover the expense of setting up the foundation. I wanted at least a billion dollars to fund the project. Now, growth will occur from this investment. I hope to get 100,000 dollars in interest a day."

Becky looked up, "Siegfried, the ten million for your bank and the gemologists is fine with us. We trust you. As you said, we consider you now part of our family."

Siegfried pushed a piece of paper to the couple, "I'll guarantee you 1.25 billion US dollars for your diamonds. It could be more, but no less."

Becky had a question, "How soon can we start drawing on this new money?"

Siegfried paused, "I'll say you can count on ten million dollars available to you now. I think it is safe to say you can depend on at least a million dollars more in your account each day here after, not counting interest dividend."

Becky nodded her understanding and took the paper, "That's fine, Siegfried. We'll leave the details in your capable hands. Can we have a car out front, please?"

Siegfried rose and shook hands with the couple. These two strange people were turning into his best clients, "The car will be waiting for you."

Becky stopped to get some walking around cash for she and Kyle. Plastic was helpful, but one needed cash for tip money. Then they walked to the car.

Their first stop was of course, The Humidor, where Kyle loaded up on boxes of his favorite cigars. Today, more than hinted to be a shopping extravaganza. He anticipated smoking a few as he waited for Becky to go on her shopping safari. She was loaded for bear, but wasn't sure what bargain or unique look she'd bag. Kyle knew enough that it was *the hunt*, that was the most fun for his wife.

Becky stopped at La Femme. She knew Kyle loved her thongs. His interest with the forty's prompted her to purchase a few garter belts and traditional stockings. She *had* to indulge him some of his fantasies.

Becky decided to call Marie, Siegfried's assistant, for some advice. Marie whispered for Becky to check out *The Parisian*. It was *the secret doorway* into the exclusive European Fashion world.

It occurred to Becky, that they'd now been catapulted into the elite international strata of technology and finance. One thing her mother had burned into her brain as she grew up, was *Dress for Success.'*

At The Parisian, Kyle arranged for Becky to have a special preview of the latest fall outfits. She knew she absolutely needed a few cocktail dresses, some formal and leisure dresses, plus pants suits. A couple of informal and lounging outfits for relaxing and the best sleep attire. Of course, it would be a sin to not have the latest shoes to go with each individual outfit as well.

A hostess seated Becky and Kyle in *a private room*, where the models strode in modeling the latest creations. As Becky oowed and aahed she instinctively reached out to feel the rich fabrics between her fingertips. In this way she knew what would feel best against her skin. She selected numerous fashions that interested her that would be presented in her size to then try on.

The hostess then escorted Becky into the large, pink, French provincial styled salon, with surrounding mirrors and *perfect* lighting. A professionally trained dreseur, a small middle-aged brunette woman, smiled invitingly and offered Becky assistance to match the fashions to her physique.

"That would be fabulous!" Becky bubbled.

WHILE BECKY WAS IN THE dressing room, Kyle called Marie. "Marie? Hi, this is Kyle Swoboda. Becky sends her *undying gratitude* for the tip on The Parisian. We've been here two hours now."

Kyle smiled, "I'm quite comfortable and appreciate the car you've provided. I can sit inside it or on the convenient benches outside the shops. Nothing like a great cigar and people watching. *I love that.*"

He listened, laughed, and then got to the point of his call. "Marie, I was wondering. Becky's having such a wonderful time this afternoon but, can you please send over a panel van? The mountain of boxes and bags are starting to pile up in the lobby. People can't get into the door of the shop. Becky found so many treasures she says she, "Simply must have!" He waited, "Right way? I'm glad you understand. It must be *a girl thing.* Yes, we want to keep the car. I have another place I want to go and, the driver told me about this quaint restaurant down by the docks on Back Bay. I want to take Becky there for a quiet dinner. I've had the limo driver make reservations for us." Kyle listened some more, then smiled, "Thanks Marie for all of your help. Yes, I feel like we're family and appreciate your advice. Keep your ears open for any unique fashion emporiums. I'd be interested to hear about them." Kyle listened to Marie, blinked and jerked, *"Really? Can you?* Oh my God, Becky *would love that!* Yes, secure a seat on the Paris Fashion Runway. Yes, *on the runway*, or not at all. My lady is going First Class. Thanks Marie, gotta run. Becky's motioning me over to look at this next dress, but we desperately need that truck," he said as he hung up.

BECKY EMERGED FROM THE PARISIAN refreshed and exhilarated. She hadn't gone shopping *like that* since she and her mother melted plastic in Zurich three years ago. The experience *was spiritual.*

Becky talked with Rinaldo, a local, who was their chauffeur this afternoon. He was born and raised in Freeport. He knew the streets like the back of his hand. He also had his finger on the pulse of the best the city had to offer.

"Rinaldo," Becky purred, "I need a sophisticated haberdasher for my husband. Do you know of something exquisite for him?"

"Oh yes, Mum," Rinaldo answered without hesitation, "Enrique's is a fine, full spectrum men's clothier. We're not far from there now. Shall we go there straight away?"

"Oh yes, please," Becky smiled. "I'd love to secure you for our guide while we're in the city, if you don't mind."

"I'm at your service, Mum," Rinaldo answered. "The man from the bank said I'm to see to your needs, you and your gentle-mon."

Rinaldo pulled the limo to a stop outside a bright blue building. "I'll come in with you. I've a mate who works here. He'll do you right, I promise."

Kyle opened his door and helped Becky step out onto the sidewalk. This allowed Rinaldo to reach and open the haberdasher's door for his passengers to walk in. Rinaldo moved around them, looking about the well appointed store.

Rinaldo saw his friend, "Yo mon, Barnabas! I've got some *special guests.* I want you to take care of them, *personally.*"

Barnabas, a tall thin islander smiled at Rinaldo, "Right you are, mate!"

Barnabas looked at Becky and Kyle, sizing up the gentleman. He was able to accurately judge his size and weight and knew what clothes to show him.

"My name is Barnabas. How my I be of service to you today?" he asked.

With Kyle's blessing, Becky took over, "I need to outfit my husband in many categories, please. Let's start off with a tuxedo. Of course: several business suits, preferably in grays, both light and dark, a dark navy-blue one also to bring out the richness in his eyes, leisure trousers, shirts, ties, sweaters, sports jackets matching the separate trousers please. All are to be in current European cut." Quickly Becky added, "We'll require matching shoes, and cuff-links."

Kyle shrugged at Barnabas, "Rinaldo says you're good. I'll trust your fashion knowledge. I want to *be presentable* in various settings."

Kyle felt himself moving upward, from the hick from the sticks, now stepping into the unknown circles of the intellectual and social elite. He trusted Becky's experience as to what was needed. He took a deep breath and let her guide him though unfamiliar territory.

Becky showed him how to dress to impress. She was careful not to overstep her boundaries, but wanted to prepare him to evolve into their new station. She let him choose colors and styles that were comfortable to him. Both Becky and Kyle knew he'd need some classes in etiquette and decorum. How that evolution would occur, was still to be determined.

Becky enjoyed seeing her man morph into an elegantly dressed male. This was a whole new side of her Monster, she hadn't seen before. His muscular body made his clothes pop. Barnabas was a maestro of elegant attire. With the help of a talented tailor, Barnabas suggested nips and tucks in Kyle's new clothing, that molded with his body, to accentuate his breath-taking masculine physique. Kyle's final look was polished, elegant, but not snooty.

As Kyle changed back into his street clothes, Becky spied bottles of cologne. He emerged from the dressing room as she inhaled from a blue opalescent flask, and sighed dreamily.

Kyle motioned to Barnabas, "I'll take *two* of those colognes as well,"

Barnabas winked at Kyle as if to say, 'Someone's going to *get lucky* tonight', as Kyle liberally splashed on the pheromone based fragrance.

As Kyle helped Becky into the car, his purchases were added to the back of the delivery van. Kyle looked at Rinaldo, "Tell the truck driver we won't need him any more today.

He can take the packages back to our room at the yacht club. I'd like to go to the next stop now, Rinaldo. You know where…"

"Right you are *Gov-Na*," Rinaldo smiled, complete with a gleaming gold toothed grin.

Becky looked inquisitively at Kyle, "Go where?" she wondered.

The twinkle in Kyle's eye quickened her heart, "Kyle Ibsen, don't you be startin something you're not going to finish," she warned.

Rinaldo didn't say a word as he silently but quickly made his way to their destination. In short order, he pulled up in front of a black and gold trimmed store. Kyle opened the door and anxiously Becky looked up at the sign over the doorway, Lichthy Jewelry.

"NO," Becky breathed in disbelief, *"not again!"*

Kyle gently took her hand and placed it into the crook of his arm, as he escorted his wide-eyed woman into the jewelry store. Rinaldo opened the store's door and enjoyed Becky's look of expectation.

Kyle confidently told Rinaldo, "Wait for us please. I'll take it from here."

Rinaldo grinned, "As you wish, Sir."

Becky's heart fluttered. She hadn't expected this stop. Kyle was beginning to surprise her *and she liked* this new change.

Kyle guided Becky over to sit at a chair at the ring counter. The proprietor recognized the couple. "Welcome back, Mr. and Mrs. Swoboda. *It's wonderful* to see you two again."

Becky was speechless. She was doe-eyed and breathless, waiting for the show to begin.

Kyle reached into his trouser pocket and produced a knotted handkerchief. He reached over for the velvet gem pad on the counter, drawing it in front of Becky. He untied the cloth and six crystals fell out onto the velvet, making the gems shine as if they were the sun itself.

Even Mr. Lichthy was mesmerized. Kyle explained, "We've enjoyed your engagement ring, but the lone emerald cut diamond has been lonely *for company*. I want your jeweler to craft a setting, bringing this family of diamonds together for my lady, while we wait.

Mr. Lichthy snapped his fingers and instantly the jeweler was at his side. They quietly conversed, exchanging ideas.

Becky gasped, "Kyle, when did you get these diamonds?"

He smiled, "This morning while you were still asleep, I went through the bag and selected a few *little guys*. I didn't think Adam would mind if I made you smile. You said I owed you *some bling*."

"Yeehaa," Becky whooped, "Right you are, cowboy."

"Tell the man," Kyle directed his princess, "how you'd like the stones to surround your center piece diamond."

This too, was something she'd dreamed about. Without hesitation, "I want the four round diamonds to snuggle with the emerald cut. Then further out, lay the two rectangular gems on either side," she beamed with excitement.

Kyle kissed her and then took out a metal cigar tube from his shirt pocked and dropped two more round diamonds, at least a caret apiece, on the cloth. "I want you to make these into post earrings for *my lady*. I'd like them made while we wait if you can."

"No problem, Mr. Swoboda. It's always a pleasure to serve you and your Mrs."

Becky watched as her ring took shape in front of her eyes. Kyle leaned over, "In time, we'll make a necklace for you, but it was just a quick trip today. I thought you needed some walking around jewelry. Hope they aren't too heavy for you."

"The ring is just gorgeous and I'll manage the size, you hunk you," she moaned.

A smiling Kyle watched her fit her new earrings into her pierced lobes. He enjoyed her excited smile as she looked into the mirror on the counter. The stones sparkled like the stars in her eyes. All the while she dreamily watched her new engagement ring take shape.

Kyle whispered, "Do you like them?"

"Oh yes," she exhaled. "They're *perfect*," she gasped, short of breath.

Within an hour, Becky left the store wearing her sparkling earrings and her new engagement, wedding ring set. She couldn't stop staring at her finger.

Kyle whispered, "I'm hungry. Is it alright with you if we get something to eat?"

Becky kept admiring her new *bling*, "Ah huh," she sighed.

Chuckling, Kyle helped his distracted woman into the limo. Looking at Rinaldo he asked, "Can we go to Mamma Jo's now? We'd also like you to join us as our guest too, Rinaldo. Consider it part of your duties," Kyle smiled.

"Well, since you put it that way, Sir, of course I'll have to oblige. It is getting towards the end of the day. The sun is *over the yardarm*, so to speak."

Kyle enjoyed seeing the quaint, tiny, pastel colored houses, as they drove closer and closer to the water front. The homes were only the size of a matchbox, as they'd been built back in the 1700s. The long ago islanders thought a small house was better than a large tent, against the wild wind and rain, from Back Bay.

Rinaldo stopped the car in front of a tall, white plank privacy fence. Without hesitation, he opened the almost hidden gate and let his clients, who were quickly becoming friends, into the private residence.

Becky looked around, "What is this place?"

Rinaldo smiled, "Dis place, it is Mamma Jo's. She de Wo-Man, who is the best cook, this side of Ja-Ma-Ca. Your Mister told me to call a place that makes barbeque for his wo-man. Mamma Jo started roasting a pig, as soon as I called her dis morning."

Becky looked at Kyle, with a serious look in her eye, "You and I, need to talk, *later…!"*

Kyle squinted at his goddess, *"Don't tease me,"* he told her firmly.

Becky gave him, *The Look.* Kyle knew his chances were pretty good that he'd sleep in paradise, tonight.

Mamma Jo came out to meet them dressed in a colorful island headdress with bright wrap and shook Becky's and Kyle's hands, "I cook for you since Rinaldo says you are *good people.* I only cook for family and I don't share secret recipes with *just anyone,*" she waved her body emotionally as she talked."

Mamma swiveled her head as she looked at her two white guests, "And what will you be havin ta fill your bellies? We've got roast pork, of course rice. I have conch chouda, and some red snapper on the grill. Whad be your *pas-sion?"*

Becky was drawn to the roasting pig. She inhaled and almost passed out from the fragrant aroma of sweet and tangy spices. Mamma mopped her secret sauce on the slowly rotating meat over a wood charcoal fire.

"I'll have the pork, Mamma. Do you pull it or slice it," she asked?

"Ooo girl! You're talkin *my language now,*" Mamma grinned. "I can do it either way for you, *precious.*"

"I'll have some of each, Mamma," Becky said with a twinkle in her eye.

Kyle answered, "I'd love a bowl of conch chowder, followed by the red snapper and rice. Do you have any dip that's spicy?"

Mamma smilingly looked at Rinaldo, who grinned back and winked. "We have some dip *straight out of Hades.* Are you feeling lucky today, *mon?"*

Rinaldo got up to help Mamma bring their dishes. Becky took a minute to whisper to Kyle. He nodded his head, as he munched on the corn chips with dip. Kyle dabbed his forehead with his handkerchief. Mamma *wasn't joking.* The dip burned its way down from the tongue to the stomach.

When Rinaldo returned and everyone started eating, Becky asked, "Rinaldo, you're a very resourceful man. If you ever get tired of working for the Bank, please let us know. We want to open a company here in Freeport. We'd like you to oversee the operation."

Rinaldo looked at the couple sitting across the table from him, "And what does your company do? I'm very particular who I work for. I'm *an independent mon.*"

"We're starting a foundation which will work towards bettering mankind. A start would be to grow inexpensive, but good food, accessible to all.

Kyle told Rinaldo, "I'm looking for a new source of plant protein as a source of food for the poor. Third world countries, heck even impoverished people within our own country, are given mainly carbohydrates to eat. This can cause health issues and doesn't allow their intelligence to rise. I was thinking if we could rent ocean or lagoon space on an outer island, we could aqua farm the protein plant. Maybe, some of this space could be used to fish farm as well."

Becky explained, "We're open to financially backing new ideas, new technology and new natural resources. I want to try to steer away from animal proteins as animals are more complicated to farm."

Both Kyle and Becky saw that Rinaldo was interested, but cautious. They offered a compromise.

"Maybe, we should start off small," Becky said. "We'd at least like to hire you as a consultant. Maybe you could offer suggestions how best to achieve our goals. We don't want to upset the natural balance in this paradise. Would that be more amenable to you?'

Rinaldo sampled his pulled pork, "I could be a consultant to you, yes. I like working at the Bank. I hear things that way. Being a chauffeur," he smiled, "many people think because I'm an Islander, that I'm stupid. That I don't hear," he winked, "but I do!"

Kyle looked at Rinaldo, "We don't consider you stupid at all. In fact, I think you're very intelligent."

Rinaldo looked at the couple, "You sit at my table. I share my food with you. I can see that you respect my way of life. Let's start off slow and see where this path leads us?"

Becky and Kyle nodded. "Sounds like a plan," Becky answered.

She looked around, "Is there something that your people need?"

Rinaldo answered, "My people are poor. There isn't much work around for mon or wo-man to do, to feed their families."

Kyle reached into his pocket and counted out five 100 dollar bills. "Take this money, and spread it around. We'd like to see you buy food for people. Maybe in the future, there's a property in the islands where we could start an industry to produce a useful product and give people reasonable jobs. We're open to new ideas. Ideas where honorable men and women can work to better themselves and their families."

Rinaldo took the money, "I'll do what I can. Father Rudolph in the local parish has a food kitchen. This will help feed many. Our people are proud and don't want charity. They want to work to sustain themselves."

Kyle counted out another five bills, "This is for you and your help this afternoon. He dropped several bills on the table for Mamma Jo's food."

Rinaldo slowly smiled, "Thank you for your kindness. I'll keep you in mind."

Mamma Jo hugged her new friends, who promised to return, the next time they were in the islands. Satisfied and full, Rinaldo drove Kyle and Becky back to the yacht club. At the entrance, they shook hands and promised to keep in touch.

Becky had called ahead to arrange a couple's massage package to relax their tired muscles. The hotel set up two massage tables in their room with two women that knew their craft well. Kyle and she came out of their bedroom wrapped in warm towels and laid face down on the leather tables.

"Ahhh," Becky moaned. "Heaven!" The masseuse knew exactly how hard to press each sore spot and make it feel great.

"I don't know where you came up this idea hon, but *it's a winner*," Kyle groaned from his table, where the tall woman was applying long strokes to his heavily muscled shoulders. He was having a wonderful time seeing Becky's skin and making plans for when the massage would be completed. Then he would take over and show her what he could do with his hands.

Becky saw the color of Kyle's eyes darken and knew what was to come. She blew him a kiss as a promise that they would be together shortly.

After an hour of pure indulgence, Becky and Kyle were completely relaxed and feeling rejuvenated. Becky tipped the women handsomely as they folded up their tables. "That was heavenly, ladies. You two are worth your weight in gold."

"Any time you need a massage, we are here for you," they told her.

As the door closed behind them, Kyle walked over to his lovely lady and wrapped her up in his arms. He planted kisses along her neck and over her jaw. She could feel his steel body against her softness and melted to him.

"This is the best part of the day," Becky breathed.

"I agree," Kyle answered as he swept her off her feet and into the bedroom.

Chapter 9

A soft lovely island morning found Becky laying against Kyle's chest as they talked softly to each other. The phone broke their reverie. Kyle whispered into her ear, *"Don't answer it."*

"It might be important as not many people have this number." Becky protested as she gave him a smoldering kiss. Kyle groaned his frustration and swatted her behind as she turned over to pick up the receiver.

"Hello? Oh hello, Laverne? *No!*"

Becky alarmingly looked at Kyle, *"Harold's been shot!"*

Kyle asked her, "How can we get back to the ranch the quickest?"

"Laverne, we'll be there as soon as we can." Becky told the frightened woman. "What is Harold's condition? Okay, good. See you soon," she told her friend.

Becky dialed quickly, "Hello Siegfried, this is Becky Swoboda. Kyle and I need to get back to the ranch at once. There's been trouble. Can we reverse our travel flight plan? Time is of the essence!"

Siegfried assured her that everything would *immediately* be handled by Marie, his assistant.

"Sorry to cut our fun time short honey, but our family is in trouble," Becky apologized to Kyle. "Harold is okay but just the same, someone out there is shooting at *our friends!*"

"Once we've taken care of the problem there, we'll finish what we started here," Kyle promised her.

Within a half hour a car took the couple to the airport. They boarded the private jet and five hours later, they were in Denver. Then a helicopter whisked them back to the ranch.

Laverne along with Harold, whose right arm was in a sling, met the helicopter landing alongside the barn. Becky ran to them, hugged them both and then they walked into the house. Kyle took the bags from the pilot and then the helicopter took off. Kyle stepped into the kitchen as the others sat at the table.

"What happened?" Becky asked as Laverne poured cups of coffee.

Harold explained, "I was in the middle pasture, checkin fences, when it felt like a mule kicked my right shoulder. I remember hearing a following report.

"They must've been aways off," Kyle calculated, by the separation of impact and sound."

Harold held his arm, "Next thing I knew, I was layin on the ground. I was wearing my pistol on my right hip, so I snaked out the 44 and waited. Sure enough, those jaspers came to check me. I was afraid they'd do me in. There were two of them. When they got close enough to spit, I shot them both dead. Then I made it back to the house and Laverne patched me up."

Laverne added, "He was lucky. It must've been a rifle, cause the wound was a through and through. I just poured some whiskey in the hole and covered 'er up."

Becky gasped, "Shouldn't we get him checked out in a hospital, or something?"

Laverne looked at her young friend, "*Darlin*, people here abouts can't take time to go to no doctor, *unless* they cut off a leg *or* somethin serious. Old Harold'll be good as new in a few days. It was just a gunshot wound. It didn't hit nothin vital."

Harold looked at Kyle, "After Laverne patched me up, we drove the jeep up there to collect the bodies, but they were gone! I've spent my whole life on this ranch and that was the first time the hairs on the back of my neck raised. We ain't done with this thing yet, I fear."

"I need to do some thinking," Kyle told them. He stood up and walked out the back door. Becky followed.

Kyle looked at her, "I'd better call Cobra and take his job. Somehow we need protection out here. It'd be one thing to lay for more snipers, but they're just the tip of the iceberg. Somebody's got to figure out who's behind all this evil."

Becky spoke up, "I don't *like this*, Kyle. I don't *want you to go*. You're done with all that killing. Now you'll open up that violent life again? We've made a new start here. To go backward to your old ways *is not* what we talked about."

Kyle ran his hand through his short hair, "I don't know what else to do, hon. Harold's right. If it were just the two men, then they'd be layin in the field, but someone came and retrieved those bodies. *That's professional*. In case you forgot, *they* started it!"

Becky remembered how Kyle allowed her to make decisions when it came to business. This situation involved killing and that was Kyle's area of expertise.

"Kyle," she breathed, "You know how I feel, but I'll bow to your decision. The job of protecting the family, I leave to you. *I hate* that you're going away."

He looked at his precious, "I don't like it either hon, but this is bigger than me. We need help with this. I want you to stay here on the ranch with Harold and Laverne. They'll take care of you while I'm gone."

Kyle picked up his phone, "I'll get right back to you with an answer."

Becky went back into the kitchen. She was on her second cup when Kyle came back inside.

He looked at Becky, then Harold and Laverne, "I need to go away for awhile. Will you keep an eye on my wife for me?"

Laverne put her hand on Becky's, "We'll watch her Kyle. She'll be ok."

"Do you know how long you'll be gone?" Harold asked.

"About two weeks. I can't tell you where I'm going, but you can contact me through my phone," he explained. "A car will pick me up shortly. I'd better go pack," he said as he headed toward the stairs leading to their second floor room.

Becky followed him. She anxiously sat in the chair with her hands on her lap, watching her husband pack for war. She was silent as she'd already told him how she felt.

Kyle threw a few changes of clothes in his backpack. He knew what he'd need, would be provided. He'd been on a countless number of these missions in the past. The thing was, he'd never had a wife, worrying about him before.

Kyle went to kneel in front of his woman, "I won't be long, hon. Cobra promised me he's set a perimeter around the ranch. That you three would be safe. That's *the only* way I'd go.

Becky blinked, "*Oh, Kyle.* I just realized what I guess every woman has felt when her husband is going into battle. That she wants a part of her husband to stay with her. She needs a piece of him to be with her always."

Kyle's jaw bone flexed. "I never dreamed it would be this hard to go," he confessed, "but then again, I've never had a woman I loved *this much.*"

Becky brushed a tear away, "*I'll be waiting*, darling. *Don't be long.*"

Kyle crushed her to him, "As fast as I can. We have unfinished business, remember!" He bruised her lips with his passionate kiss.

When the couple came back into the kitchen, Laverne was cooking food. "KIS, sit yourself down. I'm not sending you off without a good meal behind your belt. It wouldn't be right," she ordered. "I got a nice steak, well done with some charcoal on it, your favorite. Sit down and eat up"

The meal went quickly. As Laverne refilled Kyle's coffee cup, a plain sedan turned into the driveway. Harold looked out the window, "They're here."

Kyle became KIS once again, *The KIS of Death*. He put on his game face. He gently lifted the woman he loved up to him, as he kissed her tenderly. "I'll be back soon, hon. *I promise*." After setting her back down, he picked up his bag and walked to the waiting car. As it turned down the highway, he gave a wave out his window. Becky watched her husband disappear over the crest of the hill.

THE FIRST WEEK CRAWLED BY without any trouble. Just the same, Becky felt uneasy. The Beast from the Everglades Swamp had wiggled his way deeply into her heart. Now he was more important to her, than life itself.

"I need to go for a walk," she told her two companions as they sat in the front parlor.

Laverne wasn't happy, "Harold'll be glad to go with you, darlin."

Harold took the hint, "Let me grab my rifle and hat."

Becky with tears in her eyes breathed, "I just want to be alone for awhile. I need some time to think," she looked at Laverne. The look spoke volumes.

Laverne motioned Harold to stay seated. "We'll be right here ,honey. Don't be too long, it's getting toward dusk."

Becky picked up a shawl and wrapped it around her shoulders. It was starting to get chilly. "I won't be long," she promised.

A THOUSAND MILES AWAY, KIS lay in his nest, waiting for the target to show. His phone vibrated. Answering it, he whispered, "KIS…"

The tone of Harold's voice purely explained that he was upset. "Kyle, *Becky's gone!* We can't find her *anywhere!* We thought you'd better know."

"I'll get right back to you," Kyle answered. He tried to think.

It was dark in the dense jungle. Then he remembered something. He took out his medallion out and tapped it three times. Almost instantly, Adam came walking through the jungle. KIS didn't know how he'd gotten there, but he didn't care either.

"What's up?," Adam asked. "I'm surprised to hear from you in this place, Kyle. What are you doing under all that brush?" Adams face showed Kyle, that he knew exactly what he was doing, and that he was not pleased.

"Never mind that now. Someone has taken Becky from the ranch! I need you to get her back for me, Adam," Kyle urgently demanded.

Adam stroked the side of his chin, "Who's taken her?"

Deflated, Kyle explained, "There was trouble at the ranch. Someone or some organization was trying to steal the ranch from the Walters. I got into a fight to stop them when we first arrived. Later, Harold Walters was in the pasture and was shot. I turned to the government, people *I thought* could help. *They promised* that they'd protect my family, but now I found out *someone's kidnapped Becky!*"

"Why didn't you come to me about this right away, Kyle? I could have helped you," Adam sighed.

Kyle dejected looked at Adam, "I thought you were just an anthropologist, a nerdy, weird college professor. What could you do to help us against organized crime? *I thought* the people I worked for could protect us, *but I was wrong*. Now I've put Becky in danger! She's my life, Adam. Without her, *I don't want to live*."

Adam put a finger to his right temple. Then he looked at Kyle, most seriously, "Yes, I see."

"Give me a moment, Kyle. I need to meditate on this." Adam closed his eyes and breathed rhythmically. Finally opened his glowing blue eyes and sighed, "You know the saying, that trouble comes in pairs?"

Kyle blinked, "Yes," was all he said flatly.

Adam explained, "The people who want your ranch are the Hungarian Mafia. They were the ones who shot Harold. That group wants to buy into the American dream. It's all about money with them. Their first step is to acquire land, cheaply. Then they'll come up with a profitable product, probably drugs."

"And the other half of the trouble?" Kyle asked.

"The Columbian Drug Cartel have Becky. They want *revenge?* They've put her in a drug induced coma. They intend to," he pulled back, confused, *"Organ harvest her?* They seem to feel you owe them money? By selling her organs, they figure they can recoup the money they feel *you stole from them?"*

Kyle was stunned, "How did they know where to find us? I've kept under cover, since leaving Florida."

Adam explained, "When you returned to your old lifestyle, being a government sniper for Cobra, The Agency has ties with the DEA. They have leaks. That's how they found Becky at the ranch. The American government *is so big*, it's like a sieve. There're many holes in the system. It's nearly impossible to keep a secret."

Kyle let out an exaggerated sigh, "Can you get her back, *Adam? Please!"*

Adam blinked, then shook his head, "No."

"Yes, you can! You transported that bag of diamonds to Freeport, over night! It wouldn't be much more complicated to transport 100 pounds of goddess back to me," he pleaded emotionally.

"It's not that easy, Kyle," Adam protested. "I've never transported a human before. I don't know what would happen. The diamonds are silicon based, *like me*. You humans are carbon based. *There's a world of difference!"*

Adam felt Kyle's feelings shift to hopelessness. He knew he had to do something or this situation would turn from bad to worse.

"I can transport Becky," Adam explained truthfully, "but I don't know what would happen to her, *physically*. Something could go terribly wrong!" he protested.

"Would she live and breath? I just want my love back with me," Kyle moaned. *"I don't want to live*, without her, Adam."

Adam thought, then he unemotionally confessed, "I've moved smaller life forms. A serious side affect was that it affected their fine bodily functions, like their ability to reproduce. Can you live with that consequence?

Kyle's heart skipped a beat, "Will she be alive? Will she have a fairly normal life other than that?"

"Yes, she would live normally. Beyond that, I can't guarantee *anything*," Adam answered solemnly.

"*I want my wife back*, Adam. *Please*, return her to me?" Kyle begged. "She won't survive without your help. I'm powerless to get to her *in time*. I wouldn't know where to look, quickly enough. Within twenty-four hours, she'll be dead."

"I'll do my best," was all Adam reluctantly said, as he turned back into the jungle and faded into the heavy mist.

Kyle picked up his gear and walked out of the jungle and back to base camp. He angrily walked into Cobra's regional director's office and threw his equipment on the floor.

"You let them capture my wife! You promised you'd keep her safe! *You Liar.*" KIS fought back an urge to kill the guy on the spot. One shot is all it'd take, but then he remembered Becky. She wouldn't be happy with him if he killed out of anger. 'Ah Heck, this guy might have a wife and kids too,' Kyle thought. For a moment KIS fought with his instincts, but Kyle won out, as he managed to yell loudly, "*I quit.*" Kyle was a civilian. He could walk off any job that didn't suit him.

Two days later, a helicopter delivered Kyle back to the ranch. He burst into the back door, "Becky? Laverne?"

Kyle heard footsteps coming down the stairs, "Quiet, Kyle. Becky's sleeping!" Laverne cautioned.

"How is she?" he demanded.

"Later that night, after Harold called you," Laverne went on, "we heard someone banging on the back door. When we went outside, Becky was laying on the back porch. There wasn't a soul was in sight. Harold carried her up to the bed, and she's been sleeping ever since…"

Chapter 10

L averne nervously poked her head in Snowy's old room. Kyle's eyes instantly flashed open at Laverne's presence.

"Any change yet?" she whispered. "It's been *three days* since we found her. I'm startin ta worry. It's coming on to dark now. Maybe tomorrow, we'd better take her to a doc?"

Kyle slowly shook his head, "No. Her pulse is fine. She just can't seem to shake whatever drug they used to put her in this coma. Her respirations are good, pupils are reactive, she's just doesn't have any neural sensation."

He didn't tell Laverne. This would be *the perfect* condition for their butcher to remove Becky's organs from her living body. He'd heard terrible rumors about lone back-packers in South America, with this happening to them.

Kyle promised Laverne, "I'll call you if there's a change."

Laverne protested, "Kyle, *you've gotta* get some sleep. If you fall apart on us, we're done. At least let me make you some food. All you've had for the last two days is coffee and those stogies you smoke. You can't live like that."

Kyle answered Laverne slowly, "Get some sleep. I'll be ok. Thanks for all your help. *None* of this would've happened, if *I'd stayed home*."

Laverne made a twisted-lip face, like she was biting her tongue. Then she pulled her head out of the door. Kyle was entrenched in that room like a he-bear protecting his mate. Laverne slowly went to her room. She'd better catch some sleep herself. She unbuttoned her dress and curled up in bed. In two seconds, she was fast asleep, next to Harold. They were dead tired. They'd kept a vigil of their own since Becky's return.

The room grew dark. When full darkness had fallen, Kyle tapped his protective medallion three times. Suddenly there was a knock on Snowy's bedroom door. When Kyle answered it, Adam was standing in the hallway.

"What's news?" Adam asked, instantly seeing in the pitch-black room.

Kyle explained, "The Walter's found Becky lying on the back porch three days ago, unconscious. She hasn't come out of her coma since. We're getting really worried about her condition." He brought all the facts together, "I can't take Becky to the hospital. We don't have a family doctor who'd admit her, first off. Next, if I just take her to the emergency room, what am I going to tell them? That she was abducted by the Columbian Drug Cartel and put into a drug induced coma? They did this to get back the money *they say* we stole from them? So, they were gonna carve up her body and sell off her organs, piece by piece to recover their losses? *If* I told them that, there'd be cops and government agents all over us! We wouldn't be able to belch, without being caught on surveillance cameras, *for three lifetimes* after that."

Kyle sighed, "She hasn't stirred *at all* in three days. Can you do something to help? If you can't, I'm taking her to University Hospital in the morning. I don't care what'll happen. *She's got* to be cared for."

Adam stood with legs apart as he thought, "This looks *like a job for* Lawkjdghohannavzw."

"For *who?"* Kyle blurted out with a questioning look.

Adam stated, "He is the Healer of Healers, the Grand Pubah of our doctor-like stuff. He's all-seeing, all-knowing back on my, ah-home town."

"Ok, but how do you say his name? I don't want to disrespect the man who'd come here to help *my wife*."

"Yes, Lawkjdghohannavzw *is* hard to pronounce, isn't it? It *just doesn't* roll off the tongue. Adam winked with a sly smile, "ah, why don't you just call him *Doctor Mike?* He's a really down-to-earth type guy, and incredibly smart!"

Caution rose in Kyle, "You think Doctor Mike is the way to go, Adam? Would he know how to help Becky?"

Adam got serious, "Doctor Mike's *The Best*. He's my, ah-*family doctor* back home. I include you in my family now, if you don't mind."

Kyle stood up. His heart was breaking as he thought how stupid he was to go off and trust the government. Again, his decision had hurt the ones he loved.

He felt like he wanted to tear himself apart as his punishment, but that would be *too good* for himself. Becky wasn't even conscious, but if they did get her awake, she might not be able to have *their baby*, anyway! He was so selfish. He was just afraid to lose *the one person* he loved so dearly. The tiny woman who'd given herself so completely to him. It seemed like she really wanted a baby *and then again*, he'd failed her...'

A tiny hand reached out and took his massive fist, "Don't be hard on yourself, Kyle. I love you too," Becky told him in a weak voice.

Kyle was instantly by her side, "Becky? Love? *Oh my God* you gave me such a fright!"

Becky looked at Kyle with sunken eyes, "I don't want you to be angry with yourself. I'm glad you asked Adam for help. If we can't have children, *that's ok* with me. I can be happy with just *the two of us*."

"I didn't say anything, hon," Kyle confessed.

"I thought you did. It seemed as if you spoke into my ears. I heard you as clear as day," she answered.

Adam looked at his charges, "Kyle, your self-recrimination and guilt are powerful emotions. When Becky was transported, she must've picked up some, *additional abilities* from *my er-side*

136

of the family. She can now hear your thoughts. In a way, you saved her life, Kyle. She loves you also, more than life itself. You two are destined for great things together."

Without saying more, Adam straightened and went into a trance. In what seemed like seconds, there was a soft knock on the room door. Adam opened the portal. An older gentleman with gray hair stood outside in the hallway.

He walked over to Kyle and shook his hand, "Adam has told me all about you, Kyle, and your lovely wife, Becky. Please call me Doctor Mike.

Kyle anxiously asked, "Can you help her doctor? I'm extremely grateful that you came so quickly."

Doctor Mike walked over to Becky's left side and moved his open palms over her, like a Reiki Master flowing energy from themselves to another. He started at her head. As his hands moved over her face, Becky smiled. She relaxed, coming out of her darkness, back into the light. As his hands passed over her abdomen, he gasped, "Oops" then he continued down her legs to her feet.

"I didn't like the sound of *the, Oops*," Kyle frowned.

Lawkjdghohannavzw looked at Kyle and answered, "Adam told you we haven't transported humans before, right? That problems could occur?"

Kyle worriedly asked, "Can you do anything? Can you heal her, doctor?"

Doctor Mike explained, "You and your strong empathetic emotion called to her spirit, and she answered you, Kyle. *She returned* to the man *she loves*."

"What about the Oops?" Kyle asked. "What's that all about?"

Doctor Mike stirred and then looked Kyle directly in the eye, "In the transfer processes, the object's molecules are disassembled at one point and then reassembled at the home point. You can imagine how difficult it is to get all the, ah-pieces where they're supposed to go, right?"

Kyle shrugged, "Yes."

"Well, I don't want to go into details, but there was an Oops with Becky."

Kyle cringed. He didn't like the sound *of that*.

Doctor Mike looked at Adam, "I need to admit her. I can't care for her here."

Kyle stepped forward, "Doctor Mike, I want you to help Becky, *but* she doesn't *ever* leave my sight! *Only*, over my dead body."

Adam nodded to Lawkjdghohannavzw, "We'll take him too."

Instantly, Kyle felt he was in a cloud. It was soft, warm, and very clean. He seemed to hear voices talking all around him. At a point, he seemed to have lost consciousness, but strangely, he wasn't afraid. The next thing he knew, he and Becky were back in Snowy's room at the ranch, and the sun was just rising.

"HAVE YOU BEEN AWAKE LONG, darling?" Becky asked, stretching like a lioness in her bed. "I feel absolutely wonderful. Like I've been asleep for years," she confessed.

Instantly, Kyle was by her side, "Oh Becky, you scared me. *Are you ok?"*

Becky mentally checked herself, "I feel fine. A little stiff from laying on my back all night, but that'll go away."

"Do you remember anything about what's happened?" Kyle asked.

Unfazed, Becky shot back, "Oh yes. I remember Doctor Mike, the cloud-like room, with other people buzzing about, and then waking up here."

"Do you remember anything about the people who kidnapped you?" Kyle wondered.

Becky searched her memory, "Nope, not a thing," she sighed. "I feel great. I'm so relieved your back, Kyle. I missed you terribly. Please *don't ever* leave me again."

Kyle shook his head, "I need some coffee."

Becky jumped out of bed, tossed off her night gown and turned to reach for her bra. Kyle looked at her.

Becky turned around with her fists on her hips, looking at her husband, "You dirty man!" she gasped, but quickly added, "but it sounds like fun..."

Impishly she shot an idea toward Kyle. He rocked with the mental image.

He carefully walked over to the one he loved and took her in his arms, "I love you too, *and yes*, I'd love *a welcome home present*." Then he realized, "You didn't speak that, did you?"

Becky silently replied, 'Nope. Evidently, we can communicate mentally, through telepathy now. Something tells me that in this experience with Doctor Mike, our brain capacity has increased by ten percent. I remember Doctor Mike saying that if we gained more brain capacity, like them, that we couldn't tolerate humans. That people would then be aggravatingly ignorant, like bugs.'

Kyle looked at Becky and grinned, thinking, '*You hottie!* I never would've guessed you thought all those wonderful, things!'

Becky scrunched her nose, silently replying, 'Now wait a minute buddy. I want *some privacy* here! We need to set up some rules between us. Just listen to what I project to you. Don't go digging around into my mind. I don't want to be mentally naked in front of you, *all the time*.'

Kyle looked at Becky and thought, 'You're right. That wouldn't be fair, but then again, he looked at her devilishly. Becky looked shocked at the projected images. Then a cloud descended over Kyle's mind.

Kyle thought further, 'I need to find a new life and never return to my old ways. We were lucky this time. Anyone else would've been carved up for bait. Those horrors exist in the world. The world truly is evil,' Kyle saw.

Softly, Becky turned Kyle's face toward her, 'We need

to look for the good in life, or we will attract the evil. I've a feeling Adam will help us. We'll deal with the bad guys later. Don't be afraid.'

'Ok, my love. I trust you,' he thought.

Becky looked deeply in Kyle's eyes, 'And I trust you too. You did the right thing for me and it'll work out.'

Kyle's eyes widened, 'Do you really? Should we try so soon? Is it safe?'

Becky grinned, but pretended to be angry, 'You're reading my thoughts again, Kyle!' as she climbed back into bed. She made space for her husband.

Kyle quickly began undressing, but turned, embarrassed, 'Oh Becky, you're *so naugh-ty*, but I think *you're great, too!'*

Becky laughed, 'You sound like Adam at times now. You've seemed to have acquired some of his British ways.'

Kyle climbed into bed and threw the covers up over their heads and growled. Becky shrieked out loud with laughter, then thought, 'Now you're *my Monster*, my *Magnificent Beast…'*

DOWNSTAIRS IN THE KITCHEN, LAVERNE dropped the frying pan. Harold looked up at the ceiling, but didn't say a word.

Laverne sighed in relief. *"I don't know how* he did it, but God love him, *he brought her back!"*

For Laverne, Becky's coma had been as bad as when they'd gotten the letter that Snowy was killed in the frozen desert of Kuwait. She pushed that horrible memory, way back, in its dark, hidden place in her brain.

She took a steak out of the freezer, "I'd better have food ready *for that boy*. He's hard at work," she giggled.

Harold grinned as he heard the head-board. He didn't say a word. He too was relieved Becky was feeling better. She was like the daughter he'd never had.

Laverne tried to suppressed a smile, "Ooo mercy, he's getting busy," she tried to fan herself. He'll have an appetite when they come down." Then she brightened, "I still have hopes we'll have a full bassinet come spring."

Harold silently eyed Laverne, but didn't say a word. He had other worries on his mind, now that the immediate drama with Kyle and Becky was over.

"I got a call from Zeke," he told Laverne. "Zeke said he got his foreclosure notice from the Bank yesterday. He has to make a payment on his loan within thirty days, or they'll throw Judd and him off their land."

KYLE BOUNCED INTO THE KITCHEN as Harold was telling Laverne about the phone call from his cousin. Judd was Zeke's only son. He was just seventeen, but he was as big as an ox. He'd happily quit school to take a full time job, but there weren't any jobs to be had in the area. Their place was like the rest of the country, an economic desert.

Laverne looked at Kyle, "You sit yourself right down here, Mister. I bet you're plum wore out, or, maybe she is?" Laverne wasn't sure. She blinked, "I've got your steak frying in my pan there on the stove, six eggs, with flap-Jacks on the side. Will your lady be down shortly, or should I go up and check on her?"

Becky sashayed into the kitchen like a princess on a cloud. She'd had her rest. Her man was home, *and* she *knew it!* "Just coffee Laverne, please," Becky hugged her. Laverne noticed the smile on her tiny friend's face.

Laverne reached out for the coffee pot. She poured Becky a cup.

"Did you say something, Laverne?" Becky questioned. "I can walk just fine, thank you. And yes*, it sure is* a beautiful day."

"No dear. Maybe I was mumblin to myself. I do that, being alone most of the time, with Harold in the fields." Then Laverne thought, 'He's not had much to do lately, and the ranch is going ta seed.'

Kyle looked at Harold, "What does Zeke do? I know your cousin Frank is a horse man. You've never talked about Zeke or Judd before. Do they live far from here?"

Harold looked strangely at Kyle as he'd not said anything to him about his cousin. "Oh, you heard us talking," he said.

Harold reached for the coffee pot and refilled his cup, "Zeke and Judd have a cabin up yonder, on the other side of the mountain. 'Bout six miles from here. They own a small hundred acre spread. They're carpenters and masons by trade, but there ain't no work around here for a body to keep themselves alive."

Kyle sloshed some chipotle sauce on his steak for extra spice. He cut off a hunk and sat back as he chewed.

Kyle looked at Becky thinking silently, 'I want to build a workshop next to the barn. I've been getting all sorts of ideas since last night. Would you mind if we had Zeke and Judd build the workshop for us?'

Becky thought back, 'It'd help them and they'd be helping us as well.'

Kyle saw a book he hadn't seen before. He reached over and opened to the first page. He rifled though it, looking for pictures. Suddenly he realized something!

'I'm gonna want to buy that helicopter pretty soon, hon, if you don't mind,' he interjected mentally to Becky.

Becky was surprised and thought, 'You said it might take you several months to do all the studying, attend classes, and take the flight exams.'

Kyle's eyebrows went up as he projected his silent thought to Becky, 'Hon, I just read the 600 page Gone with the Breeze, *as fast* as I could rifle thought the pages! If I read all the manuals as fast as I read now, take the written test, pass it, then I can take the flight test, and then I get my license punched for the helicopter *much faster*.'

Silently Becky responded, 'License punched? That's a good thing?'

Kyle shot back thinking, '*You betcha*. I want the workshop because I have several ideas and I want to build prototypes here at the ranch. If they work, we can move them into a factory that we buy later. Can you call your attorney friend, Robert Edwards, and see if he can recommend a good patent attorney? I've some designs I want to patent, along with the seeds, so no-one can monopolize our ideas.'

Becky took a sip of her coffee and thought, 'Sure, as soon as we're finished with breakfast, I'll give him a call. No problem.'

Harold and Laverne sat quizzically watching the couple look at each other but not saying a word. Harold shrugged at Laverne's "What's going on?" look.

Suddenly, Kyle got up and ran upstairs for a large drawing pad of paper, the 18 x 24 inch kind that artists draw on. Quickly he sketched out the kind of workshop he wanted, complete with dimensions. He brought the sketch back down to the kitchen.

Showing the drawing to Harold he asked, "Can you take this drawing over to Zeke this morning, Harold? Ask him how much and how long it would take to build a workshop like this? I want to get going soon. Tell him to figure in pneumatic nailers, like a framing, roofing, and finishing tools. That'll speed up the process. He might need a chop saw and stand too, if he doesn't have one."

"It will be Zeke and Judd, as they are, Kyle," Harold confessed. "They sold all their equipment to pay down on their land. They got nothin but hope ta save them against the storm, and she's beginning ta blow."

"No sweat," Kyle said. "I'll buy the nailers, nails, and saws. Get me a figure soon so we can order the wood and supplies from the lumber yard."

Harold stood up, grabbed his wide brimmed straw hat and jeep keys. He took a moment to strap on his 44 on his right hip and then he was out the door. He was on a mission! It felt good to have a job.

Chapter 11

As Harold walked out the door, going to Zeke's place, Kyle thought to Becky, 'What do you want to do this morning? How are you feeling?'

Becky shrugged, thinking, 'I feel fine. I feel like I always do. No problem.'

Kyle looked at her, 'After all you've been though, I think we should take it easy today and not get into trouble.' He grinned, 'On the other hand, we could stay upstairs all day. I love looking at the mole on the small of your back.'

Becky's eyes flashed, *'No! Nope*. I'd better go upstairs and get dressed.'

Kyle started to protest. Becky put a finger over his lips to silence him.

She shared her thoughts with him. 'This little dolly is all danced out, at least for a while,' she smiled.

Kyle slumped, frowning glumly, 'I hope I didn't hurt you, hon. Am I being too rough?'

Becky bent down and kissed his cheek, 'No Kyle, but you're *The Beast*, and I'm the Beauty.' She turned, heading upstairs, 'I'm gonna to go get dressed. Finish your breakfast. I'll be down in a minute.' She made the mistake of looking back. Kyle gave her the biggest set of puppy-dog eyes. It took all she had, to go upstairs and get dressed, *alone*.

Once upstairs, she had a moment to herself. She looked through the closet, "Hummm, I don't have a thing to wear, except one pair of short shorts, and two pairs of blue-jeans."

She slid into a pair of jeans. It wasn't safe to wear shorts, with Kyle around, unless they were going out on a date. Otherwise, she was surely going to get scraped up. Kyle was always getting into something.

A thought perked her spirits. The clothes from Freeport would be arriving today or tomorrow by messenger. She'd heard Kyle calling the yacht club earlier, asking them to put their purchases on the next plane. All those beautiful clothes. Now all she had to do was figure out somewhere she and Kyle could wear them.

She heard the back door swing shut. She couldn't imagine where Kyle was going. Maybe he was gonna gas up the jeep or the GTO? She remembered Harold took the jeep, when he drove over to Zeke and Judd's place.

She told herself she'd better get a move on or Kyle would leave her, but then she quickly dismissed that idea. She turned and looked at her butt in the mirror, frowning. She thought she was drooping a little. Maybe she could help Laverne with the house work? That'd almost be as good as a trip to the gym.

She skimmed downstairs, entering the kitchen. Laverne was washing the breakfast dishes, "Where's Kyle, Laverne?"

Laverne was a shinning light, "*Oh*, don't you look *darling!* As pretty as newborn calf."

Becky turned around and showed Laverne her butt, "I think I'm startin to get the saggies. What do you think?"

Laverne gave her one of her stunned, 'Whadda ya mean?' looks. Then she softened, "Look suga, you've been laid up for a week. Sure you got a little soft, but you'll tighten your figure up in no time."

Laverne smiled, "That's what's nice about living away from town. *It cuts down* on the competition," she giggled. "It helps when you're *the only female* within a twenty mile circle," she grinned.

Becky blinked. "Isolation does have some benefits," she said.

Laverne broke her train of thought, "Kyle's out in the barn. You better go out and see what he's up to. I hear him tinkerin with somethin out there. Just ask him if he wants something to drink. That's what I do. That way, they don't think we're keeping tract of what they're doin," she winked, "but we are."

"Smart lady!" Becky raised her eyebrows. "I knew I could learn a lot from you," she said. She touched Laverne's arm in friendship as she headed out the door, moving towards the barn.

Now she could hear some metal on metal tapping sound. Nothing regular. As she got to the open barn door, a nice breeze hit her. Kyle had opened the rear door and there was a beautiful cross-breeze through the barn. The day was turning out *lovely*. High, thin clouds on a brilliant blue sky. The hills, in the distance, were sparsely covered with pines. The ranch was away from civilization, but it was absolutely beautiful.

She blinked. Her man had a new toy! 'What are you doing, Kyle,' Becky telepathed.

Kyle had rolled out an ancient, *huge*, red tractor. Allyson-Chalmers was emblazoned on the dusty fuel tank. "Oh-My-God, Becky! I was waiting for you to come down, and I wandered out here. I saw a huge lump covered with a canvas tarp against the back wall. I *had* to check it out. What a treasure! This tractor is *an antique.*"

Becky blinked, "You don't say?" she feigned interest.

Kyle was more animated than she'd *ever* seen him. "What's so special about this ol' tractor, Kyle?" she wondered aloud.

"I love anything mechanical but I *really love* tractors," he explained to her.

"I knew of your attraction to machinery, but what is it about tractors, that makes them so special?" Becky questioned.

Kyle remembered back, "It was two summers before my mom and dad were killed. I had worked and saved my money from my allowance and from doing odd jobs. I had almost six hundred dollars saved up. One afternoon, my mom drove me past an International Harvuster dealership. They make tractors. There were three little tractors, *just my size*, parked out front. Wow, 'to be a man', I thought. The captain of my own destiny. All I could do was dream about those tractors all summer. Finally, I couldn't take it any more, and I talked to my mom. I told her I wanted to buy one with my money"

Becky walked closer to her man. She leaned against the six foot high back tire, as he told her his story.

"Mom wasn't all that keen on the idea. She knew dad was going to have a fit. It'd take all of my savings to buy the Cub Kadet tractor. It was my ticket to freedom. My land-ship to fortune and fame!" he explained with a broad smile.

Kyle paused, reflecting, "Our family had a long driveway and when it snowed, dad had to walk the twelve blocks to the hospital. Getting a man to plow out the driveway was both expensive and they didn't do a good job."

Becky saw Kyle had touched a nerve, but she urged him on, gently. "So what did you do?"

Kyle swallowed, "When I bought the tractor, it was the end of the summer and with winter coming I got a snow plow to go with it. Oh, I pampered that little thing, changing her oil religiously, greasing her wheels. It was two months before mom felt we could bring the tractor to our house from my aunt's place where we hid it. Dad *wasn't* happy I'd spent my money this way. He never said much, but if he wasn't happy, he let you know."

"So what happened with the first snow?" Becky prompted him.

Kyle smiled, "I parked the tractor in front of dad's car. It snowed a good foot and dad would've had to walk to work. I not only plowed out the driveway *expertly*, with no problem, but also plowed the sidewalk in front of our three-quarter acre property. It was rough if you had to shovel all that snow by hand! Once our place was plowed out, I went roaming and earned almost 150 dollars that day, plowing out other people's driveways. I don't remember dad saying thanks, but he offered to buy me a set of chains for the tractor tires, so they wouldn't slip. I guess that was my dad's way of showing his approval. All in all, that little tractor helped our family."

Becky understood how it felt to not be talked to when she was growing up. Each day, she learned she and Kyle had more in common. It strengthened their bond to each other.

"Thank you for telling me about your family. Now I understand your love of machinery," Becky smiled at him.

Kyle walked over to the workbench and grabbed some tools. Then he walked back to the engine on the tractor. He made some twisting motions on one of the spark plugs. Next he went over to the GTO and drove it along side the tractor. He took out jumper cables and attached them to the tractor's battery, leaving the GTO still running. Then he jump-started the tractor. The engine coughed, then roared to life as Kyle tinkered with it. He coaxed it to settle into a steady hum rather than a rattling pile of rusting junk.

Quickly, he unhooked the electric cables from the two machines. He returned the wires to the trunk of the GTO.

"Do you feel like a driving lesson?" Kyle smiled.

Becky jerked her head in surprise, "You mean *on that thing?*"

Kyle gently put his hand on her back and one hand under her butt and effortless lifted her six feet in the air and into the driver's seat of the Allyson. He turned off the engine in the GTO. Then in two steps, he stood one foot on the rear axle housing the other on the hitch mount, standing behind Becky.

He pointed to the pedal in front of her right foot. He showed her the gear shift lever between her legs, under her seat.

"I wanted to surprise you and teach you how to drive,' Kyle explained. 'The trouble is, that all the vehicles we have are stick-shifts. With you being the FNG, *ahh*, the new guy, it's hard for you to coordinate all the actions to drive a car. When I found this tractor, *it was the answer* to our driving problem!"

Becky looked shocked. Kyle always was thinking of ways to make things fun! She listened intently. Now she knew how Kyle felt when he drove his Cub Kadet tractor. He was a good teacher. He wasn't demanding and he didn't yell if she made a mistake. She made a mental note to give him *a special surprise*, tonight, *for being so sweet*.

Kyle told her, "With the tractor, you can put it in one gear, and it's like an automatic transmission car. Here, let me show you. Put your right foot on the pedal and push down. That's called the clutch."

Kyle put his massive arm over her chest, squishing her. The next problem was she was sitting too far forward in the seat. She blinked when he put his arm briskly between her legs and yanked the gear shift lever firmly into first gear. Her eyes widened and she loved his physical strength.

"Now gently, slowly, take the pressure off the foot pedal, and we'll move outside the barn," he told her as his face was even with her's.

As she slowly lifted her foot. The tractor lurched forward and she suddenly focused on driving and not her instructor's arm. She *shrieked* with excitement.

"Oh, Kyle! This is so much fun!" she exclaimed.

Kyle didn't move his right arm, "That's what I've been *trying* to tell you." With his left hand, he helped her steer the tractor safely out of the barn and onto the road around the ancient structure, leading to the long driveway going out toward the highway.

Becky was filled with adrenaline and was having a blast. "Where are we going?" she shouted above the din of the engine.

Kyle kissed behind her ear, "Down the driveway love, towards the road. I filled the ten gallon fuel tank before we left. We can run up and down this road and probably won't see another car or truck *all morning*. Since it's a farm road, this is *a perfect* place to practice your driving."

Kyle thought he'd better behave himself. He removed his right arm. Becky looked him in the eye, *"Thank you."*

Kyle blinked, innocently, "I was just showing you where all the handles and controls were."

"Ah-huh," Becky answered blandly. *"In case* you haven't noticed, *I don't* have a handle down there."

"Oh," is all he said. However, she didn't mind his smile. She knew *she* was the one *who put it there.*

Kyle politely put his hands on her shoulders as he stood on the back of the tractor. He could stand like this all day.

He reached around and took a hair tie he knew she kept in her shirt pocket. As he balanced himself, he combed her hair with his fingers away from her neck, pulling it into a tail at the back of her head. He tied her hair up. He bent down and started kissing the back of her neck. She felt his lips wiggling, and then she felt *a pinch.*

"Kyle, don't you be giving me *a hickey!"* she warned.

"I'm just playing," he answered innocently. He pulled back and looked at his handy-work, pleased with himself.

Becky was too busy to notice. She was riding a two thousand pound monster, six feet off the ground. Kyle had set the throttle, keeping the tractor down to about fifteen miles an hour. It wasn't too fast, but it was fast enough she had to be careful what she did. Driving the tractor required all of her attention.

Kyle decided to behave himself as he rode on the back. He enjoyed watching the clouds and seeing more of the area as Becky was having the time of her life. All told, they were out driving for about three hours.

"Oh Kyle! This is as much fun as when you taught me how to drive the airboat back in The Glades," Becky exclaimed.

'I'm glad you're having fun, hon,' he told her mentally. 'I have another *surprise* planned for this afternoon.'

Becky looked up, "What is it?" she demanded aloud.

Kyle smiled, then changed the subject, "We'd better turn around and head back to the ranch. I bet Harold is there by now."

Becky, harrumphed, *"O-K"*.

Zeke, Harold and Judd were in the kitchen when the couple walked into the house. Zeke stood five foot ten, weighing about 180 pounds, had long dark blond hair and a full beard. Judd favored his Native American mother, who'd died in a freak blizzard when he was four. Judd had midnight black longish hair and a beardless face. He stood a good six foot, weighing nearly 200 pounds. Both men clearly had fallen on hard times. This was evidenced by their thread-bare jeans and shirts, but the holes and tears had been carefully repaired. The clothes were old, but meticulously clean.

Harold introduced Kyle and Becky to Zeke and Judd. Then Becky excused herself to go upstairs and get their satellite phone.

Zeke looked at Kyle, "Harold says you want to build a workshop next to the old barn. Is that true?"

"Yes," Kyle responded, "It'll need to be twenty-four feet wide, by say forty-eight feet deep. Let's make it a two story deal. The first floor ceiling will need to be twelve feet high in case I want to work on a tractor. The second floor can be the usual eight feet high. I want plenty of southern exposure windows to capture natural light in the winter. They should be triple paned and use 2x6's with R-20 insulation for the sides and in the attic. We can use normal plaster board for the interior walls. I want a sliding garage door in the back, wide and high enough so I can get attachments for the tractor into the workshop. Put down a poured concrete floor as I might be making glass or welding. No wood as it would burn."

Zeke listened, looked at Judd then decided, "We can do that."

"Do you guys usually work with a lumber yard near here

that employs people from this part of the country?" Kyle questioned.

Zeke nodded, "We use Kendal's Saw Mill. They get their wood stock from the local mountains. Then they cut the logs into boards themselves."

Becky came back into the kitchen, announcing, "I'm ready."

Kyle looked at Zeke, then Harold. "Can Zeke take the jeep home, Harold? He can bring it back in the morning when he brings the shopping list for the lumber mill. Right now, I'd like you to drive Becky and I into The Springs. We want to get a truck and another jeep. You can drive us in the GTO since you know where we're going."

Harold shrugged, "You're the boss, Kyle. We'll do as you say."

Becky looked at Laverne, "Do you need anything from the city?"

"No darlin. We're fine for now," Laverne answered.

Laverne looked at Zeke and Judd, "I need to give you two hair cuts. You both look too much like old time mountain men."

Laverne called out to Harold, "Can I give Zeke your old straight razor?" She knew both of her relatives had hocked all they could for money to pay on their ranch. They were at the end of their rope now, both with empty pockets.

Harold called back to Laverne, "Sure, hon. You know where it is. He'll need to sharpen it first or he'll rip half his face away it's that dull."

Kyle led off outside, with Becky and Harold following. Harold blew Laverne a kiss as he walked away. Zeke and Judd were staying back at the ranch for a home cooked meal. They'd been living on fat-back and oatmeal for the last two weeks. Laverne promised them both a steak. Her cooking was the best in the county so there wasn't any argument from either of the two bachelors.

Harold walked to the GTO and slid into the driver's seat. Kyle held the door open for Becky to get into the car. She scooched over to sit in the middle of the front seat. Kyle got in and shut the door. Harold started the engine. He drove down the two hundred yard front drive out to the road and then down to the highway. There he turned the GTO east, heading towards The Springs.

Becky looked at the far away mountains. "I guess if we buy a jeep today, we can bring it home, *somehow.*"

Kyle nodded. He was deep in thought.

She confessed, "I'm having fun with you teaching me to drive, Kyle."

Kyle brightened, "I wanted to let you drive around and get some practice. It's pretty desolate out here and it could be fun," he smiled. "We can learn some of the back roads and the small towns. This area is rich with history. We could pack a lunch and go on a picnic, while I teach you to drive. There are interesting ghost towns all around these mountains. It's really fascinating."

Harold looked at Becky, "Kyle's right, Becky. I've lived in this part of the country all my life. Gold and silver was the heart-beat of this neck of the woods."

Kyle explained, "I've wanted to see Cripple Creek to the east, Royal Gorge to the south, Salida over to the west, and then there's Hartsel to the northwest."

Kyle looked at Becky, "Can you call Robert Edwards? I wanted you to ask him if he knows of a good patent attorney."

Becky shrugged, "Yeah, no problem. I'm sorry I forgot. I was having so much fun driving the tractor." She took out the satellite phone and dialed Robert's office number from memory.

Her call was answered by Robert's secretary. Becky responded, "Hi, this is Mrs. Swoboda. Can I speak to Mr. Edwards, please? Ok, I'll wait," she said.

In a minute, her call was answered, "Hello Robert, Becky Swoboda here. Thanks for talking with me. We were wondering if you could recommend a good patent attorney? Kyle, my husband, has some ideas he wants to protect."

Becky laughed, "That's wonderful Robert. I didn't know *you* were a patent attorney! Oh, you just did the real estate stuff for us, as a favor to dad? I didn't know your main interest was business law. That's great!"

Becky looked at Kyle, "Should I ask Robert to check out the property I saw in the magazine? You know, the one we talked about near the park?"

"Might as well hon, while you have him on the phone," Kyle answered.

"Robert," Becky continued. "First of all, I guess we'd better set up an account with you. You seem to be doing more and more work for us. Yes, that's fine. You're worth *every penny*, I know. The second thing we want you to do for us is to check on a 21st floor condo that sits on Riverfront Park. It has walls of glass so it's very picturesque. Can you get back to us on what you find, please? Kyle and I might want to buy it, for when we want to stay in Denver. By the way, where's your office in Denver? On Wewatta Street, just north of 16th ? Okay. Call back when you find something out, please. Thanks and talk to you later."

Now that Becky was off the phone, Harold asked, "What kind of truck are you lookin for, Kyle?"

Kyle turned his head, "I know we might be haulin lumber or equipment, so one with some muscle. I was thinkin about a V-8, Cheevy Silverato, contractor crew-cab with *full sized* bed, automatic transmission, and 4x4. I might want to convert the engine to burn alcohol fuel soon. Then I want to get a jeep Wrengler with automatic transmission, so Becky can drive it comfortably. I want to buy or order a hard top, for when the weather turns cold. We can get a soft cover now, for the summer."

Harold answered, "So you want me to go to the Cheevy dealership first?"

Kyle nodded, "Sounds good. Once we buy the truck, you can take off and go where you want. We're going to go to the jeep dealership for the Wrengler after we get the truck."

Harold shrugged, "Ok. So after you buy the truck, I'll just head back to the ranch in the GTO. I don't have anything I need in The Springs and I don't want to leave Laverne alone after dark. Zeke and Judd will stay with her until I get back home. They'll protect her and they're better shots than I am with either rifle or pistol. They live on the meat they shoot up in the mountains."

Kyle silently nodded his understanding. Zeke and Judd were following the lifestyle of the mountain men of old. They lived off the land.

When they got to the truck dealership, Becky and Kyle found a nice Caribbean yellow truck with an automatic transmission.

'Oh Kyle, this is just a beautiful color,' Becky thought. 'It reminds me of Miami and all the festive spirit that goes with it.'

Kyle smiled at his princess. He enjoyed her female perspective. It was so different from how he thought. He was going to buy the truck since it fit their needs, not by its color. It was loaded. After a test drive, they settled into a quick stop at the office. Since they were paying cash, they made a good deal.

Becky placed another call to Robert Edwards, "Robert, Becky Swoboda again. Can you recommend a good insurance agent? We just bought a truck and hope to buy a jeep shortly." She thought for a minute, "We might be taking on more employees at the ranch, so there will be business insurance choices too." Becky listened, "Wow, that's wonderful. You're our one stop shopping source today. It's handy you have an insurance agent working in your office."

While Becky was giving Robert's secretary all the car information for the insurance policy, Kyle waved to Harold. Then he drove off back to the ranch. The next stop for the couple was the Wrengler dealership.

As soon as they got out of the truck, a sales man approached, "Howdy folks! What can I do ya for today?"

Kyle explained looking at Becky, "We want a six cylinder Wrengler, cruise control, automatic transmission, 4x4, soft cover, but want to buy a hard top either now or order it."

Kyle looked at Becky and thought, 'What color do you want, hon?'

Becky thought for a minute, 'We'll be using the jeep primarily on the ranch, and we use the jeep to go to the mine. In the snow, white would be a good color to stay hidden. In the summer, the mud splash will camouflage it well. My vote is for a white jeep, with a white hard top, if possible. '

Kyle looked at the sales man, "Do you have a white one?"

"Yup," he answered, *"sure do!* You caught us at a good time. We've loaded up for the winter trade. The white top isn't commonly called for. We'd have to order that. We can deliver it when it comes in."

Kyle looked at Becky thinking, 'I had an idea. Why don't we get a car trailer that we can hitch to the truck?'

Becky relaxed, telepathing back, '*I like* that idea. That way we won't hurt the jeep towing it. Also, if we want to visit some of the ghost towns around Colorado, then we can tow our jeep there and use that to get to some of the hard to reach places.' She paused for a second, 'I've heard there are jeep clubs, couples who get together, and travel to interesting destinations. It might be fun for us to get to know other people.' She shrugged, 'Just an idea.'

Kyle looked at the salesman, "Do you have a trailer that would carry the jeep behind the truck?"

"*Sure, no problem*, Sir!" the salesman answered, "We can

do that. We've a lot of military people around here who tow their second cars when they move. I can make you a right nice deal too."

Becky was making her call to Robert Edward's secretary, to add the jeep information to their insurance policy. Kyle turned to her.

"Hon, when you're finished, can I talk to Robert, please?" Kyle asked.

Becky shrugged, "Sure, no problem." Becky said Kyle wanted to talk to Robert. Becky handed Kyle the phone.

Kyle walked outside the dealership. Within a minute, Robert came on the phone and answered, "Hello?"

Kyle confidently started in, "Robert, this is Kyle Swoboda.

Robert answered, "Yes, Kyle. What can I do for you?"

"I wanted some legal advice," Kyle answered, "I used to be a military sniper. I'm used to being armed. I wanted your advice as to the laws of this state, about what is needed to carry a pistol. Do I need to apply for a permit?"

"Yes Kyle, I read your military file. I wanted to know the kind of person who married my friend's daughter. Your record is exemplary to say the least. I'm sure you know, that you still carry your right to kill clearance? Of course your Rules of Engagement are the same as law enforcement officers, but you're considered a competent and cool-headed man."

Kyle raised his eyebrows, "I was counting on that clearance. You see, Becky was kidnapped last week. I was away from home at the time. Some people took her. Luckily, we got her back. It's just that I don't want to be foolish any more and not be armed. Can you help me, Robert?"

"Kidnapped? You're serious?" Robert blurted out.

Kyle explained, "When I met Becky, she was in trouble with some people from Miami, who followed us here and kidnapped her. Fortunately I got her back. I want to protect her. Then, when we first got to the ranch, there was trouble with another group of people. I've heard they are part of the Hungarian Mafia? That sounds *too weird* to be true."

Robert answered slowly, "*No Kyle*, unfortunately *it's not*. A criminal element has moved into the west these days, much like it did just after the Civil War. But, the West has its own variation of justice. We are, ah, more open to peace-keeping initiatives, than back east. Of course we stay within the guidelines of the federal statues, but we take a broader interpretation of *self-defense*. Often there are isolated farms and areas in our state that don't have 24/7, local law enforcement. Many farmers don't bother to call 911. The average response time could be almost an hour. To protect themselves from burglars, farmers use sound to warn off criminals. They pull back the bolt on a rifle and chamber a round. If a robber wants to tangle with an armed man, *then he's* been warned. We take self-defense *very* seriously."

Kyle laughed, "This sounds like *my kind of place*, Robert!"

There was a pause as Robert thought.

"Kyle, knowing your background, what do you say if I make application to the sheriff for you to carry a concealed weapon? Of course you can wear a pistol visibly in the back country *without* a permit. I can also get a Letter of Endorsement, to any law enforcement representative you might encounter, to treat you with respect and dignity. Of course I'll represent you in any dispute, should one arise."

Kyle smiled, "Like if I have to shoot someone?"

Robert nodded, "Precisely, *or* if you have to kill someone, in self defense. Of course, Kyle, I would expect you to behave yourself. I have no doubt you are aware of the ladder of defense?"

Kyle answered, "Yes, to avoid trouble if possible, and to meet force with like force. If they use a knife, I'm limited to a knife. If they use a gun, it needs to clear their holster *before*, I can kill them."

Robert agreed, "That pretty much sums it up."

Kyle added, "Robert, I want to teach Becky how to shoot too. So she can carry a pistol without a permit as long as it is clearly visible."

Robert answered, "Yes, Kyle. It's a rule of the old west."

Kyle went on, "Since we're in The Springs, I was going to go buy some pistols today, after I take Becky to the Motor Vehicle Test Center to get her learner's permit."

Robert looked at his watch, "I can get started on the paperwork today. You'll have to visit the country sheriff to get your picture taken for your permit when you can. Is that ok?"

Kyle smiled, "Sure. I was just going to teach Becky how to shoot tomorrow. After that, I was going to take her out for a driving lesson. If we go on lonely roads, I think it would be wise to be armed, just in case."

Robert straightened, "Ok Kyle. Let me get started. For the sake of my friend and me, *please* protect his daughter. She's *very* precious to him, even if she doesn't know it."

"She's very precious to us all. Consider *it done*. Thanks for all your help, Robert. You've made everything painless. Bye," Kyle said as he disconnected the call. Just when Becky came out of the showroom, the salesman drove up to them in Kyle's new truck with the Wrengler attached behind riding on its trailer.

Kyle asked the salesman, "How can we get to the DMV Test Center?"

The salesman looked at Becky and grinned, "Out the driveway, turn right, two blocks north on the left hand side is the DMV." He had an idea, "Why don't you and your lady take one of our courtesy cars and leave your truck right here? When you've finished your errands, bring the loaner back. We close at 9 PM."

Kyle shrugged, "Sounds good to me. I'll take you up the offer. Oh, by the way, do you know a good gun store around here, with military weapons?"

The salesman laughed, "Afraid they won't pass you?"

Kyle and Becky laughed, "No. But it never hurts to be prepared, right?" Kyle grinned back.

The Gun Emporium. Three streets west, on the right from the division of motor vehicle office. They have *every-thing*," he told them.

Becky slipped a hundred dollar bill to the salesman, "Have dinner on us. You've been very helpful, Freddie."

Freddie touched the brim of his hat, "My pleasure, Mrs. Swoboda. Ya-all come back now. We're here to serve."

The salesman pulled out his radio and called for a courtesy car. In a minute, a mechanic drove up with one.

Kyle drove Becky over to the motor vehicle test center. She was nervous.

He tried to calm her, "Get the driver's laws and *scan them*. We can read *really quickly* and with your already photographic memory, you'll pass the test."

At the Center, Kyle spearheaded their visit. He told the receptionist, "My wife needs to get her driver's permit."

"Your wife's never driven before?" the secretary asked, surprised.

Becky answered, "No."

The secretary explained, "First you need to pass the law test, then we can give you a learner's permit. You need to have a licensed driver with you when you drive after that. In a month, you can come back here and take a driving test. Once you pass that, you can get your full drivers license."

The secretary handed Becky a book, "You might want to take this manual home and study it. Then you can take the test.

Becky rifled through the pages. She looked up, "Can I take the test now?"

The secretary's eyes widened, "*Sure*, right over there. The tests are given on the computer these days. Just follow the instructions."

Becky walked over to the computer. In fifteen minutes, she walked back to Kyle. She showed him her driver's permit. "I'm all ready!"

Kyle walked out to the courtesy car. He held the door open for Becky.

Next he drove to The Gun Emporium. Becky saw the sparkle in his eyes.

Becky and Kyle found The Springs to be a beautiful western town, home to many activities and places of interest. The streets were open with a south western charm and a mixture of old and new architecture. The sun was starting to cross over towards the Rockies which dominated the western skyline.

"What had you wanted to get at the store, Kyle," Becky asked.

Kyle answered, "I wanted to get a pistol for you hon, so I can teach you how to shoot and protect yourself. I talked to Robert about the right to carry a weapon laws here. We can evidently carry a pistol without a permit as long as it is visible and not in a large city. He's going send the paperwork to the county sheriff to get us permits to carry concealed pistols. I know it sounds weird, but where we live, we're out in almost a wilderness areas. We could encounter a bear or even modern day desperados. Either way, if a person can shoot, they can protect themselves."

Becky blinked, "Wow, I never thought about that, but I see your point."

KYLE PULLED UP IN FRONT of the store. He helped her inside.

Immediately, an ex-military-looking salesman came up to Kyle, "What can I do for you today?"

Kyle smiled. He noticed the ex-grunt didn't call him Sir. That was good. Kyle was an ex-Sergeant. Sergeants like to say, *they work* for a living.

"I want to get my lady fitted out. I'm thinking a 38 caliber pistol with a four inch barrel. The four inch barrel will allow the bullet to reach a high enough velocity for the hollow point to expand properly. She'll carry it in a drop, tie down holster," Kyle answered.

The salesman put a soft mat on the counter over the revolvers. He brought out three different pistols. Becky held them all and selected one she felt comfortable with in her small hand. It was a nickel plated, six shot, single-double action pistol. Kyle showed her how it worked.

Next Kyle found her a right-handed tactical nylon, thigh-length tie-down holster that fit her 38. This put her pistol where her arm reached her thigh for a quick draw if needed.

Kyle then asked, "Do you have speed-loaders for the 38, and a leather carrying case for two extras?

The salesman turned and reached into a drawer and brought out a nice selection for them to choose from in leather and nylon.

Becky leaned forward as she chose the style of a holder for the ammunition that fit her pistol. She selected the soft-brown, varnished holder with tooled leather design. It held the customary twin speed loader cylinders.

Now that she was settled away, Kyle asked to see a 44 caliber, 4 inch barreled revolver. The salesman showed him a Smith and Westen, nickel plated Mountain pistol.

Kyle asked, "Will this shoot 44 magnum and specials?"

"Both," the salesman replied. "Do you like the magnum?"

Kyle tilted his head, "No, actually I like the 44 special. It's great for follow up shots." In a minute, Kyle decided, "I'll take this pistol. Do you have a tactical drop, tie-down holster for it too? I need a left-handed one though."

The salesman nodded, "No problem, Mac. We got you covered. Is there anything else you need?"

Kyle looked around, then at Becky, 'This could get expensive,' he thought to her. 'Bringing me to a gun store is like your shopping trip in Freeport for clothes.'

Becky thought for a minute, 'Kyle, I don't mind you buying *anything* you want, but I *want it understood*, this is for pleasure or defense. I don't want you going back into the sniper *business* EVER again.'

Kyle kissed her, 'I agree.'

Becky kissed him, 'OK, then go have fun. I'll sit over here and watch.'

Kyle asked the salesman, "Do you have a 50 BMG Barett Model 82A1?"

The salesman pulled his fingers off the counter, "Ooo, now you're talkin my language, Mister. I gotta warn you, the prices aren't for the weak of heart! Like you're talking close to 9 Gs. You up for that? Each round of ammunition will cost you maybe five dollars a pop!"

Kyle smiled, "Shake out a 82A1. Let me see how she feels."

Becky noticed the rifle. It looked really familiar!

"Isn't that the one you were just shooting, Kyle?" Becky questioned.

Kyle looked over at his wife, "Yep. It's the same. Never know when I'll need to drop a coyote over 2000 yards away," he winked.

The salesman tried to suppress a smile. It was as hard now, as it was back in Boot Camp, but he managed.

Kyle decided, "I'll take it."

The salesman became serious, "*You gotta* have something to shoot."

Kyle grinned, "Oh yeah! I want Winchaster brand if I can. I want a case of 38 specials, 110 grains hollow-point, and a case of 44 specials in a 200 grain hollow point. Then I want a case of 7.62 mm, 168 grain boat-tail, in ultra match quality. Next, I need a case of tracer, and a case of 647 grain armor piercing ammo for the 50 caliber BMG."

As Kyle was talking, the sales man was getting what Kyle wanted. One last thing caught Kyle's eye.

"Let me see that little 12-gauge pump turkey shotgun will-ya?" Kyle asked the salesman. He handed it over to him.

Kyle motioned Becky over to him, "Here, hon, hold this. How does it feel?" Kyle showed her how to work the slide.

Becky held the short weapon that had a 21 inch barrel, "Wow, this is great! *Can we get this too?*" she asked excitedly. She looked at the business end of the barrel, "*Wow,* that'll chew someone up, I bet."

Kyle looked at the salesman, "Give me a case of 12-gauge OO buckshot."

The salesman looked at the shotgun and Becky, then he asked, "Where do you folks live?"

Kyle smiled, "Why?"

The clerk blinked, "*I don't* want to wander over your way by mistake. In case you two are *in a bad mood.*"

It took several trips, but Kyle carried his purchases to the courtesy car. Next they drove back to the dealership. In minutes, they loaded their arsenal into their new truck. Within the hour, Kyle and Becky were on the highway, weaving their way down to Canon City and then northwest on route 9. Kyle skirted Granite Bluff for now, taking a farm road back to the ranch.

It would've been more scenic if they drove home the northern route from The Springs. Like going through Cascade, up to Woodland Park, taking highway 24 west into Hartsel and then south on route 9. The trouble was that the northern route takes you over the mountains. Kyle didn't want to go over them in *a new truck*, haulin a Wrengler on a trailer! So he chose the southern route, but he dodged Granite Bluff just the same.

By the time they pulled into the driveway at the ranch, they saw there was a light on in the bunkhouse. Becky and Kyle knew that Laverne and Harold had moved out there. That left the house all to themselves.

After getting ready for bed and brushing their teeth, both climbed into bed and Becky was ready for sleep.

Kyle turned, asking, 'Do you really want to have a baby so fast? I'm not against it, but you're still pretty young. Maybe you don't want to get bogged down in responsibilities so quick?'

'Ahhh,' Becky thought. 'You're being sweet.' She examined her feelings then projected, 'I grew up alone, Kyle. I missed having someone to talk with, to share experiences. Laverne's here with us. She'll be a great help. IF we need to get away for a weekend, Laverne and Harold are live-in nannies. I'm being offered a wonderful opportunity. Yes, I'd like to see if we could have a baby. My grandma said women in her day had children early in life. It worked out, as long as everyone agreed, and were relaxed about the challenges that occur.'

Kyle reached out and stroked her hair, guiding his lips to her's. Becky kissed him back and reached to turn out the light. It had been a full day.

Chapter 12

The next morning, Becky awoke, feeling *absolutely perfect*. The light was softly filtering into the bedroom from the captain's watch french-doors. She was snuggly-warm. She looked at the clock on the night stand that stated 8:45 am. Songbirds chirped their songs from a near-by tree.

Becky's eyes flashed open. This was *too* perfect. *Where was Kyle?* She looked around the room. He was nowhere to be seen. The tip-off was that his jeans and cowboy boots were gone. That clinched it.

Becky threw back the covers muttering to herself, *"Men!"* she sputtered to herself. "If they aren't making a woman: achy, dirty, sweaty, then there's *something wrong*. Just like this morning. I should've known this was too good to be true. Laverne was right," she mumbled, "you gotta keep watch over them *all the time."*

'What in the name of heaven is the matter?' Cathy gasped, seeing her long-time friend in such a state.

"Oh Cathy. Am I glad you're around. I don't know *where* Kyle is," Becky blurted out. "He didn't poke or prod me this morning. He didn't wake me up putting on his pants and boots. I didn't even smell his coffee the first thing when I woke up. *Something's wrong."*

"Mercy sakes, Becky," Cathy stammered, "calm down, honey. You're gonna burst a blood vessel." Cathy thought, "I remember seeing him outside in the back yard, but I didn't pay attention to him. I sensed you were really upset and came up here straight away."

"Now take a deep breath and hold it," Cathy ordered her.

Becky was used to Cathy being pushy, so she did what she told her. In a minute, her pulse started to gain some sort of tranquility.

Cathy stood with legs apart, fists on her hips, complete with a frowning look, "Now it's time you got dressed. After your shopping extravaganza yesterday, I'd assume you're going to go to the rifle range. A proper young lady will dress causal, but elegantly. We aren't beasts of the field, *you know*."

Becky walked over to her closet in her all-together. She'd taken off her night gown. "My clothes from Freeport better get here soon, or I'll scream," Becky threatened.

Cathy had been with Becky, Rebecca Allison Wells, since she was a child. She'd seen all of Becky's moods and tantrums, but this was a new facet of her young friend. This would warrant watching."

Cathy came over and stood next to Becky, "There, there, dear. It's ok. It'll all work out. Don't get yourself into such a state. Kyle is probably out in the barn, puttering with that 'ole tractor he found. He doesn't need to see his little dolly all upset, with puffy red eyes, *does he?*"

Becky admitted back, "No, you're right as usual, Cathy."

Cathy impishly said, "Let's get you dressed in your lacey lingerie set, you know, the white ones with the thong that he likes. That brings out the Bad Boy in him," she giggled. "Then you want your jeans and the cotton shirt with a collar. You can cover up that hickey on the back of your neck. You might want to wear a scarf too. That's a hum-dinger!" Cathy chuckled. "Looks like you got attacked by a giant sucker-fish."

Becky seethed, "*I told him* not to do *that*. Wait until I see him! I'll give him a hickey he won't soon forget," she threatened.

Cathy laughed, "*No you won't*, young lady. Ladies don't do that sort of thing, at least not at your age."

"Oh! Like I'm an old spinster? Cathy, I'm only eighteen you know," Becky reminded her.

Cathy ignored her friend. She sensed Becky was changing. Something *was different* "You'd better wear the sneakers. I've a feeling you're going to be walking around and you want to be comfortable, no matter what. I've gotta go."

"Go where?" Becky demanded. "Are you still seeing, *Naughty Ned?*"

Cathy blushed, "Yes, we're trying to work out our, ahh, differences."

Becky looked shocked, "You said that old man was too kinky for you!"

"A guardian angel doesn't have that many romantic options," Cathy retorted. "

Becky blinked. She wasn't sure she wanted to continue this conversation, but her curiosity got the better of her, "How did you work things out?"

Cathy blushed, "Ned's all hands, he was like a Grabby Gus. You know, Roman Hands and Russian Fingers?"

Becky laughed. "He's spent too much time with that donkey of his!"

Cathy leaned forward, "You better not tell Harold, his ancestor is a letch."

Becky said, "I think that runs in the family. Laverne calls it Harold and Laverne's, *slap and tickle time.*"

Cathy frowned, "Ned gets grabby, and he pinches. Then I slap him silly. The trouble is, then the cycle starts all over. Brother, he's a slow learner! I keep tellin him, "Rub, don't grab! The next thing the neighbor's hear is, *whap*."

Becky wasn't going *there*. It's like talking to your mother about some things. Some subjects are just best left, unspoken. Cathy looked at her old friend deeply. Then Cathy blew a kiss to Becky and whispered, "Ciao baby," as she faded away.

Fully dressed, Becky made her way downstairs. There wasn't anyone in sight. The house was as quiet as a tomb.

Becky remembered what Laverne did. She stood and listened. She heard rustling outside in the back yard. She went out the back door and was stunned.

The white Wrengler stood proudly by the back door, all cleaned and polished. There was a huge pink ribbon hanging from the windshield. She noticed that her 12-gauge shotgun hung horizontally on the roll-bar. It was within easy reach for anyone sitting in the front seat. All of their shooting gear lay across the back seat. Kyle had pushed the canvas top back since it was such a clear and lovely day. He was sitting in the passenger side smoking a cigar, nursing his usual cup of coffee.

'Happy Anniversary,' Kyle exclaimed via telepathy.

Becky blinked, 'Is it our anniversary, already?'

Kyle smiled, 'Everyday I know you is an anniversary for me, honey. I'm just so happy we're together. I can't say it so well, in words, though I try.'

Becky ran to her man, 'I knew you were up to something. I didn't have to *fight you off* this morning. I woke up totally rested and content. I knew something was wrong!'

Kyle looked upset, 'What was wrong?'

Becky blinked her long eyelashes, *'You,* weren't in my bed.'

Kyle grabbed her, 'Well, we can remedy that real quick.'

Becky feigned anger, *'No! Nope.* We're not going back upstairs. I'm all dressed for the day. You missed your chance, Bucko. Besides, you promised to teach me how to shoot this morning, *and* you're going to give me another driver's lesson this afternoon, remember?'

Kyle liked the feel of her wrapped in his massive arms. She was so femininely soft, 'Oh, I was, was I?'

Becky nodded her head, little girl style, 'Yep, you were.'

Kyle dropped his grip a little lower, so his arm was around

the small of her back as he stood up, lifting her effortlessly with him, so they were face to face. He looked at her luscious lightly pink lips. He went to kiss her, but she teasingly pulled back.

"If I give you a kiss as tribute, *will you* teach me how to shoot?" she asked."

Kyle smiled, thinking, "Ok, but it has to be a *really* good kiss."

Becky laid into her task as she molded her soft lips to his, and she gave him, her best. Kyle's eyes flashed open as he began to smile.

Becky pulled back as if in a daze, "How was that, cowboy?"

Kyle smilingly licked his lips, "I especially liked that last part. I think we should try that again."

Becky pushed back, *"No! Nope.* You got your kiss. Now *you* deliver."

Kyle roared and threw her up over his shoulder. Becky screamed in laughter out loud. Laverne and Harold stuck their head out of the bunkhouse door, then immediately disappeared again inside.

Kyle walked around to the driver's side and moved his shoulder so it bounced her into the air and Kyle caught her, supporting her back and under her knees. Then he stole another kiss, before he deposited her gently in the driver's seat. He showed her how to adjust the seat, so she could reach the pedals. Then he walked around and got in the passenger's side.

He looked at her, "You know, I was reading this month's Cozmo. There's a thing starting, where a woman is tattooed on the small of her back, just above her hip-hugger jeans. They're calling it a tramp stamp. Also, women are getting their belly-button's pierced."

Becky gasped, "Where did you get a copy of Cozmo?"

Kyle smiled, "I ducked out when you were taking your driver's exam. They have the most *interesting* articles."

Becky was aghast, "I don't like you reading that rag, Kyle. You're gonna get the wrong impression about women that way. If you have a question, I think we should talk about whatever it is you're curious about."

Kyle smiled, kissed her and answered her generous offer, "Sounds good to me, hon. I appreciate you talking to me about all sorts of subjects."

He returned to their activity at hand. He showed her how to turn the key in the ignition and the engine started. 'The long vertical pedal is for the gas and the flat horizontal pedal is the brake. Put your foot on the break now.' Then he pointed to move the floor stick of the automatic transmission to circle D, for drive. 'When you take your foot off the brake, we should start to move.'

Becky did as Kyle instructed. Then they started to move. She drove down the path to what is now known as, Kyle's shooting range. Becky drove the jeep over to the picnic bench and then slowly pushed the brake to stop. Kyle showed her how to put the transmission in park, set the parking brake, and turn the engine off."

Becky jumped out of the jeep and met Kyle at the back of the car. He started unbuckling Becky's leather belt.

"*Not out here*, Kyle," she looked nervously around.

Kyle looked at her with astonishment in his eyes. He picked out her tactical leg holster and slid the belt through the top loop of the holster. Then he reached between her legs and pushed them apart.

"What are you doing, Kyle?" Becky fidgeted.

Kyle looked at her innocently, "I'm showing you how your holster fits on your leg. It's really great. It only took a hundred years before this style came back." He'd pressed the Velcro leg bands around her upper thigh. Next he reached in the jeep and took out her 38 caliber pistol.

"Why didn't you buy another pistol like you had when I first met you, Kyle?" Becky questioned.

Kyle, still looking at the weapon explained, "When I was in the military, I had to get used to an automatic pistol, but they weren't my first choice. Their barrels float, even the second generation autos. That instability doesn't let you accurately shoot much more than fifteen yards. I personally like a revolver. I've accurately placed shots in a bull's eye at fifty yards. The barrel on a revolver doesn't float. It's stationery and so you can really get accurate shots that way. By changing the length of the barrel, you can increase the distance you can accurately place bullets."

Kyle showed Becky how to push in the lock and swing out the cylinder. He handed her a box of ammunition. She knew how to put the cartridges into the cylinder, and then she instinctively closed it.

"You have to be careful now, hon. That weapon is ready to fire. *Always* point a loaded weapon away from you or anyone you don't want to shoot," he told her. He took an empty, plastic milk jug and threw it about twenty yards away. He also put a pair of ear muff protectors over her ears. She could hear what he said, as if his voice came through a speaker.

Kyle showed her, carefully, "Single shot means you pull the hammer back and then squeeze the trigger. I think that's the most accurate way to shoot a revolver. You can squeeze the trigger, making the hammer pull back, and then eventually fall against the cartridge. That discharges the weapon. That's called double action. I find there's too much wobble doing that. That throws the bullet off." He took a breath, "When you shoot a weapon, you need to think of throwing a stone. The bullet acts like the stone. If you can visualize how your stone is flying through the air, then you can soon sense where your bullet will strike."

Kyle stood behind Becky, "Now pull the hammer back and shoot the jug."

Becky did as she was told. Her first shot was wide.

Kyle explained, "There's a fin on the front of the pistol and a groove at the back of the barrel. You aim, by putting the front fin in the grove at the back of the barrel. Moving the front fin up or down in the grove makes the bullet hit higher or lower on a stationary target."

Kyle put his own, left-handed holster on. Then he took out his 44 caliber revolver and loaded it. Next he holstered it, tying it down, with the nylon strap over the back of the revolver.

Becky had fired all six shots from her weapon. Kyle showed her how to push in the lock, swing the cylinder out over an old coffee can, and how to push the shell extractor bar in, to eject the spent brass from the weapon.

"I guess I didn't do very well," she was disappointed with herself.

Kyle wasn't upset, "Hon, practice makes perfect. Also, lead down the barrel, is the pathway to accuracy. They're old, but wise sayings."

He pulled her slightly behind his left arm, then he unfastened the tie down strap from his holster. With measured, controlled speed, he drew his revolver, grasping it with both hands, using his right thumb to pull back the hammer. His first shot, popped the milk jug into the air. Then the other five shots jerked the milk container each time a large slug penetrated it. As the echo of the sixth shot faded, the jug thunked to the ground. Instantly, he opened the cylinder and with practiced hands, ejected the spent brass into the coffee can. He immediately reloaded his revolver.

He looked at Becky, "A weapon is a deadly tool, but it's not very lethal unloaded. Once you've fired all your rounds, eject, and immediately reload. Then holster and tie down your weapon until when you are going to shoot again."

Becky couldn't help ask, "Kyle, why do you call the revolver a weapon instead of a gun?"

Kyle said, "There's a difference, honey."

Becky was curious, "What's the difference?"

Kyle gave up and recited the creed he learned at boot camp.

He held up the revolver in his left hand and held his jewels in his right. Holding his revolver he recited the punishment, engrained in his memory forever, "This is my weapon, in his left hand, this is my gun, in his right. This is for shooting, this is for fun."

Becky blinked, "*I had* to ask, *didn't I?*"

Kyle shrugged as he holstered his weapon. Next he showed Becky how to put the speed loader holder on her left side belt. Then he handed her a round gadget, that held the six cartridges into the holder, with the release knob down and opened. When all six cartridges were in the loader, she could lock the release knob that holds the cartridges upside down.

"Once you fire the last round in your weapon, open the cylinder and ejected the spent shells. The six fresh cartridges in the speed loader fit the cartridges into the six holes of the cylinder. Twist the release knob and the cartridges drop into the cylinder holes. Close the cylinder and the revolver is ready to shoot again," Kyle instructed.

"With two speed loaders, a shooter has eighteen rounds available to fire quickly," Kyle explained. "Hon, back in the day, in the old west, when gun fights were used to settle arguments, a quick draw wasn't always the best. It was the most accurately placed, quickest shot, that was the most important."

Becky wasn't all that sure, "What if someone is as experienced as you or an experienced combat vet?"

Kyle looked at her, "There aren't that many really good shots around. Often fear of being shot will affect a shooter and their first shot can go wild. That's why it's important for your shot to be accurately placed. If you face someone as experienced as me, you have to trust that they won't shoot you unless you're a direct threat to them. There isn't much challenge in shooting a newbie. The challenge is shooting someone as expert as yourself and bettering them."

Becky could see his point. She hoped she'd never face someone as lethal as Kyle when he was mad.

Kyle stood beside the jeep, "In time and with practice, hon, you can learn to shoot pretty well." Then he pointed to the 12-gauge turkey gun hanging under the roll bar, "Grab that. This is your equalizer, until you get good with your pistol."

Becky reached above the driver's seat and pulled the little shotgun down. Kyle showed her how to use it.

She held the weapon as he explained, "There's a button to the left of the trigger, feel it?"

She felt around and found it, "Yep".

"Now push in the button and pull back on the slide," he told her.

She did as she was told and the slide opened the chamber. She saw a clear plastic cartridge with round balls the size of raisins inside, which appeared for an instant, before she instinctively thrust the slide forward until it locked.

"Always point a loaded weapon down range, hon. Push the other button behind the trigger to the right. Now it's ready to fire. Hold the weapon against your right hip. At least this way you won't get kicked with the recoil, but a 12-gauge is a very lethal weapon. Go ahead and shoot the milk jug. Try to point the barrel in the vicinity of the jug. Then squeeze the trigger."

The valved ear protectors muffled the roar of the large shotgun. It allowed Becky to hear a conversation, but an abrupt *loud* bang, closed off a diaphragm, protecting hear ears.

Maybe it was beginner's luck or maybe Becky found her weapon of choice. She obliterated the milk jug with her *first shot*. She was *a natural* at point shooting.

Kyle laughed, "I'm gonna start calling you dead-eye."

Becky was amazed at her ability, "Wow that was fun."

Kyle told her, "Pull back on the slide and eject the spent shell. Early this morning, I took out the plug in the magazine under the barrel. Now your shotgun will hold six shells and one in the chamber, if you want. I'd advise, just go with the six shots. If there are any desperados left standing when you're empty, I have an extra box of shotgun shells in the glove box." He showed her how to reload, sliding the fresh shells into the tubular magazine of the shotgun.

Kyle policed the area, cleaning up the plastic shotgun cartridges. He found what was left of the mangled milk jug. He had Becky load her speed loaders, and then he did the same. Once their revolvers were reloaded, they holstered them, locking them down with the nylon tie down strap.

He looked at Becky, "Let's go back to the house. I asked Laverne to make us a picnic lunch. I wanted to take you out on the highway and let you get some driving practice. We can clean the weapons when we get home after that."

Kyle climbed into the passenger seat as Becky climbed into the driver's side. She turned on the ignition and the engine sprang to life. Just then the phone rang. Kyle picked it up, "Hello?" he said into the satellite phone.

Kyle turned to Becky, "It's Laverne. She was wondering when we were coming back to the house."

Becky nodded as she started the jeep and put her in gear. She headed the jeep down the path and back to the ranch house.

Kyle answered, "Laverne, we're coming back to the house now. Is our picnic lunch ready? Becky and I are going to do some driving practice."

"Yep, Kyle. I'm all ready for you two. I've packed: sandwiches, chips, olives, Jewish dill pickles, Dr. Peper and sweet iced tea for the little darlin."

Kyle smiled, "We'll be right there. See-ya," and he disconnected the call.

Becky didn't say much. She was concentrating on her driving.

"How do you like the jeep, hon? Is it ok or should we take it back?" Kyle wondered.

Becky gushed, "*Oh, this is wonderful.* The jeep is just my size. I can toy around with this thing *all day.* I think the truck will be too big for me to comfortably handle.

Kyle said, "I can see that. That's why I got you this new jeep." He had her pull the four-wheel drive lever, and they felt the little jeep squat down and grab the ground firmly with all four tires.

"Ooo," Becky chuckled, "We can go *anywhere* with this."

Kyle smiled, "That's the idea, hon. I don't like to be restricted."

When they got back to the ranch, she went upstairs to freshen up. When she got back downstairs, Kyle took the picnic basket off the kitchen counter and called his thanks to Laverne for her thoughtfulness. In a minute, both she and Kyle were back in the jeep, heading west on the farm road that ran in front of the house.

Kyle explained, "We're going over to Guffy, just north of Granite Bluff. Then I figured we'd drive north on route 9, through Hartsel, past Fairplay, going towards Breckenridge. It's a really straight road. I don't want to get that complicated for our first time out. There's a gold mine north of Fairplay I wanted to see. We can stop there, find some shade, and have our picnic."

Becky was enjoying the bright sunshine and cool air. With the top down on the jeep, Laverne had insisted she wear a Southern Bell hat, with the six inch wide brim, that tied under her chin to keep the hat on.

Becky drove them through Alma, heading towards Hoosier Pass. Just after that, Kyle spotted a little pueblo with a central square. The place was called Hansen's Crossing. The town consisted of a filling station and a general store.

Kyle pointed to the store, "We can ask directions to the mine there. Want to come in with me?"

"Naw," she replied. "I'll just stay in the jeep. You won't be long, will you?"

"Nope, just in and out," Kyle answered.

Becky stopped in front of the turn of the century general store. She noticed two crew-cab pickups at the filling station. She didn't pay them much attention.

When Kyle got out of the jeep to go inside the store, Becky closed her eyes to rest, pulling the wide brim of her hat down to shield her eyes from the noonday sun. She heard footsteps on the gravel close by. She looked up. It was *Mr. Stanley*. He was the man who tried to force Harold and Laverne to sell their ranch to him, when Kyle and she first came to Colorado.

"I couldn't help seeing you from across the street," he said. "My name is Vladamir Vjeti." He held out his hand, which Becky ignored and didn't shake.

"Do I *know you?*" she asked cautiously.

Vladamir was undaunted, "No, but I am attempting to change that."

Becky looked up, "Whatever you're attempting to do *isn't working*, Mister. I'm a happily married woman and my husband is inside the store. Please leave me *alone*. I'm *not* interested."

Vladamir pretended not to hear the last part. He motioned for two of his toughs to flank the general store doorway, in case her husband decided to intervene.

Anger flared inside Vladamir as he viciously slapped Becky's face, "You American women *have much* to learn. You don't know *your place*."

Becky couldn't believe this was happening, in broad daylight, in the middle of America! She gritted her teeth, determined not to let this cur see her cry.

"I'm going to tell you to *walk away!*" she ordered him. "Walk away *now* or, you'll be sorry. My husband isn't a man to trifle with. If you leave now, I'll not press charges against you for battery."

Vladamir began to chuckle, but again, he savagely slapped Becky's other cheek, "You husband is *as good as dead*, silly woman. My men will see to that!" He reached out and savagely grabbed Becky's left breast.

Becky gasped at this outrage! She struggled to dislodge Vladamir's hand, but couldn't. He cupped her viscously.

Vladamir hissed his intentions, "My men *will kill* your

husband. I am attracted to you, so I will take you for my woman, for now. When I tire of you, I'll give you to my men. IF you survive six month's, I'll be surprised. None of the other American women we've seized, have."

The crushing sound of wrist bones caught Becky's attention, as the hand on her chest was savagely removed. Vladamir whipped out a straight razor, flicking the blade open with a distinctive snap. He moved to slash Becky, but was stopped as KIS grabbed Vladamir's right wrist. KIS reached up and took control of the blade. With an instinctive move, KIS whipped Vladamir around, his right arm forced Valdamir's right arm behind him and then up. As KIS pinned his right arm behind his back, his hand grabbed the collar of Vladamir's coat and dislocated his right arm causing *excruciating* pain. In a blink of an eye, KIS pulled the deadly straight razor from the assailant and professionally slit Vladamir's throat, slaughterhouse style. KIS held him for a minute until he felt Vladamir sag. Blood rhythmically spurt from the man's severed jugular.

Simultaneously, four men started running towards the fight. Becky *had all* she could stand. Something snapped inside her. She stood up on the driver's seat with blood in her eyes and grabbed the 12-gauge. Instinctively, she pushed the slide button release and chambered a round of double ought buckshot. She pointed the turkey gun at the oncoming herd of men. Instantly, they stopped! They now stared down the one inch wide barrel of a 12-gauge shotgun. It was held by a woman who'd been savagely abused and slapped twice in the face!

"Excuse me," came a voice from the right. Becky and KIS turned as one. Becky kept the shotgun trained on the group of men. A sheriff stood watching the scene before him. He looked at Kyle, "Did you ever rodeo?"

Kyle kept his hand close to his pistol, but he didn't draw. "No," Kyle flatly answered.

The sheriff rubbed his mouth, "You could've fooled me,

Mister. You annihilated those two henchmen as they grabbed you coming through the door. Then you bull-wrestled Vladamir and slit his throat. *Very professional*, I'd say."

Kyle turned to the group of men, "On the ground, *now*, or I'll slit open your bellies with a dull deer antler. If you look up, this angry woman will gladly blow off your heads. I call her, *Dead-Eye*. Let her *show you* how she got the name."

Kyle turned back to the sheriff, pointing to his shirt pocket. The sheriff nodded, "Ok."

Kyle took out the wallet with Robert Edward's card inside. He handed it to the sheriff who read the card. "My name's Kyle Swoboda, recently Sergeant Swoboda, not long out of the Corp. This lady is my wife, Becky.

The sheriff handed the business card back. He pushed back his hat and then shook hands, "I'm Hank Slocum. Pleased to meet cha, Sarge. I was a PFC back in the day. I got out after a four year hitch. This is my home now."

Kyle surveyed the crossroads, "Can you call for backup?"

The sheriff shook his head, "I'm all the law this hamlet has, 9 to 5, Monday through Friday, no weekends or holidays. Other times, the staties take the calls."

Kyle walked in the general store and came out with a roll of duct tape. He tied the four men's hands behind their backs. Next, he collected their wallets. The two men by the door, were dead from snapped necks. Vladamir lay dead in his own pool of blood.

Kyle handed Hank the four wallets, "Call these names into Immigration, Hank. I've got a feeling, they're illegal. Immigration might want to question these boys. We'll keep them covered until you come back."

Hank nodded, "Ok. Thanks for helping me clean up the town. This gang blew in here about four months ago. I didn't have anything on them to arrest them. I know they've been buying up ranches all around this area, mostly muscling the ranchers into selling out cheap, fearing for their lives."

Kyle nodded, "Go call them in."

Hank walked off. Kyle worriedly looked at Becky, who stepped across the seats of the jeep to her husband. She handed him the shotgun and then immediately broke down, sobbing deeply.

"I can't believe this happened to me, *again*," she wailed "Do I have a sign painted across my forehead advertising, *victim?*"

Kyle held her, "I'm sorry you were roughed up, Becky. I saw what was happening, but those two goons grabbed me when I came through the door. It took a minute to get to you."

Hank walked up to the couple, "Immigration is sending a wagon for these guys. There are several outstanding warrants for each of them."

Kyle said, "I guess I'd better call my attorney. I assume there'll be a judicial inquiry about the death of these men."

Hank twitched his mouth, deciding, "*Naw*. I saw the whole thing. Vladamir accosted your woman. On my official report, I'm going to list the cause of death as *Shaving Accident*. My uncle is the Justice of the Peace, and the mortician is my brother-in-law. Justice was served. I have the phone number of your attorney if there should be a problem, but I don't think there will be."

Kyle was surprised, "Do you need us to stick around?"

Hank looked with concern toward Becky, "You better get her home. I'd recommend a shot of whiskey. I know that's what I'm gonna have the minute I'm off duty. It's been an *interesting day!*"

Kyle shook Hanks hand. We have a ranch east of Granite Bluff. Our table is always open to a fellow gyreen and the coffee's free. Drive by and say howdy, sometime. Becky and I have come *to stay*. This is our home now too." Hank nodded, "I'll do that, Sarge. Until we meet again. *Vaya con dios.*"

Chapter 13

The next month flew by. Everyday was action-packed. Challenges arose, but with determination, Becky and Kyle found solutions.

Zeke and Judd came by with their materials list for the new building. Becky felt lost not being able to just fax the list over to the lumber yard. Kyle drove the two builders over to order the supplies they'd need to erect their workshop.

Becky called Robert Edwards in Denver. She was getting on a first name basis with Robert's secretary, Brian.

"Brian," Becky began, "we need to set up hospitalization on the four employees we have plus, worker's comp, and the usual insurances."

"Ok, Mrs. Swoboda," Brian answered efficiently, "What's the name of your corporation or company?"

Becky laughed, "We hadn't stopped to think about that, Brian. Hold on a minute," she requested.

"*Holding*," Brian sighed, a tinge of exasperation in his voice.

Becky threw out her thought to Kyle. She hadn't ever projected this far before, 'Kyle?'

Miles away, Kyle walked away from the contractor counter at the lumber yard, 'Yes, love, is something the matter?'

'No, no,' Becky reassured him, 'no problem. Brian, Robert Edward's secretary is asking me what our corporation name is. I'm sure Robert will file papers forming a corporation using the name we come up with.'

Kyle thought for a minute, but had to confess, 'I don't have a good name in mind.'

Becky smiled, *'Let a woman do this'*, she thought, 'We met mysteriously and under miraculous circumstances. Then there was our unusual encounter with Adam. What do you think if we called our company, the *Mystique Corporation?* You'll be the President and I'll be the VP, treasurer, and secretary? Other than you being listed as the corporation president, we'll ghost my name as the officer for the other positions? That will keep my identity confidential and protect me from being bothered by sales persons.'

'Works for me, hon,' Kyle smiled, 'You've got such a great head for business. I'd be at a loss without you! *I'm serious.* Kisses to ya, suga.'

Becky mentally gave her Beast a kiss back. Then she quickly got back to Brian, who was still holding.

"Brian, are you still there?" Becky questioned.

"Still holding, Mrs. Swoboda," Brian piped up.

"We're going to call our company the Mystique Corporation," she said.

Brian said, "Very good. Also, Mr. Edwards would like to speak with Madam, if you would, please."

"Of course, put him on," Becky responded.

"Becky? Robert. How are you today, darling?" Robert gushed.

Becky half-laughed, half-cried, "Robert, I'm having *a horrid day*. All I have to work with is this old telephone made back in the 1950s!"

"No, no! We simply cannot have you fighting that situation," he paused, as he thought. "I have a friend, Julian, who's *a genius* with office décor. I could drive him down this afternoon?"

Becky laughed, "Robert, how about I send a helicopter to pick you and Julian up there in Riverfront Park? The pilot can fly you from Denver to us at the ranch in half an hour. Then we can let Julian see just what antiquated equipment I'm working with. I'm sure he can suggest a solution to my office problem for now. We can plan an ultra modern office when the new house is built or the old ranch house is remodeled."

Robert frowned, "Rebecca, you are such a wet blanket. I was planning on *an over night junket*, but you are too practical, by far."

Becky blinked, "I just don't want to tempt you, Robert. I thought you were going exclusive, last week?"

Robert frowned, "No dear, *that* was last week. Out in the wilderness like you are, you're so out of touch. I'm a *play-ya*, love. I roam the field."

"O-K," Becky laughed, rolling her eyes. "I'm not going there, Robert. Call me and let me know when the chopper can pick you both up?"

Robert's eyes widened, "Ooo *chopper*? Can we wear *lea-tha*?"

Becky sat up, "No, Robert. This is business, *not pleasure*. I've a feeling you'd like leather chaps too much," she laughed wickedly.

"Ok, da-ling. You are worse than my mother," he fumed. "I'll have Brian call you back with a pick-up time. Lata, *princess*."

Becky put down the phone. She laughed, *"Wow."*

'You know why you can talk to Robert so easily, Becky?" Cathy asked.

Becky jerked around, surprised, "Cathy? *Oh my God*, *Am I* glad you came back. How's it going with Ned?"

Cathy frowned, "He's getting so possessive. He's been back in the woods too long with Jezebel, I think. I needed some space, to let him cool his jets."

Becky closed off her mind. She didn't want Cathy reading her thoughts. Then she realized what Cathy had said.

"Why can I talk to Robert so easily?" Becky wondered.

Cathy stood over one hip, "Because of your father, *silly*.

You're used to people from all different walks of life. You have your life the way you choose, and they have their lives. It's wonderful how you accept people as they are."

The phone rang. It was Brian, "Can you pick Mr. Edwards and Mr. Fleming up, in an hour, at the foot of 16th street and Chestnut, in the park?"

"Yes, Brian. I'll call the helicopter company to give them the address and pick up time. Thanks for coordinating everything."

"No problem. That's *what I do*, Mrs. Swoboda. I work *miracles*," Brian quipped softly.

Becky hung up the phone and turned to Cathy, "Oh, my God, *so much* has happened. I need to bring you up to date."

In two hours, Becky and Cathy were interrupted by the sound of the helicopter landing beside the barn. This coincided with Kyle driving up in the truck. Robert and Julian got out of the helicopter and bent over, moving quickly to where Becky stood, waiting to greet her guests. Kyle got out of the truck and stood beside his wife.

Robert was dressed impeccably, in a light brown sports jacket, open-necked blue starched cotton button-down shirt, beige cashmere trousers and cordovan penny loafers. Julian, in contrast, had beautiful, dark-brown hair, growing just past his shoulders. His hair was elegantly gathered in a long pony-tail, tied in a brilliant red silk kerchief, that was color coordinated to match his ascot. He wore a powder blue sports coat, white dick pants, with open toed leather sandals.

Becky turned to Kyle thinking, 'I asked Robert to bring a friend to see what could be done to create a temporary office. I *simply can't* work like this. I feel like I'm repressed. *I can't* communicate with the rest of the world,' she complained.

'Ok, love,' Kyle thought back. '*Whatever* you need.' He wanted his goddess happy.

Robert handled the introductions, "Becky, Kyle, this is my friend and colleague, Julian Fleming. He's an *ar-teest* when it comes to interior design."

Becky and Kyle shook hands with Julian. Kyle was careful not to crush hands when he greeted their guests. Becky motioned to the house.

"Julian, Robert, this way please," she directed.

Kyle waved his hand at the group, "I've got things to do out here, folks. I'll leave you to work out a solution to Becky's problem. Thanks for helping us."

Kyle turned and walked away toward the barn. Becky had arranged for the helicopter to wait while they had their meeting. When it was over, Robert and Julian could be flown back to Denver, in time for afternoon tea.

Julian watched Kyle walk away. His mouth fell open. He breathed, "*A Northern Saxon Knight*. He can ravage me, *any-time*."

Robert frowned, "Julian, you are such a hussy!"

Becky moved all of her five feet, 100 pound frame in front of Julian, demanding his attention. "*That knight*," she said emphatically, batting her eyelashes, perturbed by the blatant display, "*is* already taken!"

Julian weaved, "Well, one can at least, look…"

Becky narrowed her eyes. Robert took Julian's arm, urging him along, "We've got work to do, dear heart. We don't want to offend our hostess."

Kyle enjoyed getting close to the helicopter, looking inside. It was a civilianized, military helicopter. He'd seen these a thousand times before.

"You want a cup of coffee while you wait?" Kyle asked the pilot.

"Thanks, but no. I'll just sit in the cockpit. I was told their meeting shouldn't be long," the pilot responded. If you want, you can sit in the copilot's seat, while we wait."

Kyle didn't have to be asked twice. "That'd be great. I've

been thinking about buying a helicopter myself. I thought it would be handy, living way out here."

The pilot checked the setting on his radio, "The maintenance on these birds *is horrific*. You might do better leasing one or contracting with a share service. That way you have the availability of the craft without the extra hassle."

Kyle nodded, "I understand, but if I can afford it, I'd like to indulge myself. I'm just in the thinking stage right now. Flying is a passion of mine."

The pilot's attention was drawn to the back door. Julian emerged from the house howling in displeasure, "*You poor dear. I pity you, Becky,*" he moaned. He looked at Robert, "I need to get back to civilization and converse with Alfred. We'll put our heads together and find solutions to her problems."

Julian drew himself fully upright, "*Don't you worry,* Becky. Julian, is on the case. We'll drag you out of the Stone Age and into the new millennium in no time." He put a fist on his right hip, "I'll have state of the art phones, computer links, cushy chairs, maybe a French Provincial desk, for you to govern *your realm.*"

Robert took Julian's arm, "Come on, darling. Tomorrow is another day. If we don't shake a leg, we'll miss our reservations at Antonio's."

Julian blinked in dismay, "Well in that case, *let's go.*"

Kyle and the chopper pilot witnessed creation in progress. Kyle looked at the pilot, "Show-time," he said as he opened the copilot's door. The Pilot flicked a series of switches and toggles, then watched the dials, as his bird came alive.

Kyle held the rear door while he helped Julian into the helicopter. Julian leaned into Kyle's ear, "You have an adorable wife, Kyle. I could just eat her up. She's too sweet for words."

Kyle smiled back at Julian, "Watch your step, and yes, I could eat her up too," Kyle winked back, grinning broadly.

Julian gasped at Kyle's naturalness, as he twirled to Robert, "Heavens, he's such a magnificent *beast.*"

Robert turned to Kyle and shook his hand, motioning to Julian, "He's really very talented. I hope he didn't upset you, Kyle?"

Kyle shook Robert's hand, "No, not at all. Thanks for coming on such short notice, Robert. You know that woman is my life. I'll do *anything* for her."

Kyle helped Robert seat himself in the helicopter. Robert leaned forward, "And so you should, dear man. I'm glad you two are so close. I'll relay your best wishes to Becky's father, Jeffrey. He was so worried Becky wouldn't turn out alright, living with that *evil witch*, Angela."

Kyle smiled, "Thanks for all your help, Robert. You've been a very kind friend to us both. Thanks for being there for us."

Robert was visibly touched. He looked at Becky handing her a business card. "Here's my personal cell phone number. Please feel free to call me with *any* question you may have. *If ever* you need help, *please* don't hesitate to call me."

Robert watched Kyle hug Becky, and she hugged her giant back, while the helicopter lifted off the ground. Robert thought, 'If I'd been fortunate enough to have a daughter and son in law like these two, I'd consider myself a lucky man.' At the same time Robert realized that they had become very important to him. He now considered Becky and Kyle, a part of his inner circle of friends, even though they weren't part of his lifestyle.

Robert didn't see Becky grasp Kyle's arm as she whispered into his ear. Kyle raised his hand and waved to the chopper. He also was a happy man.

Becky and Kyle walked around the side of the barn. Zeke had staked out the new workshop. It was starting to take shape. He and Judd were to start work on the foundation in the morning.

Becky stopped as if stuck by lighting. She took out her ever-present satellite phone and dialed Robert's number, "Robert, it's Becky. I thought of another question." She laughed, "Yes, yes, I'm full of them." She persisted, "I was wondering. There are so many regulations about growing food, but we have a grain and a seed pod we'd like to grow here on the farm. Is there a way around all the red-tape? We want to get food to the starving poor and homeless people."

There was a pause. Becky listened closely. Finally, she said, "Thanks Robert. Also, Kyle and I want to patent these seeds. Yes, I can Fed-X some samples to you tomorrow, to start the process. I knew I could count on you. Talk to you later and I hope you have a lovely dinner tonight. Yes, you know I'll keep in touch. G'bye."

Becky took Kyle's hand and walked him around the barn. She pointed to the pasture on a southern slope just behind the barn.

'Remember you were worried about all the regulations about raising the grain?' Becky thought to Kyle.

'Yup," he thought back.

Becky wriggled with excitement, 'Robert said we can grow our grain and seed pods *if* we call them *organic*. We can sell the grain or food in Health Food Stores. I was also thinking we can offer our grain, ground into flour, to the soup kitchens. They'd at least try the food. They could use it to feed the homeless.'

'It's worth a try,' Kyle thought back.

Becky wondered, 'Can you give me a few weeks? I'd like to clear and plant 100 acres of the grain and plant some of the seed pods along the riverbank of the stream, that runs through the center part of our land. Would that be enough time to do all of that?'

Kyle thought, 'It'll take Zeke and Judd at least that long to pour the foundation and let it cure. Zeke was going to subcontract, pouring the floor, to a separate company who puts in floors for warehouses. They have special tools and workers just for that. And yes, with modern machinery, we could clear and plant two fields in that amount of time. No problem.'

Becky perked up, 'We can rent the tractor and implements we'll need to clear and plant our fields. We could also rent a combine and harvest the grain ourselves when it's ready,' she grinned. 'One of the problems with farm families is, that they are equipment rich, high in debt, due to all the tools they need to farm and produce their crop. A farmer can't always contract a company to harvest their grain, because the crop could ripen very quickly. Scheduling an expensive harvester to bring in the grain might not be possible. The farmer could lose the year's crop. So, they buy their own expensive machinery. Most just break even every year. Being a farmer, you're rarely going to get rich.'

Becky stood up straight and projected, 'Adam? Are you there?'

'Yes, Becky, I'm always here,' Adam projected to both Kyle and Becky.

Becky asked, 'We want to grow the grain here on the ranch. To plant a hundred acres as a test. Can you get us enough seed to plant that much?'

Adam chuckled lightly, 'Yes. Seed for 100 acres isn't a problem. If you wanted to plant 100 square miles, that would take some effort.'

Kyle asked, 'Can you put the seeds in the barn tonight?'

'No problem. Is there any other questions while I'm here?' Adam asked.

Becky double checked, 'Are there any plant diseases or pests we need to plan for, when we grow the crops? I don't want to introduce any problems into the state.'

Adam answered quickly, 'No. The plants are healthy and disease free. They are perennial. They also are superior to any kind of food being offered to humans today by your food industry, but that's a whole other subject.'

Kyle asked, 'We just clear the land, plow it, disc and then rake the soil to prepare it for planting? Then we plant by broadcasting the seed onto the soil with a spreader?'

'Yes, Kyle. That's how we did it with the Mayans,' Adam agreed. 'Of course, they did it all by hand, back then.'

Becky thought, 'Thanks for your help, Adam. We want to start preparing the land tomorrow.'

'Don't worry, I'll have the seed in the barn tonight. Let me know how it goes,' Adam answered as his thoughts faded.

Becky looked at Kyle, "I'll go in the house and see about renting the equipment for tomorrow."

Kyle nodded his head, "I'll come inside in a minute. I just want to make sure the cars are gassed up." That gave him an idea. "Can you ask the tractor company if they can deliver some sugar beet seeds with the equipment tomorrow? I want to plant a small patch of beets, to see if I can grow some, to make alcohol fuel from them?"

Becky turned to the house, "I'll see what I can do."

The next morning, just before dawn, Becky and Kyle were roused by the sound of several large trucks coming up the driveway. Kyle jumped out of bed, threw on his pants and boots, and was out the door. Becky quickly followed.

The agricultural, "ag" rental company delivered the *huge*, dual wheeled tractor, wide plows, discs, and rakes. Next there was a broadcast spreader with a hopper that could hold fifty 100 pound sacks of grain seeds. Once the equipment was offloaded from the delivery truck, the driver got Kyle to sign for the rental. Next he explained the tractor controls to him.

"I'll be back in two weeks to pick this stuff up," the driver explained. "If you finish your planting early, call us. The rental price will end at sunset of the day you call. Ok?"

Kyle nodded, "Sounds fair. See you then, unless we call sooner."

The driver got back into his tractor-trailer, waved, and drove off.

Kyle was like a kid with a new toy. He climbed into the beautiful green tractor. The tractor was *huge!* Becky was surprised there was space for her to join him in the luxury cab. Kyle started up the diesel engine and drove off to their intended field.

Yesterday, he'd marked out a hundred acres. Now he needed to wrap a stout chain around some of the scrub brush that littered the land from years of over grazing. Becky hadn't ever seen how land was prepared for planting. She enjoyed being with Kyle while he worked. Kyle liked having his woman with him too. She was his best friend now, his soul mate. They were becoming inseparable.

It took some time to clear the field, and pull the brush into a pile, then chip it into compost. Next the field was plowed, then disked to break up the soil, and finally raked to smooth the dirt. Finally it was ready and they seeded the field. Kyle did the same operation to prepare the twenty acre plot down by the river, for the pod plants. At the end of the two weeks, the Ag company came to collect their equipment.

After dinner, Kyle and Becky went to the second story balcony to watch the sunset and enjoy some time under the brilliant, star-filled, sky. Becky thought, 'Life can't get any better *than this.*'

Chapter 14

Becky snuggled close to Kyle as he enjoyed his evening cigar. The couple relaxed on the soft sofa Kyle had hoisted up to the balcony. It was becoming their evening routine. Becky didn't mind this way of ending the day. This gave them the chance to touch in with each other before sleep. The sky overhead was *crystal clear*. Suddenly, they both saw a shooting star.

Kyle looked down at Becky, thinking, 'Make a wish.'

Becky smiled, looked up, thinking back, 'What do you mean?'

'It's an old saying, to make a wish upon a star,' Kyle pointed towards the shooting star.

She thought for a minute then decided. 'I wish for a peaceful place, where we can enjoy life, not only for us, but for our family as well.'

Kyle turned slightly, "I don't understand, hon."

Becky tenderly placed her hand over Kyle's heart, explaining, 'We need to start planning not for *just us*, Kyle, but for our baby as well.'

'*Baby*?' Kyle gasped in his head as he tried to sit up straight.

Becky kept Kyle where he was, but she couldn't help seeing his broad grin. 'You know, Kyle, this is the first time I've seen your teeth when you smiled?' She put her head on his broad chest. 'Can I believe, you're as happy as I am?'

Kyle nodded a silent *yes*, but then hesitated, 'Are you sure?'

Becky confessed, 'I'm late. I'm usually like clock-work. A woman *knows* about these things.'

Kyle hugged his tiny lady closely. Never in his wildest dreams had he envisioned being so happy! He wondered what Becky would look like with a big tummy.

Becky sat up and looked at Kyle, 'If our baby is a boy, I'd like to call him Kyle Ibsen Jr. What I'm not sure is, if we have a girl. What name you'd like?'

Kyle smiled, 'I guess Rebecca Allison Jr wouldn't work?'

Becky laughed, 'No, I don't think that's how it goes.' In a minute her eyes brightened, 'What do you think about Alexandra or Alexa? We could call her Lexy for short?"

Kyle nodded, 'Alex or Alexa, would be wonderful. Lexy is cute also. Can we at least make her middle name Rebecca?'

Becky's heart melted, but she frowned, 'Alexandra Rebecca just doesn't just roll off your tongue, and besides, a woman likes to be an individual.' She shifted her weight, 'How about Alexa Christine Swoboda, if we have a girl?"

"Alexa, Christine," Kyle tasted the name, "Hmmm, I like that."

There was a gust of wind and a presence entered Kyle and Becky's mind. 'Do you mind if I intrude?' Adam telepathed.

Kyle looked at Becky, then looked into the darkness of the night, 'Please, Adam, join us,' Kyle telepathed back.

Adam walked from the bedroom and out onto the balcony. 'I understand *congratulations* are in order for you two.' Adam looked at Becky's middle, 'I see a human growing inside of you, Becky. I'm so happy for both of you.'

'Thanks,' Kyle and Becky both echoed in thought.

Adam frowned a little, '*You know*, you two have unfinished business that needs to be addressed.'

Becky looked questioningly at Adam, 'What do you mean?'

Adam leaned against the balcony railing, 'Those men from Florida? The Columbian Drug Cartel? They claim you two owe them money. A *lot* of money. You know, they won't let you alone until you pay them back. Now with the baby, you can't afford to ignore that threat.' Adam shifted his weight, 'Since you have enough money, you can pay these people back, and be done with them. Fair is Fair.'

Becky seethed, 'Those people *are ruthless*, Adam. They'll kill both Kyle and myself, just to show others, not to take anything from the Cartel.'

Adam moved his head, 'I view them as businessmen, Becky. What I'm asking you to do, is to approach them, offer to pay them back their money, and then their claim against you two *should* be satisfied.'

Kyle sat up, 'Adam, I'm not sure they'll leave it simply as settling a debt. These folks like to make examples of people who *they consider* have wronged them. Even if we pay them back, I'd bet, they'll try to kill us.'

Adam looked at Kyle seriously, 'That is a possibility. What I'm asking you to do, is to approach these people, offer to pay them what you took from them, for *whatever reason*. I wish to dispel their claim against you.'

Becky looked amazed, 'How can we do that, Adam?'

'Simple, my dear,' Adam smiled. 'Just ring them and offer to meet them in Miami. Offer to settle your debt, so that they'll leave you and your family in peace. Then you can travel the world, unafraid. To be able to enjoy life. To go out dancing. To have dinner unconcerned about your safety. Please, *trust me*.'

Becky stood, walked into the room and then returned with the satellite phone. She pressed the phone number of the El Toro night club. She remembered the front desk number with her photographic mind.

"Hello, Ricardo? This is Becky Wolefski. May I ask who is running the club, now that Raul has gone to his reward?"

In a moment, her question was answered, "Ah, Don Miguel. He'd be a wonderful choice. May I speak with him, please?"

Becky looked at Adam and Kyle while she waited. In a moment, her call was answered,

"Hello, Don Miguel, this is Becky Wolefski. Yes, I can imagine you'd be surprised to hear from me," she stated somewhat stiffly. "I want to settle any bad blood between the Cartel and myself. Is that possible?"

Becky listened closely, "Whoa, I have *two million dollars* of yours. The third bag was torn up in the Everglades *by an alligator*. For that bag, you'll have to discuss that issue *with him*. I had nothing to do with that."

Becky laughed, incredulously, "What do you mean, I caused the Cartel to lose all that money? Raul and Carlos were going to sexually assault me on the airplane that night, and then sell me as a sex slave to someone in Bogotá. Did you expect me to just sit calmly *and allow* those atrocities to happen?" She tried to settle herself, "I'm offering to discuss the return of one million nine hundred thousand dollars, in a cash transfer."

Her eyes narrowed, "*No*. Not two million dollars! I had one hundred thousand dollars in the offshore bank account which *you* no doubt siphoned off. So, I consider what is outstanding between us is one million nine hundred thousand. The other million dollars is the cost for a *bad business idea*."

Becky listened closely, "Yes, I realize you're tracing this call, but you already know where I live."

She looked at Adam. He answered her telepathically.

'They will kill us Adam!' Becky seethed.

Adam looked at Becky softly, 'My dear, you are as close to me as family. I wouldn't let *anything* happen to either you or Kyle. *Trust me*.'

Becky wouldn't let it go, 'But Adam, I've seen the kind of men who protect this mob. They're vicious and ruthless.

You're *only* an anthropologist, a college professor. No offense, but I don't want to trust my husband to a ninety pound weakling."

Adam smiled, 'I *know* what I am, Becky, but looks can be deceiving. I come from a warrior race who evolved into academic endeavors. Our society was close to total annihilation from our fierce evil tempers. I *am* capable of terrible destruction *if angered*. I will be with you both at your meeting.'

Becky searched Adams eyes. Something in Adams words, in his soul quelled her fear. Adam was *more* than he appeared. Her feminine intuition told her. She relaxed and returned to her phone call.

"Don Miguel, you've always been a reasonable man. I enjoyed serving you, but, I have friends too. They will look *for you*, should *anything* happen to myself or my husband. I can promise you *that*."

She smiled, "No, I'm not threatening you at all. I'm just stating a fact."

There was a long pause. It was as though Don Miguel was consulting with his lieutenants.

Becky listened closely. Then she answered, looking at Kyle, "Yes, my husband and I can be in Miami tomorrow night, at the club. Say, 9 PM?" She waited, "We'll be there. Good night." Then she disconnected the call.

Kyle looked at Adam, "Will we be safe at this meeting?"

Adam nodded, *"Yes,"* as he disappeared into the house.

Kyle got up to get another cigar as Becky called to make their usual travel arrangements. She was getting used to doing this. She thought she might as well have everyone on speed dial. Later, she went to pack for both Kyle and herself.

She opened the overflowing closet in her room filled with *beautiful* clothes that *finally* arrived yesterday. She wanted to enjoy wearing some of her new clothes. 'What good are clothes, if one doesn't have an event to wear them?'

The next afternoon, at 2 pm, Becky and Kyle boarded the

helicopter at their ranch, bound for the Denver Airport. This time they boarded a smaller corporate jet and settled in for the flight in the passenger's section. At Miami airport, a contract limo picked them up and drove them to South Beach. On one of the back roads, the limo pulled into the parking lot of the El Toro nightclub. Kyle and Becky were quickly and politely ushered into Don Miguel's office. Kyle wasn't the *least bit surprised* when he was confronted by six huge body guards all standing around Don Miguel's desk.

Don Miguel stood, "It is good to see you again, Becky. We thought we had you the last time, *but strangely*, inexplicably, you escaped from us."

Becky wore a black, sleeveless, open neck cocktail dress, with a necklace of diamonds, and black high heels. Kyle wore a charcoal double breasted suit, starched white cotton shirt, black polished shoes, and a powder blue silk tie.

Don Miguel remarked, "It looks like you're doing well since you worked for the club, Becky. I hope it's not from spending *my money?*"

Kyle stood with outstretched arms as two of the body guards frisked him for hidden weapons. The guards were surprised that he was unarmed. All six guards surrounded the couple.

Becky looked at Don Miguel with cool confidence, "Our wealth, *is none* of your business. You would be overly arrogant to think The Cartel is the *only* successful business venture in this world. We're here tonight to transfer the one point nine million dollars from our offshore account to yours. Are you interested?"

Don Miguel smiled, "*Oh yes!*"

Becky saw his computer and asked, "May I?"

Don Miguel moved aside, "Please, be my guest."

Becky paused, "I will want a Paid In Full letter from you Don Miguel. To insure, we'll not be bothered by your men in the future."

Don Miguel smiled, "You two won't be bothered in the future. You have my word on that, Becky."

Becky looked at Kyle, who answered her, mentally, *'Trust, Adam.'*

Becky took the piece of paper from Don Miguel that listed his account number. She typed in their account number and made the transfer command. She waited as Don Miguel hand wrote his receipt. Becky read it and then punched in three more numbers. At that point, the one point nine million was transferred.

Don Miguel looked at his account. Satisfied, he looked at Don Antonio and said, "*Kill them.*"

Instantly, the room lights *went out.* Kyle grabbed Becky, protecting her as he felt a *powerful* electric current surge all around him. An eerie buzzing crescendoed inside the room. Gun shots were fired and some of the men screamed in terror as they were cut down. The room shook like they were in the middle of an earthquake. Points of glowing lights, the size of domino cubes, began to appear where the bodyguards had been.

As the lights in the room slowly brightened and the commotion settled, Kyle and Becky cautiously looked about. Don Miguel's head appeared above his desk. Like a little child, when the conflagration began, he dove under his massive mahogany desk for cover. He shakily stood up. The cubes of metal glowed with radiant energy and then slowly disappeared. It was as if the bodyguards' life energy and bodies were reduced into their metal components and heat. The glow was as if the life energy from their body, left the cube, to dissipate into space. This proved the Law of Physics, that energy can neither be created nor destroyed, only transferred.

Instantly, Don Miguel froze, as a message was telepathed into his brain. 'IF you ever come after *my people* again, I'll come after *you* and *yours!* Hell will look good after I'm finished with you. Inform the miscreants in your business community, the same can happen *to them*. This couple and their family are *not* to be disturbed. You saw what happened to those who wished to harm them. Now go, tell the criminal world!'

Don Miguel shouted, "*Go. Get away from me!*" he screamed at Becky and Kyle.

Kyle stood calmly, letting Becky stand on her own. The lid on Don Miguel's humidor lifted as if by magic. Silently, a large, expensive cigar mysteriously floated over to Kyle.

Kyle smiled as he took the cigar and sniffed the Churchill sized delectable. "Mmmm Cubano," he savored. "Though I favor Dominican, I always wanted to try a bona fide Cuban cigar." He looked at the amazed, wide-eyed Don Miguel. "Thanks, I'll enjoy this later if you don't mind." Then Kyle walked Becky through the club. A stunned Don Miguel walked behind them, insuring the couple wasn't delayed as they left. As soon as they left the club, Don Miguel started making phone calls, advising his business associates *not to mess* with Kyle Ibsen Swoboda or his family. To do so, would be a *deadly mistake!* This Diablo has mystical powers.

Once Becky and Kyle were in the limo, Kyle thought, 'Thanks, Adam. We trusted you and you didn't let us down.'

"I wonder how he did that," Becky remarked.

"All I know," Kyle said, "is that with his protection, we'll never have to worry about the drug cartel or their henchmen ever again. It's a great feeling."

Becky turned to Kyle, "Would you mind staying over night? Since we're in Miami and safe, there's someone I'd like you to meet."

Kyle relaxed back in the plush seat, "I'm game. This is your town, lead on."

Excited, Becky leaned forward, talking to the driver, "Take us to the Wellsley Hotel, please."

"Yes Ma'am," the driver replied.

Becky picked up her trusty phone and dialed the hotel's front desk. "This is Mrs. Becky Swoboda. My husband and I would love to stay overnight. Do you have an ocean front suite, we could reserve?" She waited a minute, "That would be lovely. We'll be at the hotel in a few minutes. Right, see you then."

Becky sat back and snuggled against her Monster. She smiled.

Kyle raised his eyebrows, "You seem pleased with yourself," he laughed.

She nodded, "Yes. I always wanted to stay at that hotel. I heard they had a marvelous dinning room and adjoining dance floor for late night entertainment."

Kyle stiffened, "You mean, like dancing?"

Becky sat up, "Yes. I love to dance."

"That's what I was afraid you'd say," he moaned.

"Why? What's wrong?" Becky wondered.

Kyle hesitated, "I never danced before. I don't know how," he said shyly.

Becky smiled, "Well, I'll just have to teach you. It'll be fun! We'll keep to the slow numbers. Just shuffle your feet so you won't step on my toes. I'm wearing open toed high heels," she laughed.

Kyle brightened a touch, "My mom started to teach me how to slow dance, just before they passed away. So I do know how to dance a little, if you'll be patient with me."

Becky smiled and thought, 'Ah, you must be a country-boy! This city-girl will be gentle with you. Trust me,' she smiled, with a twinkle in her eye.

Kyle told himself to relax as the limo pulled up in front of the hotel. The bell hop came and collected their bags. Becky confidently walked through the amazing lobby. It was simply opulent. The décor was modern, but still retained some lavish 1940s charm.

Kyle looked around in awe. He'd never seen a hotel this grand.

Becky was in her element as she bantered with the front desk manager and learned what was available.

The bell hop took them to the twelfth floor and opened their room door. It was a grand suit with an entertainment area, a sitting section facing the fabulous ocean view, and was completed with a lush bedroom suite with a marble bathroom.

Becky opened her purse and tipped the bellman. He took the money and strangely looked at Kyle, then left.

Becky laughed once the door was closed, "Darling, I'm going to have to teach you the finer points of living. You'll also need to carry cash to tip the help."

She thrust a wad of twenty dollar bills into Kyle's hand. "I'll hold up one finger for one bill, two for two bills, etc. Follow?"

Kyle smiled, "I can do that." He looked around, "Where to next?"

Becky grabbed Kyle's arm, "I'm famished. Let's go to the dinning room."

Kyle pulled the room door closed and both walked to the elevator. They were quickly whisked to the main lobby. Becky led the way. When they got to the dining room, Becky explained to the Maitre d' what she wanted. Looking at Kyle, she held up three fingers.

The couple was ushered to a table close to the dance floor. Becky explained, "This way we can watch the couples dancing. After dinner, they'll clear the table. We can stay right here and dance when we like the songs."

The waiter brought menus. The couples perused the broad section of food. Becky asked mentally, 'Are you ready to order our appetizer?'

Kyle nodded, 'Yep, but I'm not sure what I want for the entrée.'

Becky shrugged, 'That's ok. When I go out, I like *to graze* and leisurely sample different foods. Must of all, I want to enjoy the experience.'

She motioned for the waiter. He quickly responded.

"Are you ready to order?" he asked.

Becky smiled, "Yes. I'd like to start off with sliced brisket, a chefs salad, and iced tea for my appetizer. For my main course, I want a two inch thick filet minion, medium rare, French style mashed potatoes algot, with cheese and garlic whipped in, plus string beans."

Kyle was amazed that his little angel was that hungry but then remembered why and smiled. He looked at the waiter.

"I'll start off with the jumbo shrimp cocktail, *heavy* on the *hot* cocktail sauce, with iced tea also for my appetizer." He looked up, "Do you have a fresh baked loaf of bread?"

"Yes, sir," the waiter answered, "We have a bread chef."

"Do you have a small Italian loaf?" Kyle wondered.

The waiter hesitated, "No, but we have French baguettes."

Kyle smiled, "Those'll do. I'll have a loaf now and another with the meal please with whipped butter. Then I'll have the surf and turf, the twenty ounce Maine lobster along with the sixteen ounce porterhouse steak. I'll have two baked potatoes *with the works*, and a chief's salad with Thousand Island dressing. I'll order desert later," he smiled.

The waiter rolled his eyes as he collected the menus. Becky gasped, "Oh Kyle! I'll be right back!"

Kyle stood while Becky ran over to a table and stood before an older gentleman and his friend. Becky took the hand of the white-haired man and pulled him over to Kyle. The other gentleman followed with petite steps.

Kyle motioned to the waiter to bring two other chairs. He clearly understood these guests were special to Becky. That she was excited, was clearly evident.

As Becky approached Kyle, she announced carefully, unsure how this all would go, "Jeffrey, this is *my husband* Kyle. Kyle, this is *my father* Jeffrey, and *his significant other*, William."

Kyle extended his hand warmly, first to Jeffrey and then

to William. "We were just about to have dinner. Would you both like to join us?"

Jeffrey blinked, "Certainly, if you wouldn't mind!" he put his hand over his heart. He announced, "Please forgive me," he trembled. "I've *not* been allowed to see or speak to my daughter, since she was a small child. I was simply stunned when you walked in Rebecca. You were next to the last person I'd expected to see here."

Becky made sure William was comfortable before she replied, "Please call me, Becky, Jeffrey. I detest formality. I think you can understand why."

Jeffrey nodded. He understood. They both had an unpleasant memory of a protocol fanatic.

"Oh, ok. I'll call you Becky, *if* you'll call me father?" Jeffrey hesitated.

"Do you mind me calling you dad or daddy?" Becky countered. "Father sounds too cold to me," Becky said.

Jeffrey motioned to the waiter as he answered Becky, "Dad or daddy is fine with me, honey. *Whatever* makes you happy."

Jeffrey told the waiter, "I'll have a double tanqueree gin down on the rocks, with olives. William will have a whisky sour." He looked at Kyle and Becky, who shook their heads, but then Becky told the waiter, "I'd like a bottle of champagne, please. This is a night *to celebrate!*"

Becky asked, "Would you both like anything to eat? Do you mind if we start? I'm famished."

Jeffrey gestured, "*Please.* Don't let us interrupt. I'm just so happy, to be in the same room with you, Becky! You don't know how I've dreamed of this day." He spoke, "I was crushed when I heard you'd run away from Angela and possibly, had been killed. I was beyond distraught."

William took his drink and admitted, "Jeffrey was so thrilled, Becky, when you called him about your ranch. Robert Edwards has been keeping us up to date on you and your husband's progress. It's all *so exciting!*"

The waiter brought their appetizers and placed them on the table. Kyle began on his jumbo shrimp. His face lit up when he tasted the hot cocktail sauce. He saw William eyeing his shrimp and Kyle offered the dish to their guests. William couldn't resist and he dipped the delicacy into the sauce.

Kyle warned, "I like things hot. You might want to be careful."

William looked at Jeffrey, "*I love* hot things too." William motioned for the waiter, "A large dish of sour cream, please."

The waiter nodded. He went to get the order.

William's eyes widened, but excitedly fanned himself, "OH, that *is hot*. How delicious," he said as his eyes watered.

Everyone was settling in as they became comfortable with one another.

Becky looked at Jeffrey, "I was so surprised to see you here. I didn't know you came to Miami."

Jeffrey looked around, "I've been coming to this hotel, since I was a little boy. My father's family owned this place, until a corporation took control, sixteen years ago."

Becky stopped, "I didn't know your family owned this place, Daddy. I knew you were from New England, but Mother never tell me much about you."

Jeffrey frowned and twisted his lips tersely, "Yes, Angela would be like that, wouldn't she. She loves to control everyone and everything!"

William touched Jeffrey's arm, "Now honey, don't get yourself upset."

Jeffrey visually tried to put unpleasant memories aside. This was, the day *he'd dreamed about*. William was right, he didn't want to miss a moment.

"Tell us Becky, Kyle, what have you been up to?" Jeffrey urged.

Becky couldn't contain herself as she first looked at Kyle and then back to Jeffrey, "Daddy, would you be upset if I told you, you were going to be a Grand Daddy?"

With that, William leaped into the air and cut loose an ear-splitting scream of joy. "*ATTENTION, ATTENTION* everyone!" Once William had center stage in the dining room he reverently announced, "Jeffrey is going to be a Grand Daddy!" Williams started clapping openly and unashamedly to Jeffrey, Becky, and Kyle. Tears of joy rolled down his plump cheeks.

Not to be undone, Jeffrey stood and announced to the room, "The drinks are on me tonight. We're going to have *a party* to celebrate this wonderful event! Jeffrey joined in and began clapping to congratulate the you couple's wonderful news. The room erupted in applause.

Becky beamed in total joy as she hugged her Monster from the Black Lagoon. Kyle wasn't used to all the attention, but he knew Becky was. He let her have her well deserved moment of recognition and well wishes.

Kyle stood up and whispered to Jeffrey, who nodded. Jeffrey walked to the band leader and Kyle walked over to Becky. He tenderly took her hand and pulled her up, then guided her to the empty dance floor, nodding to the band leader, who began playing, "There's a Moon Out Tonight…. and they danced their first dance, together."

Kyle took Becky in his arms and began to move from side to side. Becky motioned for Jeffrey, who took William's hand, and joined them on the dance floor. Other couples filtered onto the dance floor as everyone shared in the celebration.

After the dance was over, Kyle took Becky back to their table. Jeffrey and William followed. A middle-aged female couple began walking over. William jumped up in excitement, "Sybill and Yvonne! You both look simply darling to night. Ravishing!" as he mock kissed each side of the women's faces, careful not to smudge their makeup.

Jeffrey hugged Sybill, "Becky, Kyle, I'd like to introduce Sybill and Yvonne. They are very old and dear friends, from the other neighborhood of our shunned community. William and I respect their bond, as they do ours."

Sybill smoothly moved to Becky, "Oh Jeffrey, she's simply darling," she said as she carefully hugged her. "Why did you keep such a precious secret, Jeffrey? You never brought her *to any* of our gatherings."

Jeffrey's stony face spoke volumes, "Angela forbade me to contact my daughter at all. It was simply by chance that we met Becky and her husband here in the dining room." He brightened, "Maybe it was fate?"

Sybill put her fists on her hips, "Angela, *that Witch*. She is enough to give womanhood a bad name." As an after thought, Sybill gasped, looking at Becky, "I hope you know Angela is in a breed all her own. She doesn't represent the feminine gender *at all*." She looked accusingly at Jeffrey, "Angela is like a male in a female body. She has all that horrible male energy, oozing from every pour."

Jeffrey broke out laughing, "Sybill, there you go with that Male Energy theory of yours…"

Sybill smirked at Jeffrey and then she turned her attention on William, "Can they come to our wine tasting party in the Hampdens next month? *We must* spread the news of this wonderful event!" Accusingly she eyed Jeffrey, "You just can't monopolize their time, Jeffrey, you beast. Please bring them to some of our social gatherings. Despite any claim to the contrary, our social events are similar to those in the common community."

William brightened as he looked at Yvonne, "Yes, you and Sybill *must* attend our grand opening gala in Watervillle. We are debuting our condo megaplex there in two weeks. Jeffrey has been a juggernaut working on that project. I had to drag him down here to get him away from all those details."

Becky told Kyle to sit and enjoy his meal as she motioned to the waiter to bring their dinner entrée. Small conversations sprang up everywhere. Everyone seemed to surprisingly know everyone.

Jeffrey spoke to Kyle, "I hope we aren't bothering you.

I wouldn't *dream* of offending you, Kyle. Becky seems to understand our lifestyle."

Kyle laughed, "No Jeffrey, you and your friends don't bother me. Everyone here is like an extended family. I love Becky and we're happy together. Who am I to judge other people, if everyone agrees and no harm is done?"

Jeffrey moved to Becky, almost shouting over the din of surrounding conversation, "I'm going to like your husband, Becky. He's a wonderful chap."

Becky eyed Kyle, with a smile on her face, "He grows on you each day."

Jeffrey nodded his head. There was a scent of respect in the air. It smelled refreshing.

It wasn't long after dinner that Becky asked Kyle if he minded if they said their good nights?

"I'm happy, full of food, and content that our lives are on course," Becky smiled.

Chapter 15

The next morning Becky was awakened by the phone. She picked it up as she knew Kyle wouldn't, "Hello?" "Good morning, darling. This is William," the voice on the phone replied.

Becky rolled over and smiled, "Hi William. How are you today, dear?"

William tried to rein in his normal exuberance, "*Oh darling*, I can't tell you how happy you've made your father! I wanted to call and invite you and Kyle to join us for breakfast in the dining room. Can you come down, or do you two have to rush back to Colorado?"

Kyle was already dressed and sitting in a soft reading chair. A silver coffee service sat on a cart in the middle of the living room. Becky covered the phone. She looked at Kyle, who questioningly asked who was calling, "It's William. He and Daddy are inviting us for breakfast? Is that OK with you?"

"As long as you're with me, I'm happy, Becky. I do want to stop by and visit Wela before we head back to Colorado," Kyle answered. "Other than that, I'm free."

"There is someone I'd like you to meet," Becky added. "Can we do that this morning and then drive over to see Wela this afternoon? We can catch an evening flight back to Denver and be back home to sleep in our own bed tonight?" she offered.

"Ok," Kyle moved to freshen his coffee. "When you're ready,

we can go downstairs. After you've finished with the phone, I'll call Wela and ask if we can come over later today."

"William?" she waited, "We'll be down in twenty minutes. Wonderful, we'll see you both then," and she hung up the phone.

She threw back the covers and sauntered over to her hubby in her lacy bra and panty set. Her eyes glowed with excitement.

Kyle feasted on his beauty in her finery, "Rebecca Allison, Don't you…"

Becky put a finger to his lips, "I'm just teasing you a little Kyle Ibsen. I'll pay my bill *tonight* when we get home." With that she kissed her hunk and sauntered off to the bathroom, purposely swaying her hips as she walked.

Kyle knew better than to attempt to get the last word with his woman. He groaned to himself, "It's gonna be a long day…"

In thirty minutes, Becky waltzed into the dining room of the Wellsley Hotel, fashionably late. William clapped his hands excitedly, appreciating her effort, "She's being *so bad*, Jeffrey. She's a girl after my own heart!"

Jeffrey double flashed a look at his mate and then back at his daughter. She was absolutely radiant. Jeffrey kissed her softly and then extended his hand to Kyle, "We appreciate your time. We know you have to get back home, but I was jealous and wanted to see you two again, before you left. I'm like a thirsty man, greedy for another glass of water after a long dry spell."

Kyle laughed, understanding, "Thanks for inviting us."

William lightly touched Kyle's hand, "Hopefully this will be the first of many social engagements we can share, together? We'd hoped that we could begin a friendship with you two, if you wouldn't mind?"

Kyle looked at William, "If it's ok with Becky, it's ok with me."

Kyle seated Becky while Jeffrey motioned for the waiter to take their order. William's eyes widened when Kyle ordered. "Can he fit all that into his tummy, Becky?" William giggled.

Becky smiled, then told the waiter, "Just orange juice please."

Jeffrey sat forward, "Are you *alright*, my dear? You aren't sick or should I call Dr. Henderson at the University Hospital to examine you? I knew you shouldn't have had that glass of champagne last night." He was starting on a roll, "While you're carrying my grandchild, *no more* alcohol *for you*."

William gasped and leaned forward, "Control yourself, Jeffrey. She isn't the first woman to have a child, you know. There'll be no double standards at my table. You know my rules," he said with a huff.

William softly turned to Becky, "Please excuse the beast, my dear. You've brought out the protective instinct in your father, I fear."

Becky laughed, "Everyone, just relax. I'm fine. It's just a touch of morning sickness. I'm getting used to it." She sat back smugly and looked at William, "Don't worry dear, I have my protector with me, *nearly* all the time."

William looked confused, "And who is your protector, my precious?"

Becky laid her hand on Kyle's, "He's right here. He's promised me he won't leave me alone *ever again*. That he'll *always* be within arms reach."

William looked at Kyle, who was shoveling in mouthfuls of egg and fried potatoes. When Kyle swallowed, he said stone faced, "William, I haven't been ordered to kill anyone yet today, but the day's still young," he winked.

William flicked open his elaborately painted fan, as his eyes widened, "I'm glad to hear that, suga," he said as he nervously looked at Jeffrey.

Jeffrey considered Kyle closely, "A report I read said you've taken good care of my daughter. I wanted to thank you for your kindness."

Kyle wasn't surprised, "No thanks are needed, Jeffrey. Becky is *very* precious to me, more than I can express. I'm not very good with words, but it is my pleasure being with her."

In short order, William coordinated with Becky their contact information. William sat forward, "Maybe we can meet here again, the next time you are in Miami? Just give us a call saying you're going to Florida and we'll make a point of being here too. If not here, maybe you'd like to visit our home in Watervillle, New Hampshire? We'd both love to have you come visit. We have so much to catch up on. Of course, I have some wonderful shops in mind, Becky, for maternity clothes. I'd *love* to help you pick out some darlin outfits. Oh, and Jeffrey, we *must* convert one of the guest rooms into a nursery!"

Becky hugged William, "We'll keep in touch. You know where we live too. Soon we hope to rebuild the farmhouse. We have some business to conclude, then we'll have more time. Robert Edwards is helping us with some patents on inventions Kyle is working on. Hopefully, we'll be ready to introduce them to the academic and business community soon."

William jumped with joy, "Oh goody! A gala introduction. I'd love to help you organize that event."

Jeffrey leaned towards Becky whispering, "William is an absolute genius when it comes to marketing and interior decoration. He's so creative."

Becky's eyes twinkled, "Yes, William. I'd love your help. I'll call you darling. We'll do lunch in Denver, soon?"

William looked at Jeffrey, "I can see the private jet was a wise move on your part. Did you have a premonition?"

Jeffrey just smiled. He didn't say a thing. When Becky called him about her ranch, he felt he might have a chance to be with her, now that she was away from Angela. A big problem was that they lived so far apart! He immediately contracted a corporate jet service, something like a time-share for passenger jets of all sizes. The company had him fill out a questionnaire, so they would know his preferences as far as food, sleeping arrangements, down to the kind of music he enjoyed. All he had to do was call a central phone number, tell the receptionist he wanted to fly from point A to point B, and at what time. The company would arrange the appropriate aircraft and the flight crew for the client, at a fraction of the cost of owning a jet yourself.

William tingled with excitement. Ideas raced around his head. He stopped long enough to shake everyone's hand. After Becky hugged and lightly kissed Jeffrey on the cheek, she and Kyle left also.

Kyle walked over to the front desk to pay their bill. Becky was close by his side. The desk manager was *very* courteous, *very* respectful.

"There is no bill, Mr. and Mrs. Swoboda. Your room and all your expenses at this hotel, have been compted," he explained.

Kyle was stunned, "I don't understand, compted?"

Becky understood, but interjected, "This is all very kind, sir, that our bill has been complimentary paid, *but by whom?*" She thought she knew.

The manager softly replied, "By the hotel directors, Madam. That's all I'm at liberty to stay. I am instructed to inform you, should you *ever* be in Miami, the Wellsley Hotel would consider *it an honor*, if you'd choose to stay with us. Please consider this hotel, part of your family."

Becky blinked, but wasn't about to look a gift horse in the mouth. "Please convey our gratitude for this kindness to the hotel directors."

The manager nodded, but added pleasantly, "Please, don't be confused, Mrs. Swoboda. This isn't a singular gesture. This is an *open invitation*. Your needs are to be catered to, Madam. Those are *my instructions*."

Becky coughed, "You run a marvelous hotel here, sir. Until next time."

The manager explained, "I've taken the liberty to order you a limousine, which is waiting for you out front, compliments of the hotel. The driver is instructed to take you where ever you wish to go. Your bags are already on board."

Becky took Kyle's arm as she walked through the lobby, "Something *very strange* is going on here. At first I thought Daddy had paid our bill, but I sense something larger is lurking in the shadows. I just can't put my finger on it *yet.*"

Kyle looked down, "It seems too good to be true, but I think it's wonderful. This hotel is centrally located and beautiful. The food is excellent and they have a dance floor! I'm sold," he smiled, enjoying his new station in life.

Once Becky was seated in the limo, she told Kyle, "If you're happy, I'm happy." She then leaned forward to the driver, "Please take us to the bus terminal. Let us off, but wait."

"Yes, Ma'am," the driver answered.

Kyle looked confused. Becky patted his arm excitedly.

"I want you to buy me some red roses," she handed him a bill. "Pay for the flowers with this," she grinned, handing Kyle a one thousand dollar bill.

Kyle looked at the bill, raised his eyebrows, and then smiled, "Ok, hon."

Inside the bus terminal Becky hid behind her giant husband. Kyle walked into the florist shop and looked for the gray haired lady behind the counter who glanced up at her new customer.

"I'd like a dozen red roses please," he said and handed the bill to the woman.

Blanche looked at the bill and choked, *"I can't cash this,* sir."

Without allowing any further conversation, Becky jumped out from behind Kyle. "Well then! I guess you'll just have to keep the change, right?"

Blanche thrust a hand over her heart, "Damn girl! You about gave me a heart attack! I thought you were dead! Blanche and Becky moved to hug each other.

Becky grinned, "Not hardly. Here," she indicated to Kyle, "Blanche, I want you to meet my husband. Kyle," Becky explained to Kyle, "I'd like you to meet Blanche. She helped me when I ran away from home and arrived here in Miami. She knows *everyone!*"

Blanche nervously looked around, "Are they still looking for you? But wait, I heard some rumor that you showed up last night at the El Toro with Diablo himself. Diablo is Kyle? Your Husband?" Blanche gasped, laughing to herself.

Becky said, "We needed to clear up the dispute about the money, so Kyle and I can come and go in Miami without worrying about the drug gang."

Blanche nodded, "Well whatever you two did, you scared the bejesus out of them! The word has passed that you two *are not* to be approached, or toyed with at all. Otherwise, they and their families could suffer a excruciating death."

Blanche blinked. All of this was happening too fast.

She stood back, "Let me look at you little girl," Blanche told Becky. Then Blanche shook her head, "Oh my! You've grown so much since I saw you last. You have your man, you are evidently successful, but wait," Blanche ordered as she scanned Becky's eyes and face, then her gaze dropped down to Becky's belly. "You're not!? Are you?" Blanche happily giggled.

Becky half laughed, half cried as she nodded her head, "*yes*".

Blanche moved back and sat down on her chair. She tapped out an unfiltered cigarette. Kyle moved forward to light it for her. She didn't miss a thing!

Kyle took out a cigar, punched a hole in the closed end and then lit his own. Becky looked around.

"Are you happy here, Blanche? Was owning your own shop all that you hoped it would be?" Becky questioned.

Blanche took a long drag on her cigarette and exhaled, *"No*, not really," she confessed. "I thought it'd be lovely to be surrounded by beauty all day and not deal with so many unhappy people. No more smell of ham hash and burnt toast. But I miss seeing the different people and my friends regularly. Today, no one has money for flowers. I watch my inventory fade and die in silence," Blanche sat silently. The cigarette ash grew long as if Blanche was in a trance.

"Blanche?" Becky tried to break though, but she was unsuccessful.

Blanche was viewing her life on fast forward. Becky had seemed a disaster waiting to happen. The only apparent things she had going for her was her body and sharp mind. Now Becky appeared to have *everything*, even *a baby.*

Becky tenderly touched Blanche's shoulder, "Blanche?"

Becky touching her, broke the spell. Blanche looked up, "Yes?"

"I need your help again," Becky said softly.

Blanche laughed, *"Honey*, you don't need *my help.* I should take lessons from you. You're the girl with all the treasures!"

Becky hugged her dear friend. That seemed to break through to Blanche.

Blanche cried, *"Oh*, how I've missed you, Becky. I was so worried that they'd killed you too. But then, you sent the money for the flower shop, I knew you were alive somewhere. You couldn't ever come back to Miami, or they'd find you fast. I didn't want to think what would happen next."

Becky kissed Blanche's weathered cheek, "I've been really lucky and have had oodles of help. Kyle and I are starting a foundation to help people. I, we'd," she looked at Kyle, who shook his head yes, "would you like to head up our office in Miami?"

Blanche dropped her cigarette on the floor. She crushed it out.

"You mean you want to help the people of Miami? The poor? Doing what?" Blanche wondered aloud.

Becky smiled, "That's what I want you to tell us. Food is always an obvious need. We also want to find or create jobs for people if we can. I don't know what else."

Blanche felt helpless, "I can't leave here. I have to finish out the year's lease. It would cost nine thousand to buy myself out of the place, I checked."

Becky took out her checkbook. She thought to Kyle.

'Is it ok to free Blanche, to head up our Miami office?' Becky thought.

Kyle thought back, 'You say she knows this city and its people like the back of her hand. She'd be wonderful. She'd be like a guardian mother.' Kyle thought to Becky, 'I want an office with a water view. Somewhere we can see boats, like on an inlet, a lagoon, or on the intercoastal waterway, is all I ask.'

Becky looked at Blanche, "Ok, there's nine thousand to buy you out of the lease. We'll pay twenty-thousand for your inventory, and twenty-thousand advance pay. We want you to locate an office building, nothing too elaborate, but *it must* have a water view, for Kyle."

Becky took out her phone and called Robert Edwards in Denver. In a minute, he picked up.

"Hello, Becky! Great to hear from you. Where are you now?" Robert asked.

"Kyle and I are still in Miami. We saw Daddy last night, and met William," she giggled.

"Yes, I heard. Jeffrey and William are beyond themselves. They're so happy to have met you finally and your new husband too." Robert paused, "I sense you need something. What can I do for you today, sweetheart?"

"Kyle and I want to start an office for our foundation, here in Miami. I was wondering if you had an attorney you trust *here?* Do you have someone I could have my people contact for legal help? Someone who hasn't been bought out by the Cartel?"

Robert thought for a minute, "I know of a person. Actually, my recommendation is a female, an *extremely intelligent* woman. I respect her opinion greatly. Her name is Samantha Hindall. She's called Sam for short. She's impeccably honest and well connected with the State Legislature. She'll know what will be allowed and not. She has her finger on the pulse of south Florida. She knows what industries will succeed and which ones will fail."

Becky answered, "Kyle and I are organizing our people here. We need someone on retainer to handle legal issues as they arise. I want an old friend to look for an office building in Miami. A small place that we can buy, that's easily accessible to the people." Robert gave Becky, Sam's office phone number.

Robert shrugged, "*What-ever*. Samantha is your person. She has the patience for people issues. I'm more into business."

Kyle asked for the phone, "Robert? Kyle here. I have an idea I want to patent when we get back. What will you need to proceed with that?"

Robert smiled, but was surprised, "Nice to hear from you Kyle. I'll need drawings of your product. Are you going to manufacture it?"

Kyle answered, "It's a different kind of battery and yes, I want to start a factory to manufacture them when I can. I need to select a location not far from desert sand, but close to a railroad freight line."

Robert appeared interested, "When you two come through Denver, call ahead. We can discuss the details over lunch. I know the perfect place."

"Ok, we should be in Denver tomorrow. How about lunch, say around noon?" Kyle looked at Becky, who nodded her head, but then she had a troubled look on her face. She took the phone from Kyle.

"Robert, we're flying into Denver tonight. Do you have a hotel you can recommend? That way we can sleep in and meet you for lunch," Becky asked.

Robert smiled, "I'd recommend the Wellsley Hotel. I think it'd be *perfect* for you and Kyle."

Becky jerked back in surprise, "I didn't know there was a Wellsley Hotel in Denver!"

Kyle smiled, "I'm up for it. I'd like to see what's on the menu in that hotel. This one in Miami is great."

"Ok, Robert. Can Brian your secretary, make a reservation for us over night?" Becky wondered.

Robert smiled, looking down, "Yes Brian would be pleased to help. He's such a miracle worker. Here's the hotel phone number in case you want to call them with your arrival time. They could send a limo to pick you two up."

Becky blinked, "OK, Robert. Thanks for all of your help. You're a lifesaver, as usual."

Robert sobered, "*Anything* for you, Becky. You know that."

Becky felt the caring, "Thanks for your friendship, Robert. You're a prince!" and she disconnected the call.

Becky made out the check in Blanche's name. She gave her Samantha Hindall's phone number and Becky's phone number too.

"Call me if you have a question. Right now I want to find a building, maybe an old warehouse, but *it needs* to have a nice water and boat view, please," she explained to Blanche.

Becky brushed a kiss against Blanche's face. I hope this is ok with you?"

Blanche beamed, "Seeing you again sunshine, has made my day. All of this sounds so lovely and exciting."

Becky didn't want to hold Kyle up. She took his hand and led him towards the door, "Gotta run, Blanche, but keep in touch. We'll be back off and on now that we've straightened out our troubles with the Cartel.

Blanche looked at the check, made out to herself. It was for seventy thousand dollars! She smiled, "First things first. I want to get out of this lease, close up this experience, and then get my hair done. I've got my friends back and money in my pocket. I want to get ready for the next chapter in my life. I call that a pretty nice start of a day!"

Kyle helped Becky into the limo and gave the driver directions to Wela's village. They were pretty isolated from the main roads.

The drive took awhile but finally the limo drove down an old dirt road he'd traveled many times. Kyle was coming home. He pointed Wela's store out to the driver who parked the limo along side the Quonset hut.

As Kyle helped Becky from the limo, a worried Wela came out of the store. "Kyle! Becky! Are you two *crazy?* The drug people have searched this area with a fine tooth comb looking for you."

Kyle calmly walked over to Wela, his tribal older sister, "It's nice to see you too, Wela." In a minute he took pity on the woman who cared so much for him. "Becky and I settled our differences with the drug people last night. They'll be leaving us alone, from now on. Actually, I'd say they'll keep their distance from us."

Wela looked amazed. She tenderly kissed Becky on the cheek and hugged her. Then she looked caustically at Kyle, "*Ok, who'd you kill* this time?"

Kyle laughed a good belly laugh, "I've changed, Wela. Becky's taught me I can't solve all my arguments with a gun. She's trying to civilize me. I'm a rancher now. We bought Snowy's parent's ranch from them, out in Colorado. You'll have to come visit us. Is all ok with school?"

Wela put her hand over her heart and then grabbed Becky in a bear hug, "I knew you were a Goddess when we first met! You've worked *a miracle*. You are the answer to my prayers, my angel."

Kyle quickly, but gently separated Becky from Wela's fierce hug. His eyes went to her tummy.

Wela didn't miss a thing, NO! *You're NOT?!*"

Becky smiled, "We've been blessed many times, Wela. I just found out."

Kyle sobered, "How have things been going around here?" he wondered.

Wela frowned, "I'm not happy! The elders want to build a casino on tribal land. They say it's a way to pay for schools, hospitals, and medical care for our people."

Kyle saw it in her eyes, "And you don't like that?

"Definitely not!" she seethed. "I think we're stealing from the people who come here to bet. Those people, most of them, can't afford to gamble! They do it despite their family's needs. I think it's a mortal sin. But, I'm almost alone in this. Pima agrees with me, but that's about it. He's done well with the tourist business you helped him start."

Kyle looked at Becky, 'Can I help our tribe too? Like you helped Blanche?'

Becky melted, '*Of course,*' she thought back. 'I wouldn't deny your family help, who want to better themselves.'

Kyle looked back at Wela, "I have an idea, an alternative suggestion to make money. Since you're going to school, do you have someone here in the tribe who'd be willing to run this business?"

Wela smiled, but remembered KIS wanted to be called Kyle now that he wasn't killing people routinely any more. "Kyle, you'd be proud of Pima. He's done so well with the tourist business of his. He's matured and stepped into Osola's responsibilities in the tribe."

Kyle looked around, "Is he here? Can we talk to him?"

Wela slumped a little in disappointment, "No, he won't be back for hours. Henry, one of our airboat drivers, called off sick. Pima took his group of tourists on the afternoon excursion."

Kyle said, "We're a little short on time today, but I want to invest, to help start the alligator farm Osola wanted to run, here on tribal land. The farm could employ tribal members, provide food and money. When Pima comes back, can you ask him if he's interested in managing the farm?"

Wela looked relieved. "Sure, I'll ask Pima. I feel so much better we might have an alternative source of income for the tribe, other than gambling."

Kyle looked at Becky and thought, 'If there's extra meat, we could truck it to Miami and offer it to the poor? Alligator soup is tasty, if spiced right.'

Becky thought, 'I'll run it by Blanche, but I think it'd be a good idea.'

Wela had to get back to the store. Kyle and Becky kissed Wela as they got back into the limo.

Kyle rolled down the window as he looked at his adopted sister, "Becky and I can come back more often now. You have my phone number. Wela waved as the couple in the limo drove away.

WITHIN SIX HOURS, BECKY AND Kyle were standing in the lobby of the Wellsley Hotel in Denver. It was in the old, business part of town.

Becky walked up to the desk, "I'm Becky Swoboda. Do you have a room for my husband and I?"

The desk person waved the desk manager over. "Yes, Mrs. Swoboda," the manager smiled broadly, "We've been expecting you! We have the penthouse suite ready for you. We keep this room available for *visiting dignitaries.*"

"Dignitaries?" Becky questioned.

The desk manager, utterly composed, blinked as she answered, "Yes, Mrs. Swoboda. We are honored you chose our hotel for your stay. The penthouse is steeped in tradition. Our staff hopes you will enjoy your stay with us tonight and will return as *often as you like*. We are here *to serve you.*"

Becky didn't know what to say. Kyle stood alongside her and heard the same explanation. Instantly, their luggage was whisked away to their room. After a quick meal from room service, they retired.

Chapter 16

The phone rang and amazingly Kyle answered it. "Becky," Kyle said softly as he bent over her while she lay sleeping in their huge king-sized bed.

Becky opened her eyes, "Who is it?" she groaned. "Its still night."

Kyle gave her the phone, "It's Robert". He went to a wall switch. Slowly, the light-blocking window shades retracted upward, allowing brilliant sunshine into the modern-style bedroom. A beautiful vista of the Front Range of the Rocky Mountains to the west came into view. Becky was awed as she sat up in bed.

Becky ran her hand through her chin length hair as she pulled her baby doll top down over her chest. "Good morning, Robert," she answered the phone. "Are we going to meet at noon?"

"No, honey. Brian, Julian, and I are down stairs. We want to have breakfast sent up. We can start our meeting early. I'm excited to hear what Kyle has in mind," Robert replied.

Becky looked at Kyle thinking, 'Do you want breakfast or lunch?'

'Breakfast is fine. I'm always ready for steak and eggs,' he grinned.

"Sure, Robert. Come up. Kyle said he'd like steak, eggs, and fried potatoes. I prefer fruit for breakfast, myself. Besides, I want to take a quick shower and put on my makeup," Becky said. She was worried she wouldn't have as much time to prepare for their meeting as she'd hoped.

Robert sighed, *"Yes dear,* I had five older sisters who controlled the bathroom, as if it were Fort Knox." He brightened, "We boys can have our breakfast while you make yourself presentable." He added, "As if *you aren't* beautiful enough, without all the primping and fussing that women do."

The door bell rang. Kyle left the bedroom, closing the portal, as he went to the suite entrance to answer it.

An army of servants smiled and nodded as they invaded the massive, open floor-plan penthouse of the Wellsley Hotel Denver. Kyle previously noted that this luxurious grand suit occupied a good portion of the twenty-fifth floor. The room was divided. The sitting area, where the servants were setting up a six person round table was near the foyer. A fully stocked bar, which they didn't use, sat on the eastern side of the room. Finally, a TV area, complete with gas fireplace ran against the southern wall. Floor to ceiling windows showcased the western wall with a breath-taking view of the Rockies.

A chef and a maitre d' followed the food to supervise the event. Robert evidently was accustomed to conducting business this way. He seated Julian at the table, and then he chose a seat, offering Kyle the seat to his right.

Kyle made himself comfortable. A plate of steaming, well-done charcoal steaks were offered to him. He selected two rib-eyes as the chef began frying Kyle's half-dozen eggs, over medium, with his potatoes. A waitress poured cups of steaming coffee all around. Brian, sat in an easy chair, off to Roberts left.

Once everyone had their food, Robert began the meeting. "Kyle, what do you want to patent?"

Kyle reached over and opened his portfolio he'd brought with him. He took several schematic drawings and handed them to Robert.

Robert took a napkin and dabbed his mouth as he looked at the plans. He became more and more excited the further he went. "I see a battery, but what is this inside? There *aren't* metal plates or acid, like normal batteries?"

Kyle finished chewing, "No, my battery, which can be adapted to *any* size or shape by the way, is filled with a silicon based gel. The battery is a fraction of the weight of traditional ones and is environmentally friendly. There is no acid inside and they have a ten year life expectancy. After that, the gel hardens into a solid block like stone. Then it can be separated from the traditional plastic cover and crushed back into silicon powder, capable of being reused. This process can be repeated, endlessly…"

Robert tossed his napkin down on the table as he looked at the last drawing. "Kyle! This is *revolutionary!*"

He took a sip of his coffee as he thought. His right eyebrow raised and Julian giggled. "I can see that Robert has a *naugh-ty* idea. He gets *that look* when his genius comes out."

"There's nothing special here, Kyle," Robert began, "over conventional batteries, *except* the silicon gel. Of course, there is a myriad of uses for unconventionally shaped batteries. The green material is a welcome revolution, but this final step, the process of turning *sand, any sand*, into electrical storing material is simply, out of this world! This process is the key element of your invention, *and*, we can copyright it, *not* patent it!"

Brian sat up. Robert nodded with a sly smile.

Kyle looked around at his business associates, "Please explain to a simple farm boy, the difference between a patent and a copyright."

Robert poured Kyle a fresh cup of coffee and warmed his own, "Kyle, a patent protects an idea for *maybe* seventeen years. We try to extend the product's exclusivity, by saying an invention is *patent pending.* That way we can maybe eliminate patent infringement for a total of twenty years."

Robert sat back, "The process you describe, that turns desert sand or any sand, for that matter, silica, into *both* an electricity generating *and* storing gel, *is narrative!* Your invention is a stated action, not a product! Therefore, I assert, your idea should be copyrighted and not patented. Without this stated action, sand is still, just sand. By going through your process, you rearrange the molecules in such a way, that the crystals of the sand then act as positive and negative fields. The alcohol gel, used to suspend the crystals, acts as the plasma holding element, for the generated electrical charge. *It's brilliant!*"

Kyle nodded, "I know the process, but what's so special about a copyright?"

Robert looked slyly, "A copyright is good for the author's *lifetime.* When you die, you can *will* your copyrighted process to the person(s) you wish for another seventy years!" Robert smiled, "Kyle, what this means is that you, Becky, your children and their children, will not have a financial worry *ever again*. You can buy the most worthless piece of property as long as there is sand on it, mine the sand, and make your product. Mankind, is assured a remarkably good battery, that is environmentally friendly, recyclable, and replacing the need *for petroleum* as a fuel for transportation, heating our homes, or manufacturing. *A-mazing!*" Robert slumped back in his seat.

In the master bedroom attached bath, Becky stood before the mirror putting on her make up. She was frustratingly trying to apply her mascara, muttering to herself, *'Why do boys have eye lashes a girl would kill for?* They don't even care!'

"Having trouble?" Cathy chirped.

Becky jumped from surprise and fear, "I *hate* when you do that, Cathy. Can't you just knock or call out before appearing?"

Cathy leaned against the double-sink marble vanity. She crossed her arms over her modest chest, "We'll I would, but you and Mr. Giant are attached at the hip. Slipping into the bathroom with you is about the only time I can get you alone."

Becky squinted and smirked, *"Well*, I love my husband. He and I are becoming best friends. Is there anything wrong with that?"

Cathy frowned, but shook her head, "No, of course not, but *yes*, I've been with you for a lot of years. I don't like being dethroned, too much, by your husband. Then again, that should be expected. Just don't forget your home-girls, now that you've *made it big*."

Becky looked surprised at Cathy. She couldn't stay mad at her long. They were more like sisters than imaginary friends or spirits. *What-ever!*

Becky looked surprised, "What do you mean? Who are my home-girls?"

Cathy rolled her eyes in disgust, *"I'm one* of them for starters, but also, *there's Laverne*. How fast we forget the ones who love us?"

"I didn't forget Laverne," Becky protested.

"Did too!" Cathy shot back. "You no sooner told Kyle about the baby, and then you blew off back to Miami. *You know* Laverne dreamed about you having a baby! She stuck by you when you were sick. You gave Laverne and I more gray hairs than we can afford, when you were kidnapped!"

Becky shifted over to her other hip as she stood before the mirror. She couldn't look at her reflection. *She knew* she'd blown it with Laverne.

"Oh, Cath," Becky sighed, "how do I fix this mess? You're right, Laverne has sacrificed and worried more than any woman should, and you too, for that matter." Becky mentally hugged Cathy, "You can come in the bathroom any time, just call through the door first, *ok*?"

Cathy looked surprised at Becky's offer, but then she got to think about Laverne. She brightened, "You could fly Laverne and Harold here to the Wellsley. Put them up in a room for a few days? Give them some walking around cash, then take Laverne shopping for nursery things?"

Becky looked concerned, "William wants to help me too. How do I manage both high-spirited people? I don't want to hurt either of them."

Cathy relaxed, "Well, cruise around the maternity shops, just don't buy anything. You get her input on buying the crib? You can't buy it until you ask Kyle. Unless it is too feminine, I don't think he'd mind, one way or the other, but *you never know*. Then let William help you with the nursery room décor and buying the other furniture. Remember, don't buy anything until you consult with Kyle. It's *his baby* too. You have to remember *protocol*, girlfriend."

Becky smiled, "I'm going to have to keep you around, so I don't get into trouble and offend anyone."

Cathy faded off, *"Oh thanks!* I feel like the street sweeper at the end of the circus parade. How I love, shoveling up messes.

Becky called out, "Keep in touch."

"Yeah, yeah," Cathy echoed as she disappeared.

Becky mentally called out to Kyle, 'Darling, can I interrupt?'

Kyle sat up straight, thinking back, 'Sure, hon. What's up?'

'Cathy was just here and explained that I probably hurt Laverne's feelings *by not telling her* about the baby until this late date. Cathy suggested that we fly Laverne and Harold up here, put them up in the hotel. Laverne and I can go shopping for a crib, but then ask you before I buy it. What do you think?'

Kyle shrugged, 'Sounds fine with me, but come out soon. My business with Robert is finished and Julian is itching to talk to you about the house.'

Becky looked around, 'It'll just take me a minute. I'll set it up, then be out. I don't see a reason Laverne and Harold can't be here by this afternoon.'

Kyle answered back, 'Have Zeke watch the place. He and

Judd are almost living at the ranch anyway. When they stay there, they at least have food to eat.'

Becky frowned, 'I'll be out in a minute.'

Becky called the ranch number, "Hello Laverne? Becky here. Kyle and I are in Denver. We'd love for you to join us here, as our guests. How about it?"

Laverne said, *"I don't know*, darlin, I need to ask Harold first. *What's up?"*

Becky mischievously smiled, *"It's a surprise*, Laverne. I can't tell you until you get here. I'll send a helicopter for you and Harold in an hour. Just pack for a few days. If you need something else, we can buy it here.

Laverne's eye grew wide as saucers and yelled, "Harold! WE'RE GOING *to Denver.* Tell Zeke. Move it buster, Becky wants to tell us A *SURPRISE.*

ROBERT LOOKED AT KYLE, "ARE you alright?"

Kyle smiled weakly, "I was just thinking about Becky. If she isn't here in a minute, I'll go get her."

Becky came waltzing out from the master bedroom. She wore a white cotton A-line sun dress with white three inch heels with open toes, "I'm here."

Julian jumped up and ran over to her, "Oh Becky! You look *marvelous.* I'm jealous, You're so full of color. I can see it in your face… *You're not, are you?"*

Becky batted her long eye-lashes. She didn't say a thing.

Julian blinked, but kept her secret. She had *The Look.*

Everyone at the table stood as Becky approached. Kyle held a chair for her to be seated. Their special guest had finally arrived, fashionably late.

Kyle motioned for a waiter to bring a humidor, "Would anyone care for a cigar. Do you mind if I smoke?"

Robert looked inside the box at the expensive assortment of hand-rolled beauties. He selected one to his liking. Kyle did the same. Julian held up his hand in passing and Brian choked back his revulsion. Now that everyone was comfortable, phase two of their meeting commenced.

Julian looked at Becky, *"Darling*, I've been thinking about your office and came to a conclusion."

Becky cocked her head, *"Which is?"*

"I think we should just demolish that old farmhouse and start over. *Everything* is wrong with that dwelling. It's 1930s construction!" Julian sighed in exasperation.

Kyle blew out a thin stream of smoke as he looked at Becky. He silently awaited her reaction.

Becky took a moment to wrap her thoughts around the problem. After a few heartbeats of silence, she replied.

"I don't want to demolish the old house. *I can't.* Laverne had Snowy in that house. Harold's mother and father died in that house. There's *history* there. *I can't* do that to them, as long as they're alive," she looked at Kyle.

Kyle nodded, but offered, "What if we build a new house, between the farmhouse and the road? There's close to two hundred yards of land between the two. Laverne and Harold can stay in their house. A first floor bedroom could be added to their house. We could make the bunkhouse into a guest house, for like when Zeke and Judd need to stay over if they're working on the ranch?"

Julian raised his eyebrows. "There certainly would be ample space to build you *new* house that way!"

Becky looked at Julian, "What kind of house did you have in mind? We're so cut off from civilization out there. It's beautiful, but it'll be a problem hauling building materials out there. Then also, I don't want our daily lives intruded on by strange workmen, who *aren't family*," she protested.

Julian answered, "I was thinking about going modular. Cruise ships are using this kind of construction when each cabin is added to a luxury liner. The house is fully drawn on paper before we start. You get a chance to *taste it* before a single nail is hammered. Once you approve the architecture, each room is fully built, all wiring, lights, plumbing, etc., at a warehouse near Boulder. A foundation is built on your lot. When the whole house is completed at the factory, it is trucked to your building site. Then each cubicle is hoisted into place like building blocks. What do you think about that?"

Becky looked at her watch. That will be fine Julian. Start the drawings and we can collaborate as we go along. *Call me* when you have something down on paper, ok? Then Kyle and I can come over to your office, or we can do lunch here in town."

Robert stood up as their meeting concluded. "Kyle, I'll start with the paperwork. Once we submit this to the copyright office in Washington, we can schedule a gala to unveil this idea to both the business and academic communities. There wouldn't be major retooling, so existing factories can make your batteries, under license to you, of course. Have you thought of a name of your company or corporation?"

Becky didn't hesitate, looking at Kyle, she answered, "We're calling our company the Mystique Corporation." Kyle smiled his agreement.

Becky looked at Robert, "William said he wanted to help organize the gala. Is that alright with you?"

Robert raised his eyes, "I couldn't have suggested a better person. William used to work on Madison Avenue, before he retired, to be with Jeffrey full time. He's a shrewd marketing person. I'll have Brian give him a call this afternoon. That way, we can start compiling a guest list, to be approved by yourself and Kyle, of course."

Kyle walked everyone over to the front door. Then all their guests left. For a moment, he and Becky were alone.

The phone rang and Becky went to answer it. Then she announced to Kyle, "The helicopter is about five minutes out. They'll land on the heliport above us on the roof."

Kyle walked with Becky to the elevator and in a moment

the couple stood in the heliport office atop of the hotel. He looked down at his wife.

"Are you and Laverne going shopping this afternoon? Will you be gone *long?*"

"Yes, we're going shopping and I don't know *how long* we'll be gone. We girls want to have some play time. What are you boys going to do this afternoon?" she asked.

Kyle grinned, "Well, since Harold and I are *being abandoned* by you girls, I thought he and I'd go over to the Fallen Angel Saloon. We'll do shots of anejo tequila, while watching the ladies in the strip bar." Kyle said with a straight face. He appeared dead serious.

Becky did a double take. Kyle *never* talked to her *like that!*

"Whaa?" she looked at him incredulously. "Kyle, you *don't drink* and from what you told me, the time you went to a Hoo-Hoo Bar after Boot Camp, you didn't sleep well for a week after. You thought the girls looked like hookers."

Kyle grinned and winked, "That was when I was young and innocent. Now that I'm a married man, you've whet my appetite, for a woman's charm."

Becky stood up to her Beast and was going to give him the talking to of his life, but Kyle reached out and whisked her off her feet. He lifted her briskly to him with the force of a grizzly bear. *Now* she could look him directly in the eye.

"What, were you saying, *Wo-Mon?"* he growled, almost blowing her hair away from her face with his breathe.

"Oooo Kyle! I've never seen you this way. *So Rug-Ged,"* Becky gasped.

Kyle grinned at her, as he held her almost two feet off the ground. He wasn't amused, *"Well darlin*, I just want you to know, that when the game of life is over, and the cards are counted, *this Dawg* wants to be known as a *Pit-Bull* rather than an ankle-biter."

"Kyle Ibsen, don't you..." Becky started to say, but Kyle

abruptly set her down on her three inch high heels, without breaking them off. Then, he left her alone, gasping for breath, with fire in her blue eyes. Kyle looked away from her with indifference.

Anger grew in her mind as a growl escaped from her lips. Then she turned timid, explaining in frustration, *"I need* to take Laverne shopping, to make it up to her, that I didn't tell her about the baby *before* everyone else! *What was I do?"*

Kyle gave her a steely stare, "I asked you politely how long you would be gone. You indifferently said you didn't know." He didn't offer an apology. "I don't like being taken for granted," he groused.

Becky put her hands behind her back and rocked on her heels, "Do we have time for me to make it up to you?"

Kyle looked at the landing helicopter, *"No"* he said gruffly.

Wow, this definitely wasn't the Kyle, Becky thought she knew. But then, she saw the twinkle in his eye. She leaped up and he caught her. He held her gently to him, giving her a curl your toes kiss. When he set her back down on the floor carefully, her legs were rubbery.

Kyle smiled, "I thought Harold and I would go over to the Western Tack shop. I want to look at some mountain saddles for the horses we've bought. I'll take a limo. They'll have a phone in the car. *Just call us* when you and Laverne are finished, *"OK?"*

Becky took a step back and slapped his arm, "You were *teasing me!* You weren't going to any *strip club* and to *drink tequila."*

Kyle slyly looked at his pretty wife, *"Well, I could*, if you left me."

Becky thought, 'Well, I guess I can't leave you, can I?"

Kyle looked at her soberly, 'I'm *A MAN*, Becky, not some *lap dog.* I have lava in my veins. *I've allowed you* to tame me, *a little.* Be assured, just under the surface, I am who I was. I'm still the Beast, who killed in the Everglades Swamp.'

Becky looked up, nodding her head, 'Okay, I'll remember that.'

The landing helicopter ended their conversation. As the copter touched down, the hotel staff opened the door and helped Laverne and Harold walk to the office in a bent-over fashion. A bell-hop put their luggage on a dolly and followed close behind.

Laverne was trying to settle her hair she'd wrapped in a pink scarf, in the early 1960s style. She was flustered, "Goodness, Becky! That was the first time we've been in a helicopter! What's all the fuss about?"

Becky took Laverne's arm and then walked to the elevator, that took them down two floors to their room. Kyle shook Harold's hand as Harold tried to hold his straw hat on his head from the turbulent prop wash of the departing helicopter.

"Good to see you again, Harold," Kyle shouted nonchalantly.

"What's going on, Kyle? What's all the fuss?" Harold asked concerned.

Kyle shook his head, "No big thing, Harold. Becky just wanted to take Laverne shopping, to thank her for all her help." Kyle laughed, "Becky wasn't amused when I told her I was going to take you to a strip club, then do shots of tequila, while they were out shopping.."

Harold stopped, *"Dang Kyle*, that sounds *like fun!* Why, I haven't been to a good strip club since…"

Kyle slapped Harold's shoulder, "Did you forget, Harold, I don't drink? Besides, if I wanted a lap dance, I think my little darlin would prefer to give me one herself."

Harold's face dropped, "You were just teasing me! No fair getting my hopes up like that!"

Kyle moved his jaw around, "I am taking you to a good saddle maker here in town. We need to fit the two mountain bred horses we're getting next week from Frank, remember?"

Harold saw the value in that. Lookin at a new saddle was *close* to goin to a stripper club, although *not quite* as exciting.

Kyle grinned a naughty smile, "There's a café next door to the leather shop. I can have a cup of coffee and a cigar while you have a shot or two of tequila. What-da-you say? I bet the booze we buy here will taste better than the moonshine you make back at the ranch."

Harold put an arm around Kyle, "Sounds like a plan, son. At least until the girls return."

Kyle winked, "That's the second part of my plan. After their shopping trip, I'm taking us to the Tilted Kilt Lounge. Man, they have beef steaks of all kinds, then there's chicken fried steaks, and pan fried chicken that'll make your mouth water. Or, if you like Italian, we can go over to Wagees Pizza and have some thin crust, if you'd like."

Harold couldn't resist, *"Does everyone* at the restaurant wear Kilts? Men and women?

Kyle laughed, "I guess we'll find out right? But hey, maybe the girls will get lucky, and see up some guy's skirt, for a change?"

Harold revolted at that thought. The picture of hairy legs in a skirt just didn't do it for him. "Na!"

"After that," Kyle continued, "I thought we'd go over to the Apaloosa Bar and Grill. They have music for dancing, and their kitchen stays open until 1 am. We could make a night of it and howl at the moon?"

Harold squinted, "I knew I'd like you, *even before* you beat the puke out of those mercenaries when we first met. I like how you think, Mister!"

Once Laverne saw where their room was, her nest, Becky gave her the key. Quickly, Laverne gave Harold a peck on the cheek. She was excited to be off.

Becky fixed Kyle with a squinted stare, then called over her shoulder as she turned to leave. *"Ok boys*, we ladies are going shopping! See ya later *and* you two *behave!"*

Kyle surprised Becky. He stuck out his tongue at her.

Becky tingled with excitement. This was a Kyle she *hadn't seen before.*

Laverne sang, "*We're going SSSSShopping……!*"

Once inside the limo, Becky leaned forward to the driver, "Take us to Chery Street Mall please."

Laverne couldn't wait any longer, "What's this all about, Becky? What's the surprise?"

Becky blinked, "You and Harold have been so nice to Kyle and I, we just wanted to take you shopping. Our home is on the ranch, but I'd love to get a townhouse here in Denver. I'm a city girl at heart. I love the dining, shopping, and yes the night life too."

Laverne's eyes were as wide as saucers, "I've never been to Denver. I guess they have more things to sell, than Zeswik's Country Store, back in Granite Bluff or even The Springs, for that matter?"

Becky looked at the huge mall as the limo pulled up, "*Yes*, Laverne, this megaplex is supposed to have *160 stores*. I'd say we can find *almost anything* we want here."

Laverne was agog with the sheer size of the complex. Becky told the limo driver to be close by for a phone call when they were finished shopping. Then she pulled a stunned Laverne into the mall. Laverne was like a kid on Christmas morning.

Becky guided her into one of the major department stores, "We need to get you a new handbag, woman."

Laverne clutched her old bag close to her, "*Nothin wrong* with this one. She's got another good ten years in her, just like me."

Becky pulled Laverne over to the leather handbag section. Laverne thrust her old bag at Becky. She was now, '*on the hunt!*'

Laverne was a born shopper like Becky. After two outfits, her nails being done, and a new hair-do, Laverne was in heaven. She didn't even notice the name of the store Becky was leading her into next. Laverne looked up and read, Tum-Tum – Infant Wear and Furniture?

It finally hit Laverne, then she shrieked, "Are *we* going to have *a baby*?"

Becky started crying. She shook her head, *YES*. Laverne started singing, "Becky's got - Biscuits in the Oven! We've got - Biscuits in the Oven!"

Chapter 17

The next three months passed quickly. William, true to his word, organized the unveiling of not one, but three products of the Mystique Corporation. The gala was held in the grand ballroom of the Wellsley Denver Hotel. The room was decorated beautifully, in a combination of iridescent-green for product one, heather-tan for product two, and milky-white for product number three. Becky was amazed at the confirmed guest list. Major executives from all facets of life converged to learn more about this revolutionary new corporation.

Becky looked at William, "How did you *ever* compile such an impressive guest list?"

William smiled gently, "Darling, I've known most of these people for decades." Then he whispered, "There are powers under the surface of publicized society. Many of the *other* people secretly know each other. We keep in touch and quietly network business opportunities."

"I don't understand," Becky admitted.

William showed his amazing intellect beyond his outward appearance. "Becky, for years, life has been *controlled* by *certain groups* of people. As far back as the 1920s, the news media has been tightly directed. They only report *certain* news that follows a preplanned agenda. The auto and the oil industry are two major players. However, there are other brokers of power and influence, who stand silently in the shadows. They hope one day to come out into the light."

Becky started to understand. "And *you*, William, being among an unpopular minority, see the total picture?" Becky guessed.

William didn't answer, but he wore a knowing smile. He escorted Becky around the ballroom, "There are people I want you to meet, love. They're movers and shakers who can help you. You're a tolerant person. To them, you are precious entity, someone to nurture and protect."

The ballroom was filling up with invited guests. The gathering was scheduled to begin at noon, October 19th, 1993.

Robert Edwards introduced Kyle to many of the elite guests. All were anxious to meet the president of this innovative new corporation.

The doors to the hall were about to be sealed. A blond woman with dark eyebrows, not physically remarkable, standing only five feet four, in her mid-forties, with smoldering authority, confidently strolled up to the entrance podium. She was flanked on both sides by two *huge* male bodyguards. The woman reached for the door knob of the closed room.

"Excuse me, Ma'am. This meeting is by invitation *only*. May I see your invitation, please?"

"I never heard of such ridiculousness in all my life!" she blustered. "I'm attorney Angela Wells from Chicago. Some *idiot* forgot to send me one," she complained. "Now *get out* of my way," she ordered.

The door manager, flustered, but undeterred, barred her entrance. "I'm sorry, Ms. Wells. I can't allow you to enter without an invitation."

Angela looked to her right and smiled, "Antonio, do we have *an invitation?*"

Antonio reached out and clamped his massive hand over the manager's collar bone and squeezed, guiding the manager outside the hotel. The other body guard, opened the door to the ballroom for his employer.

Angela smiled. As she passed, she softly said, "Thank you *Anton.*"

A Bedouin woman, garbed completely in flowing black robes from head to toe, the lower part of her face was veiled by convention, who wore sunglasses, *didn't miss* Angela's entrance. That she was accompanied by her pair of sophisticated toughs, caught the robed woman's eye.

As if an invisible pair of hands, placed on the bodyguard's chest, pushed them roughly back through the ballroom door and the door slammed shut. Angela now stood *alone*, but the meeting was about to begin. Her cell phone rang.

"*Yes!* Oh, it's *you*. Do I have to go through with this? I don't wish to enter a conversation with *a cow farmer*!" She listened, "What do you mean the process can't be duplicated? You say, *technology such as this, doesn't exist?* You've got to be mistaken!"

Angela straightened, "Yes Sir. I'm in the convention room, but my body guards, Antonio and Anton, *both* abandoned me. I'm *all alone* in here!" She smiled, "Yes, *please* deal *with them*. I don't wish to *ever* see them again."

She steeled herself, "Yes, I'll meet with *this idiot*. I'll do my best. Have I failed you yet?" she asked as she snapped her phone shut.

Angela gasped as a hand *dared* touch her arm, "*Mother?* What are *you* doing here?"

Angela turned and looked at a young woman, dressed demurely in an elegant maternity dress. She stiffened. "*Rebecca?* Is that *YOU?* I consider you *dead*, since you ran away from me last year."

Becky was the picture of motherhood. She proudly wore her maternity dress, although her tummy was just beginning to show. She wore a just above the knee, empire waist, deep blue-velvet maternity dress, with a high neck and collar, plus long sleeves that ended below her elbows. She wore matching three inch high heels with rounded toes. She was elegant, but announced her state.

Angela's eyes settled on Becky's midsection. "*Oh!* I see you've done well by yourself," she smirked. "*And WHO* do I have to thank, for *knocking you up?* Some lounge lizard, no doubt. You always craved physical attention. In my day, girls like you would've been called *a slut.*"

Becky's eyes widened, but Cathy intervened, "*Put up your shield!* She can read your mind! *Protect yourself.*"

Becky reconfigured her thoughts and closed the doorway into her mind. Instantly, Angela winced in both pain and frustration. She put a hand to her head. Angela felt out of control. She turned, but Becky raced after her mother.

"I see into your mind, Mother. How long have you been psychic?" Becky gasped. She jerked in surprise as a picture unfolded in Becky's mind, that which was inside her mother's head. Now Becky was reading her mother's thoughts!

Angela wouldn't look Becky in the face, "Your grandmother had the gift. On my thirteenth birthday, she told me how to use my power of sight. My mother refused to use the power, to help our family. *What a waste.* I, on the other hand, had the courage to use my ability and elevate myself to global influence. Soon I'll be a billionaire. Then I'll consider retiring to a quiet island in the Aegean. I've made many Mediterranean friends."

Becky blurted out, "What is *the Guardian Brotherhood*?" She paused as the picture opened in her mind. "They're a fraternity? They buy or otherwise gain control of inventions, even through violent means, and hide them from society? They prevent the inventions use? They control civilization from advancing any further than where they want the masses positioned?" Becky blurted out.

Angela stiffly confronted her daughter. For all of Rebecca's life, Angela had been able to read her daughter's mind. She even knew of Rebecca's stupid plan to run away. She knew Rebecca would come whimpering home in less than a month, but then, she jumped into the Everglades. For some strange reason, Rebecca's thoughts had become veiled, against every attempt to read her mind from then on. It was as if Rebecca had ceased to exist to Angela.

Angela fumed, "It's taken me *all* my professional life, to network into the inner circle of this fraternal hierarchy. To go beyond the World Bank, the façade it is. I am the first female deemed worthy of admission to the Guardian Brotherhood." She angrily answered her daughter back, "The Brotherhood acquires inventions. *We safeguard* them. *We control* the release of information to the unwashed masses, the cattle of this world. We protect the world *from itself.*"

Becky smiled, politely, "Mother, we view life *so differently.* I want to share new ideas, new inventions with the world, *not sequester them!*"

Angela glared into her daughter's eyes, "How naïve. You're like your grandmother, gutless, a common person without ambition. Her gift *was wasted.*"

Becky blinked as anger flared within her. Something had changed in her. "Angela, I'm glad you consider me like her. I couldn't have asked for a sweeter compliment, than to have it said, *I'm like grandmother.* Thank you!"

Angela looked at her watch, "Do you know *this pig farmer,* Kyle Swoboda? He's supposed to have invented a process. My oil friends find this *threatening* to stability and the natural order of the world. They worry *he is a revolutionary!*"

Becky smiled angelically and pointed to an unlikely pair, the Bedouin woman and Kyle. Kyle wore an impeccably tailored Matone' Navy-blue, double breasted suit, with cuffed trousers. His tie was silk, with navy and white oblique checks. A sky-blue handkerchief was thrust into his breast pocket for added color. He wore chestnut brown, smooth grained, Italian shoes. "I think that's *your pig farmer,*" Becky smiled stiffly. "The one in the expensive business suit. She leaned closer to Angela, "But I wouldn't tell him that. I heard he used to kill people for a living. I think he's turned to another avocation these days. I suspect, *the KIS of Death*, doesn't lay far below the surface," she warned.

Angela whirled and winced again. She was unsuccessful in reading Rebecca's thoughts. "You've changed, Rebecca. What is it? What's different?"

"Angela," Becky answered, "I've evolved. I'm no longer the innocent young girl you imprisoned in your gilded cage, to dance to your dictates like a puppet on your strings. I wish you – *Good Luck* – in your negotiation with Mr. Swoboda."

Angela was caught off balance. She gasped, *"Do you know this man?"*

Becky saw a couple approaching from the corner of her eye. She turned and kissed first one and then the other man, "Hello Daddy, and William. This is so beautiful, so elegant. Your efforts are beyond words, William."

Angela snapped, "You now call *me* Angela, but yet you greet this, this f.. as Daddy?"

Jeffrey intervened, "Tsk, Tsk, Angela. We don't use that term. Have you been in outer space or in a deep freeze that matches your heart?"

Becky restrained herself, but was bolder with the presence of her loved ones. "Angela, you were ruthless all my life. The little I've known my father and his significant other, they've been wonderfully sweet to me. When they heard that I was with child, they didn't ask, like you did, *who knocked me up!*"

William shocked, looking fiercely at Angela, "You *BIACHE*, you *DIDN'T!*"

Angela's eyes narrowed, "Oh, he has *you* with him does he?"

William's eyes narrowed like a cat ready to pounce and growled, "Grrrrr Angela, *watch* your claws. *Two* can play *that game* when it comes to family! I don't see your usual Tweedle Dee and Tweedle Dumb with you today. You must feel absolutely naked without those lap dogs hanging all over you *like a two dollar dress.*" Fire blazed in William's eyes.

Becky blew both Jeffrey and William a kiss. Then she turned and walked away from the group.

William softly said to Jeffrey, "Doesn't she *look beautiful?* I took her to the Bellie Shop, and then to Stephen, to have it altered. Oh, and those high heels are so stunning! I'd kill to be able to wear those."

Angela looked at William in disgust. Jeffrey didn't miss a thing.

"It is a shame, Angela, that you never could appreciate Rebecca. I learned she prefers to be called, Becky. I thank my lucky stars that our paths have crossed again. I feel like a new man," Jeffrey confessed.

Angela tried to salvage this trip, "*How quaint!* Jeffrey, make yourself *useful*, since I have to be in the same room with you. Who is this *no-body* in the fancy suit, *this Kyle Swoboda?*"

Jeffrey's eyes squinted almost imperceptibly, as he asked, "Becky, *doesn't know,* Mr. Swoboda?"

Angela thought out loud, "She didn't say. You two so rudely interrupted my questioning."

William laughed, "I feel so bad for you, Angela. I love to watch your black schemes go wrong."

William didn't wait for Angela's caustic comment. He gave Jeffrey a peck on his cheek and then said as he walked off, "I'm going to see to our guests, Jeffrey. Don't be long with the *Ice Queen*. Robert is due to speak any minute."

Jeffrey smooched back at his departing other. Angela's look would have removed paint from metal.

"*You two* are *disgusting*, and in public! *Have you no shame?*" she growled.

Jeffrey smiled, "William says the same about you too, Angela." Then a thought occurred to him, "You now Angela, all your life you've scratched and clawed your way to supposed fame and fortune. Do you realize, that little girl *you just insulted to the core*, could *buy you out* completely, with change from her purse?"

The color in Angela's face drained, as she hesitated, "*The trust fund?*"

Jeffrey smiled with complete satisfaction. This was *the* announcement he'd waited sixteen years, to deliver to Angela. With Becky out of Angela's control, Angela wouldn't get even a sniff at this fund.

"Yes, the trust fund," he nodded, "but, Becky is something special. She has wisdom and the instinct to find wealth on her own. She's like you, Angela, but *unlike you*. Becky is a true angel. You, on the other hand, have a special corner in Hell *waiting for you*. Please enjoy what life you have left. I see an eternity of reward for you, *bless your heart*," Jeffrey sneered as he left her also.

Kyle stood across the room from Angela. He laughed at the Bedouin, thinking, 'Adam! I'm glad you came. Hiding your skin from the sunlight in your disguise is brilliant. Bravo!'

Adam telepathed back, 'I wouldn't have missed this inaugural meeting of our foundation. It's a dream come true *and* the end of *a long wait* for me.'

Kyle looked at Adam, 'I don't understand.'

Adam smiled beneath his veil, 'Kyle, I've stayed hidden for nearly three hundred years waiting for your civilization to mature You and Becky are *very close* to me. You're like my children. I felt the same way towards Snowy, but then he was killed. You are much like Snowy, having a clean spirit and a pure heart. Your mind is a book yet to be written. I'd like us to write a book together. To make a positive mark in history. To help mankind.' He paused, then added, 'You both were open to me. You said this world was *so screwed up*, it needed *alien intervention*. How could I *refuse* such an *eloquent invitation?'*

Kyle moved his foot embarrassed, 'It's true, Adam. There are so many special interest groups in the world today, so many conflicting regulations, but I sense a master hand behind all of this. Someone or some group is controlling our destinies and I don't think they have the common man's best interest at heart.'

Adam nodded his head, 'Yes, you're right, Kyle.' Then Adam announced, 'I better be getting back to my home, or I'll miss tea.'

Kyle's head snapped around. For an instant, he glimpsed a thought in Adams's mind, '*No…*'

Adam slapped Kyle's arm, 'I shouldn't have thought that. Your evolving Kyle. I'm going to have to watch myself.'

Kyle couldn't help himself laughing, 'You don't watch the soaps, do you?'

Adam blustered. He wouldn't answer.

Kyle laughed, 'As the World Spins? General Horsepital? All my Kids?'

Adam looked serious as he countered, 'Colleen wants to go to the prom, but doesn't have a thing to wear. Her bootie is getting too big! Billy needs a new kidney. His Aunt Shirley will share one of her's with Billy, since she's close to kicking the bucket. Then there's Brent, who has a crush on Sally, but Alice loves Brent. Alice is going to have Brent's baby in two months, but can't find a prom-dress in her size, either. On the other hand, George is a peeping-Tom who watches Sally get ready for bed.' Adam looked at Kyle seriously, '*All this* is really *good stuff*. A credit to fine literature, but with an earthy appeal,' Adam winked.

May I have your attention, please," Robert's voice boomed over the sound system from the podium. Kyle turned to listen as Adam silently moved towards the ladies' room, to escape unnoticed.

Everyone turned to listen. It was precisely twelve noon.

"First of all, I'd like to welcome, Mr. Secretary, Madame Chairperson, and everyone *equally*. The *Mystique Corporation* hopes today is a day *for the common person,* and also, for the world in general."

Robert paused. He let everyone settle in.

The primary intent of the Mystique Corporation is to help all people of the world, from the G-7 down to the smallest country. They feel that it's better to give a person a full belly, then to kill them in a war. They believe that with our global oil reserves dwindling, we need an alternative source of energy for: transportation, for light, and to heat or cool our homes. This corporation wishes to promote ideas and research, that will protect our world from ecological harm."

Robert looked around the room, "I know it's almost twenty year away, but some experts are fearful in the not to distant future, in the year 2012, the end of the Mayan calendar, all sorts of destruction will occur and end all we've known."

He paused, "Some intellectuals, on the other hand, view the year 2012, as a year to rejoice! They think it marks the end of death and destruction, the end of aggressive *male energy*. Some believe 2012 is the evolving of gentle *female energy*. Some experts describe *this energy* as the energy of harmony, of peace, and of nurturing. This thought pattern sees a softer side of civilization, where war, famine, greed, and abuse, *will no longer* be tolerated. The Mystique Corporation wishes to help our world climb onto this peaceful plane."

There was a murmur in the crowd. One man yelled, "I've heard that before! *Talk is cheap.*"

Robert smiled. He was like a professor with a sense of the theatrics. He liked to interact with his audience.

"Ah, we have a skeptic in our midst!" Robert grinned, "That's OK. The Mystique Corporation welcomes constructive dialog with its peers."

Robert relaxed. Then confidently pointed over to the booths to the side of the room. "The Mystique Corporation is unveiling three products today."

He took a breath, "First, we are announcing a revolutionary process we've copyrighted, that turns a light-weight silicon gel into a battery, with endless shapes and size possibilities. Our battery is essentially made from sand. Through our special process, sand or silica molecules are polarized through isomerization. In short, after a minimal exposure to an initial energy field at the factory, our batteries will last ten years, guaranteed. They need no further electrical charging, and will generate their own power, to the level advertised."

Again, the room was alive with murmured voices. Robert waited.

"To the auto industry," Robert continued, "this means we can have electric cars, lighter than ever and won't ever need a gas fill up! We can build a battery that will heat a house, energy free for ten years, once past the initial investment. Since our battery is made from plain sand, we want to keep our purchase price within the grasp of the average person."

He took a sip of water. Then he looked around.

"The price of a battery is based on its size. It's like buying an outboard motor for a boat. The higher the horsepower of the outboard engine, the more it costs. The same principle applies to our batteries. For a small house, well insulated, our battery can run a heater or air conditioner."

"Our product is available for license," Robert explained, "so any battery company can make our product with minimal retooling. You can keep your same workforce. We feel that the broader use of batteries, will offset the need for large royalties. Price gauging of our customers will not be tolerated."

The crowd was stunned. Robert knew he was reestablishing the principle of discount selling. That is, if you keep the price of your product low, you'll make the same amount money by selling more, putting more people to work, who in turn, have the money to buy your product.

"The second product," Robert continued, "is a protein grain, much like wheat, but without the allergic component of gluten. With some innovative planning, we can make bread or protein bars. The cost, is similar to a loaf of wheat bread. We don't want to put wheat farmers out of business. We're working with agricultural extension services to show farmers how to convert their wheat fields into our new grain. The plant is perennial, saving yearly planting and insecticide investment.

Our plant is disease resistant, so it can be grown organically, which is healthier for our customers. The chemical plants that now make insecticides, can be converted, to make silicon gel for our batteries."

A woman from the audience shouted, "It seems you don't want to put people *out of work?"*

Robert responded passionately, "This corporation *is committed to people.* The Mystique Corporation believes people are intelligent. If we can show them a better product, that is cheaper and easier to make, made in a factory where they work, then they'll naturally gravitate to the new product."

"Folks," Robert said to the audience, "our world is growing up. We're running out of natural resources. We need to be looking at how we make products today, using what we have, cheaper, and cleaner. This corporation thinks if they aren't trying to pad their bank accounts, that they'll be successful. They're *ready* to *put their money* where their mouth is."

Robert announced, "The third product is a luxury item. It's a large plant seed in the shape of a pod. It can be flavored with natural ingredients, mixtures of spices, to make a plant protein, taste and chew like animal flesh for those people who desire this type of food." He pointed over to the wall, "Please stop by the booths to sample our foods and see our battery. The foods will be priced inexpensively, but are patent protected."

Again the audience was alive with conversation. All of these products were revolutionary.

Robert held up his hand as he concluded his address, "I want to thank each of you for coming today. Have a great day and a safe trip home."

Kyle was standing alone. A woman approached, innocently.

"Are you Kyle Swoboda?" Angela asked.

Kyle looked at her, "Yes, that's me."

Angela smoothly took Kyle's arm and began to lead him towards an exit, "I'd like to talk to you in private, about your products. I represent a consortium of businessmen, who are extremely interested in learning *more about you.*"

Kyle didn't know what to make of this sophisticated woman, but she seemed sweet enough. Something in her face put him off guard.

Robert swooped around to block their path, "Angela, *what a surprise!* I don't believe *you* were invited to this event."

Kyle pulled his arm from the woman's grasp, "Angela? As in Angela Wells?"

Robert raised an eyebrow to Kyle, "*The one and ONLY.*" Robert turned to an angry Angela, "Shame on you, darling, trying to monopolize our guest of honor. Your usual intent is to monopolize and control all that is around you, or has the leopard changed her spots?" he smiled.

Angela stiffened with smoldering anger, "*Robert*, you still have the knack of showing up when *least welcome*," she growled. "Don't you have some young boy hidden somewhere, who is begging for your attention?"

Robert smiled, but stood his ground. Becky saw what was happening and approached the trio.

Angela groused, frustratingly, "*Not YOU too, Rebecca!* Angela looked down at Becky's belly. Doesn't the father of *your bastard*, need you somewhere? We're having a business meeting here. *Go away.*"

Kyle stiffened and stood stock still. Becky had seen this stance before. Her pit-bull was about to bite her mother's head off. She took Kyle's left hand in her's.

Kyle felt her warm touch. *He knew* what she was doing.

Kyle looked at Angela and in a whisper, announced, "Angela Wells, I take great pleasure to introducing *my wife,….* Mrs. Becky Swoboda. Since *I'm* the father *of her baby*, she is exactly where she's wanted. She's *at my side,* being *my intellectual equal.*" He leaned down and kissed Becky gently, smiling, "And a beautiful distraction, she is too."

Angela blinked, realizing her mistake.

Becky smiled at Angela, then explained to Kyle, "Angela represents a group of business men who buy up inventions. They safeguard and control them *from the unwashed masses*. They care about nothing except money and the power it holds over citizens. They are a dangerous group. They think you are a revolutionary. A threat to their global control."

Angela opened her mouth to reply, but nothing came out. She shifted her weight, annoyed at this interjection.

Becky told Kyle, "When mother said she was interested in buying patents, from *a pig farmer* named *Kyle Swoboda*, I just said, good luck."

Kyle looked at Becky, then at Angela, "That about sums it up for me too, Angela," he said as he walked off with Becky.

Angela unleashed a tirade on Robert, "You've blocked my way *once too often,* Robert. You'd better sleep *with eyes behind your head."*

Kyle let Becky's hand go as he whipped around, *"Woman,* I used to kill people for a living. I'm *really good* at it too. It doesn't matter to me, *who* I kill. If they need it, I'm your man. It's been said, I have a mean streak a mile wide. Right now, you're on my expendable list. *Don't* tempt me!" he growled.

Angela's face went white. Something in this giant of a man scared her.

Kyle looked her directly in the eye. His eyes glowed with death. "You better pray nothing happens to my family, or *any* of my friends. I'm telling you now. If they are so much as bumped on the street, I'm gonna come gunning for you. You can try to run away, but you'll just be tired when you die."

Angela seethed, "That's a threat! I'm gonna press charges!"

Robert smiled softly, "I just heard Kyle complimenting you on your dress, Angela. I didn't hear any threat, did you Becky?"

Becky took Kyle's right hand, "I didn't hear a thing." She looked at Robert, "Can we arrange a Restraining Order, or Peace Bond against this woman? I heard her speaking threatening remarks toward my baby. Can I get a court order like she put on my father years ago? I don't *ever* want to *see* or *hear* from this viper again, *ev-er*!"

Robert smiled, "I'll have the papers for you to sign within the hour. I can do that." Robert smiled at Angela. "I think you have a plane to catch, counselor. I'll give you a running start. The Chief of Police and I are on the same team for the Fraternal Order Benefit golf tournament each year. I'd love for you to meet him."

Angela knew when she was out maneuvered. She raised her chin and stalked out of the room. She tried to retain her air of superiority as she left.

After Angela left, Robert directed Kyle and Becky toward a group of businessmen. Robert explained, "I want you both to meet some people."

Kyle slowly walked over to the group. He held Becky's hand tightly in his as he had a protective arm around her.

Jeffrey stepped forward, "Kyle, Becky, I'd like you to meet Mr. Morgan of the Wells Trust Corporation."

Mr. Morgan shook Becky's and Kyle's hand, "It's wonderful to meet you, *at last*. When you disappeared last winter, Becky, I was truly worried. I'd like to make an appointment for lunch, so we can discuss some matters of importance."

Becky looked at Jeffrey, "Daddy, I don't understand?"

William came up to Jeffrey, and they held hands. Jeffrey explained, "Becky, after your mother rejected me, I met my boyhood friend, William. Our families were very close to each other, for many years."

Jeffrey shifted nervously, "I found solace and peace with William, but we were going against convention. My parents and William's, were very formal people. Our families were steeped in tradition for nearly two centuries."

William interceded, "When Jeffrey and I joined as a couple, both our families disinherited us. The two families knew Jeffrey had a daughter. We both were the last of our families. I never married and was childless."

Jeffrey had regained his composure, "Our families gave us an ultimatum. They vowed that if we didn't stop seeing each other, they'd put our inheritance in a trust corporation. The families financial holdings would be run until you, my daughter, became of age. At which time, you would inherit our families *vast* and *total* accumulated wealth."

Becky couldn't bear this, "I don't want *your money*, Daddy, William."

Jeffrey looked at William, "We want you to have it, Becky. William and I have been fortunate in business, to more than care for our needs."

William started to cry, "We're just happy that you and Kyle, haven't shunned us too. We feel like lepers. Like we're *terrible people*," he sobbed.

Jeffrey comforted William, as he looked at Becky and Kyle, "Our crime against society is, that we loved."

Kyle took Becky's hand. He was her rock during troubled times.

Mr. Morgan explained, "Becky, just part of this inheritance is the sixty-eight Wellsley Hotels *worldwide*. That's not to mention the one hundred and twenty resorts. These profitable investments are just the tip of the iceberg of your inherited fortune. I would estimate its total value in the multi billions."

Jeffrey explained, "Our families' money is *old money*. They've been in business together, since before the original gold rush, in the 1800s. My father, grew up before World War II and foresaw America's desire to play. He invested heavily in hotels and resorts. He was *very* business savvy."

Becky gasped, "Is this hotel, what I'd be inheriting?"

Mr. Morgan laughed softly, "This is *just one* of *many* hotels, Becky. You surely can have *any* room in this hotel you wish," he smiled.

Becky sagged against Kyle. It was too much, "I need to go home, Kyle."

Mr. Morgan gave Kyle a business card, "Give me a call when she has rested. I can imagine this afternoon has been a strain on her, in her condition."

William rushed to Becky, "Are you alright, sugarplum? Do you need Jeffrey to call the doctor?" he asked worriedly.

Becky kissed William's cheek, "I'm fine. I just need to go home to the ranch, William. I'll call you, honey. We'll do lunch soon, ok?"

William nodded. Supreme concern was written all over his face.

Kyle thought to Becky, 'Montana and his wife are here. Are you alright for a few minutes? We need to say hello, but I don't want to hurt *you or* the baby."

Becky straightened. She was needed.

'Yes, we must say hello,' Becky replied. 'It wouldn't be polite to leave yet.'

Kyle thought, 'I want Montana to be our head honcho, the Chief of Staff of our new companies. We'll think up the ideas and Montana will bring them into reality. He can hire a lot of people, supervisors and such, who are ex-military. They're trained to lead people, to accomplish goals.'

Becky recovered. She felt somewhat uncomfortable in that she didn't know Montana's last name. She guessed Montana was his Air Force call sign. She waved at him, "Hello! We're glad you could come today."

Kyle shook Montana's hand, "And I'm glad you brought Mrs. Snydar too."

Becky felt relieved. She wasn't about to call a woman, *Mrs. Montana*.

Montana introduced his wife, "Kyle, Becky, may I present my wife, Abigail. We left our two teenage kids back at the base. We're so happy, that you've done so well for yourselves, in such a short period of time. It seems just yesterday, I was standing with you two at your wedding in Florida."

Kyle smiled confidently as he explained, "Montana, Abigail, I asked you here because I want to offer you a job. It'd mean a lot to Becky and me, if you were working for us. I trust you, Montana, *like family*. You'd take a lot of pressure off our shoulders."

Montana didn't know what to say. That Kyle had saved his life back in the Kuwait Desert almost two years ago, forged a tremendous bond between both men. Kyle had been wounded severely, rescuing him, and that wasn't forgotten by John 'Montana' Snydar either.

Abigail gushed as she shook her husband's arm, *"Oh Johnny!* This is what we've hoped for. To live in one place! To buy a home of our own *for our children."*

John looked at his wife, "We haven't even heard what the job is. I'm *a pilot* for cripes sake, Gailey! I've spent my entire adult life in the military. I don't know *anything else."*

Gail looked at her husband sternly, "And they've passed you over for light colonel two times. Honey, *that's* the kiss of death! We're four years away from retirement! So close, yet so far. I think we should get out while we have this job offer. You've spoken highly of KIS. *You know* you can trust him."

Kyle knew how Montana felt. He tried to help.

Kyle spoke to both of them, "Becky and I have started a corporation. You heard about our three products, and we have more in the pipeline. I, we, need a good Chief of Staff to run our corporation's operations from here in Denver. You would be like a Wing Commander, Montana. This would be a good place to raise a family. You're centrally located. You can go anywhere in the world, easily from here. Your job would to be keep us informed at our ranch, just west of Colorado Springs."

Abigail jumped for joy, "Our oldest son wants to go to the Academy."

Kyle winked, "There you go. The school's just down the road! You can visit him as much as you like."

Becky offered, "Montana, we can set you up in an office here in the hotel. If you want a whole floor for your staff, just say the word. You would run the day to day business of the Mystique Corporation for us. You wouldn't be far from our ranch either. Kyle and I would love to become friends with Abigail and you."

Kyle looked at Becky, then back to Montana and Abigail, "We'll offer you four hundred thousand a year salary."

Abigail about passed out. She slapped her hands before her face, as if in prayer. John took two minutes and a deep breath, before he shook Kyle's hand, "You've got yourself a Chief of Staff, Kyle, Becky," Montana said.

Becky took a breathless Abigail by the arm and led her over to Brian, Robert Edward's secretary. Becky stated, "Brian, I need you to set Mrs. Snydar up with an executive relocation service, *top shelf*. Nothing but *The Best* for her. *I want this lady…happy,* got it?"

Under her breath, she whispered to Brian, "Make sure she and her family are happy and settled in a good home. If you do this, I'll make sure there's something nice in your Christmas stocking, this year."

Brian winked, "I *like presents*. I'll work my magic, Mrs. Swoboda."

Becky turned to Abigail, "Brain will take good care of you. Call me if you have any problems. The Lobby will know how to get in touch with me."

Becky held out her hand to Kyle, "Cowboy, *I've gotta go.*"

Kyle understood. His princess didn't use *that tone* of voice, *often*.

Kyle called to Jeffrey, "Need helicopter, on the pad, *now please.*"

Jeffrey was on it! He knew his daughter was exhausted. There was a helicopter waiting for them, by the time the couple reached the hotel's heliport.

Their pilot was Hank. He'd ferried them from their ranch to Denver and back, several times. He knew where they were going without being told.

Kyle sat in the back with Becky. He got a chance to talk to her. To be there, for her

Becky was feeling her tummy, gently thinking, 'I had my exam this morning, Kyle. The doctor was pleased with our progress. He even ordered an ultrasound.'

Kyle looked at her expectantly, '*And?*'

Becky sighed, 'I'm not far enough along for them to know the gender of our baby. I'm sorry, Kyle.' She held her breath, waiting for Kyle's reaction.

Kyle looked at Becky tenderly, 'Hon, whatever we have, it's fine with me. All I care about is *that you and the baby* are healthy.' He hugged his precious, 'Whatever we have, I know one thing,' he thought to her.

Becky looked up with tears in her eyes, 'What is that?'

Kyle smiled, 'I know I'm in love with our baby's mother.' Then he winked and added softly, 'I guess we'll have to wait and see what happens. I bet it'll be exciting…'